9017322535

 KU-540-572

The Table of Less
Valued Knights

ALSO BY MARIE PHILLIPS

Gods Behaving Badly

The Table of Less Valued Knights

MARIE PHILLIPS

JONATHAN CAPE
LONDON

Published by Jonathan Cape 2014

2 4 6 8 10 9 7 5 3 1

First published in Great Britain in 2014 by
Jonathan Cape
Random House, 20 Vauxhall Bridge Road,
London SW1V 2SA

www.vintage-books.co.uk

Addresses for companies within The Random House Group Limited can be found at:
www.randomhouse.co.uk/offices.htm

The Random House Group Limited Reg. No. 954009

A CIP catalogue record for this book is available from the British Library

ISBN 9780224093422

The Random House Group Limited supports the Forest Stewardship Council® (FSC®),
the leading international forest-certification organisation. Our books carrying the FSC
label are printed on FSC®-certified paper. FSC is the only forest-certification scheme
supported by the leading environmental organisations, including Greenpeace. Our paper
procurement policy can be found at www.randomhouse.co.uk/environment

MIX
Paper from
responsible sources
FSC® C016897

Typeset in Dante MT by Palimpsest Book Production Limited,
Falkirk, Stirlingshire
Printed and Bound in Great Britain by
CPI Group (UK) Ltd, Croydon CR0 4YY

For Sophie, Jean-Yves and Rebecca

Know that there were three tables there. The first was the Round Table, with King Arthur as companion and lord. The second, the Table of Errant Companions, was for those who went seeking adventure and waited to become companions of the Round Table. Those of the third table never left court and did not go on quests or in search of adventures, either because of illness or because they lacked courage. These knights were called the Less Valued Knights.

– Suite du Merlin, the post-Vulgate cycle

PART ONE

PART ONE

One

It was the feast of Pentecost at Camelot, and the air thrummed with anticipation. All of King Arthur's knights had gathered together to re-speak their vows, to celebrate the successes of the year, and to toast the future. Pentecost was also when the most prestigious of quests came to the castle door, and the knights were waiting for this year's to arrive.

In the centre of the Great Hall of the castle, the Round Table gleamed by the light of a thousand candles, though nothing shone brighter than the faces of the good men who surrounded it. On a modest wooden throne sat Arthur, a simple circlet of gold atop his brow, telling the assembled knights the familiar tale of how he pulled the sword from the stone, a story as lengthy as it was uninteresting. On Arthur's left sat loyal Lancelot, smiling at his liege's tale, and wondering if he could feign the need to relieve himself so that he could go and visit Queen Guinevere (eating alone in her room tonight, as befitted a woman). On Arthur's right was the Siege Perilous, said to bring instant death to anyone who sat in it, though this was rumoured to be a lie invented by Sir Kay so that he'd have somewhere to put his coat. The rest of the knights were arranged in what, in a less outspokenly egalitarian court, one might have called a hierarchy, with the best and most famous sitting nearest their king, and the ones furthest away casting nervous glances at the other tables in the hall, wondering if that was where their fate lay.

For there were two other tables in the Great Hall of Camelot, two tables less sung of by storytellers and balladeers, in fact barely mentioned at all. One was known as the Table of Errant Companions. Oval in shape, tucked in the shadowy space beneath the minstrels' gallery, it housed those young upstarts who aspired to the Round Table, who busied themselves with minor quests and prayed for a precious chair in proximity to Arthur. The other table, to be found in the draughtiest corner furthest away from either of the fires, was rectangular, and had one leg shorter than the other so that it always had to be propped up with a folded napkin to stop it from rocking. It was home to the elderly, the infirm, the cowardly, the incompetent and the disgraced, and was called the Table of Less Valued Knights.

Amongst these Less Valued Knights was one Sir Humphrey du Val, a handsome if rumple-faced man, with hair on the turn from dark, and eyes that were tired and guarded. Sir Humphrey was bored. Bored and hungry. By tradition, nobody was allowed to eat until the Pentecost quest turned up, and this year, the quest was late. It was like waiting for the speeches to end at a long-winded wedding, and for Humphrey the wait was barely going to be worth it. The Table of Less Valued Knights was served last, the food was always cold, and if the kitchens had miscalculated how thick to slice the roast, as they often did, the portions would be smaller. Humphrey was fairly certain that they watered down the wine too, after an unfortunate incident a few years ago involving a confused retired knight who'd spent many years captive in a witch's dungeon, and thought he was still there.

He watched the Knights of the Round Table as they showed off to one another, pretending to share news but actually competing as to who had killed the most fearsome monster or rescued the most dazzling maiden. Humphrey's days of monster-killing and maiden-rescuing were behind him. Knights of Lesser Value were forbidden from going on quests. He was doomed to live out the rest of his decades sitting at this table, with toothless Sir Benedict to one side, who began every conversation with the words, 'Have I ever told you about the time I fought the bear?', and shivering Sir Malcolm on the other, who had a phobia of armour, and spent every meal staring fixedly at his plate muttering, 'I'm alone in a beautiful meadow, I'm alone in a beautiful meadow, I'm alone in a beautiful meadow.' Humphrey's stomach rumbled. There was no bread, but he wondered whether anybody would mind, or even notice, if he took a swipe from the butter dish. He sighed. Sometimes he disgusted even himself.

Meanwhile, at the Round Table, King Arthur had finally finished his story, and the knights had subtly shifted their chairs to get a better view of the door.

'Have I ever told you about the time I fought the bear?' said Sir Benedict.

'Never,' said Humphrey. 'Do fill me in.'

'I was a much younger man then,' said Sir Benedict. 'It's probably hard for you to imagine . . .'

Just then, the door to the Great Hall burst open at last. Everyone craned their necks to see who it was. Framed in the carved stone arch was a young man, tall, handsome and fair, clad in red velvet and wearing a crown several times more ostentatious than Arthur's. A few coins discreetly changed hands on the Table of Errant Companions, where bets had been placed over whether or not it would be a damsel this year.

Arthur stood. 'Welcome, traveller,' he said.

The man bowed and smiled. There was an audible gasp in the room, quickly suppressed: the man had the most astonishingly colossal teeth, which ruined his otherwise impeccable good looks.

'I am Edwin,' said the large-toothed man. 'King of Puddock, and next in line to the throne of Tuft.'

King of Puddock? Humphrey frowned. The last King of Puddock had died only recently, and he'd left no living male heir – his only son had been a Knight of the Round Table himself,

5

and had been killed a number of years ago. Puddock had a queen now. So this must be her husband. But surely that made him Prince Consort? As for Tuft, King Leo sat on the throne there, and he was young and unmarried. This Edwin must be his brother, and only next in line to the throne until Leo took a wife and begat an heir.

'Good sirs,' the self-proclaimed king continued, 'I am in need of your most urgent assistance. Six days ago, on our wedding night, my beloved wife, Queen Martha, was snatched from our marital bed by miscreants unknown.'

So it was to be kidnap. A few of the knights nodded knowingly. Kidnap was a classic quest scenario.

'I was asleep at the time, and, alas, saw nothing,' continued Edwin.

That's convenient, thought Humphrey.

'Our village crone, however, said that she found a strange man in her cottage in the early hours of that morning, whom I can only assume was one of the gang involved in taking my bride. But unfortunately he absconded before he could be apprehended.'

Edwin, Humphrey noted, spoke as if each of his words was going to be taken down for posterity.

'Please,' finished Edwin, 'would one of you gentlemen be good enough to assist me in finding my beloved?' He held out his arms beseechingly.

As soon as he'd finished speaking, most of the Round Table knights jumped up to accept the quest. Whoever volunteered the fastest would be given the task, and in the weeks leading up to Pentecost, many of the knights practised leaping, so that they would be the first to their feet. There was a special eminence attached to the Pentecost quest, the successful completion of which might move you up the table a few seats closer to the King.

To Humphrey's disgust, though not his surprise, the swiftest to rise was Sir Dorian Pendoggett. Sir Dorian was the Errant

6

Companion who had taken Humphrey's spot at the Round Table when Humphrey was demoted to Less Valued status. Humphrey was therefore predisposed to disliking him, but even so, he was convinced Dorian was genuinely insufferable, swaggering through Camelot as if he was Percival himself, and always bowing with an exaggerated flourish to Humphrey when they passed in the corridors of the castle, which was worse than not bowing at all. He hung around Gareth, Gaheris and Gawain, who Humphrey assumed tolerated him out of politeness, and claimed to be 'like a brother' to them, which was patently untrue. He'd tried to flirt with the Grail Maiden, who was a virgin inviolate. And he was always looking out for the quest that would get him into a poem.

Well, it seemed that he had found it. And with the Pentecost quest underneath his gold-buckled belt, he would be clawing his way still further up the Round Table hierarchy, while Humphrey continued to plummet inexorably downwards.

'Thank you, good Sir Dorian,' said King Arthur, 'and best of courage to you!'

Sir Dorian glowed with smugness. 'I live to serve,' he said, with a bow. Edwin returned the bow, though his was not quite so low as Dorian's.

'And now,' Arthur announced to the room, 'we dine!'

The assembled knights cheered as the roast swan was brought out, but Humphrey found that he had lost his appetite.

Two

After the other knights had gone to their beds, or, in Lancelot's case, to the Queen's, Humphrey lingered in the empty hall. With everyone gone, it seemed impossibly huge, with its double-height ceiling, the long eyelet windows, the minstrels' gallery above, and the twin fireplaces at either end of the room, each bigger than most of the peasant huts on the Camelot estate. He had belonged here once, truly belonged, before Castle Maudit and everything that had happened there. He'd been proud to be a Knight of the Round Table, had sent excitable letters full of his adventures home to his mother, may she rest in peace. That was a long time ago. He made his way over to his old seat, about a third of the way down the east side of the circle, not a bad position by any means. He sat down. It was more comfortable than his chair now – the Round Table knights got cushions. Humphrey ran his finger along a scratch on the table in front of him, softened with age but still deep, from the time that Sir Kay had thrown a knife during an argument with Lancelot, after the latter had nicked his armour. If Sir Kay hadn't been the King's brother, he'd have been busted down to Less Valued Knight a long time ago.

The door to the Great Hall opened with a bang, and Humphrey started, embarrassed to be caught sitting at the forbidden table. But it wasn't a knight, or even a servant. It was a girl. She was wearing a long grey cloak with the hood thrown back, revealing her windswept golden hair. She was pretty, he noticed, though she looked tired, and she was staring around the room with an expression of dismay.

'I missed it,' she said. 'I was told they would wait.'

'Can I help you?' said Humphrey, standing.

'I rode as fast as I could,' said the girl.

'You came here alone? A maiden shouldn't be riding alone, especially not at night.'

'So they say,' said the girl. 'Though I've noticed that if you do ride alone, other people tend to give you a wide berth. They probably think only a witch would go out by herself. So really it's fine.' She smiled, then sighed. 'Anyway, it looks like there was no point. I got lost in the dark – I've never been to Camelot before – it's big, isn't it? And now everyone's gone.'

'I'm not gone,' said Humphrey. 'Sir Humphrey du Val.' He bowed.

The girl's eyes widened.

'Humphrey? Really? That's such an old man's name.'

'It was my father's. And his father's, and his father's, and so on.'

'And have you blessed your son with this fine name too?'

Humphrey hesitated. 'I don't have a son,' he said. 'What's your name?'

'I'm Elaine. Another Elaine.' Every second maiden in the land was called Elaine. 'Lady Elaine du Mont, of Tuft.'

Humphrey nodded. He'd heard of the du Monts – they were a good family, but were known to have fallen on hard times. He looked more closely at the girl. Her cloak was well cut but faded, and some tears had been neatly repaired.

'I was told that, if I came tonight, somebody would be sure to take on my quest,' Elaine continued.

Her quest? Her *quest*? This new piece of information made the world shift just enough to make sense, like the jiggle that you gave a poorly cut key to make it turn in the lock. An arrogant prince consort who was pretending to be a king couldn't possibly be the bringer of the Pentecost quest. The court had simply assumed that he was, because he'd happened to arrive on Pentecost. What if it was just coincidence? Humphrey thought of Sir Dorian and chuckled to himself. He'd been so quick to jump up! And now here Humphrey was, alone on Pentecost night with a damsel in distress, a damsel with a quest. Though of course he wasn't supposed to go on quests. What he was supposed to do was wake Arthur, so that a Round Table knight could be assigned.

'Would you like to sit down?' said Humphrey. 'You must be tired from your journey.'

'Thank you, that's very kind,' said Elaine.

She pulled up one of the chairs at the Round Table – Sir Gaheris's – examined a few of the leftover jugs of wine, and helped herself to a healthy cupful.

'Do you want some?' she said. 'There's loads left.'

'Um, yes, I suppose so,' said Humphrey, slightly taken aback.

Elaine poured him a glass. He had a mouthful. This wine was definitely not watered down.

'You mentioned a quest,' he prompted.

Elaine nodded, her face pinched with anxiety. 'I'm supposed to be getting married,' she said. 'My parents held a tournament for my hand, just under a week ago. It was awful. It started with a melee, this horrible free-for-all fight, dozens of people were hurt, you can't imagine how terrible it was. Well, I suppose you can, being a knight. But I could hardly bear to watch. Then after that there was a joust for those left standing, to decide the ultimate victor. So many knights were riding with my colours that I might as well have ripped up my whole dress and handed it out as streamers.'

'Who won?' said Humphrey.

'This is the thing,' said Elaine. 'All those men got injured, in my name, but the winner was always going to be Sir Alistair Gilbert. He's not a Sir by birth, he's a knight at King Leo's court.

His family have money but no name. That was the exchange. It was prearranged, the tourney was just for show.'

'So if I'd entered, I couldn't have won?'

'Luckily for you, no, because otherwise in two weeks' time I'd be your wife.' Elaine smiled for a moment, then her sombre look returned.

'And you don't want to marry this Sir Alistair?' said Humphrey.

'It's not that,' said Elaine. 'He'd be a good husband, I think. I mean, I barely know him. But he's from a wealthy family, which is all that matters as far as my parents are concerned. And he seems kind, which is all that matters to me. Well, not all, but . . . Under the circumstances, it's enough.'

'He sounds like a good choice. And Alistair is a better name than Humphrey.' He was trying to get her to smile again. 'You could call him Al. If you married me, you'd have to call me Humph.'

Elaine did smile again, but her face seemed strained.

'So what went wrong?' said Humphrey, more seriously.

'Sir Alistair got kidnapped. Right at the end of the tournament. After he won, he dismounted and came over to the stands. I was presented to him, as if I were some kind of cup. He took my hands in his, looked into my eyes – very romantic, if you're not the prize in a competition.' A note of bitterness had entered Elaine's voice. 'We pledged our troth. And then out of nowhere comes this knight in black armour, visor down of course. He gallops up, smacks Sir Alistair on the back of the head with the hilt of his sword, knocks him out cold, picks up his body before it has a chance to fall to the ground, throws him over the front of his horse, and gallops away. I was terrified. The other knights tried to stop him, but they were all so exhausted from the tourney that they couldn't catch up with him. So the Black Knight got away.'

'Any hint of where he went? Ransom demands, anything?'

'Nothing. We waited and waited, we were sure we'd hear

something, but no word came. And I need to find him. Urgently. Our family – we're not a wealthy family, Sir Humphrey. And I'm the only daughter. My parents are relying on me. And . . .' Elaine stopped. She took a breath and composed her face. 'Well, that's enough, isn't it?'

It was more than enough. A proper quest for a proper damsel in distress. The Pentecost quest, no less. If Humphrey found this Sir Alistair, if he reunited these lovers, that was exactly the kind of thing that might get him back onto the Round Table, or at least onto the Table of Errant Companions. He had to get this girl out of Camelot before anybody else spotted her.

'We must leave right away,' said Humphrey.

'You're taking on my quest?' said Elaine.

'Of course. I have vowed to give all maidens succour. In fact I retook that very vow today. We'll ride through the night. Time is of the essence when it comes to a kidnap.' He glossed over the fact that it had already been almost a week since Sir Alistair had disappeared.

'Thank you.' Now Elaine smiled, a true smile which lit up her eyes, unlike all the smiles that had gone before. Then she tipped back the rest of her wine, shoved a couple of bread rolls in the pockets of her cloak, and jumped from her chair. 'Let's go,' she said.

Three

Under the Pentecost moon, round and lovely as a baby's cheek, they crept together across the deserted stable yard at the back of the castle.

'Wait for me in here,' said Sir Humphrey, opening the door to one of the stables.

Elaine went inside. Moments later, she screamed and came running back out.

'What is that monster?' she said.

'What monster? Oh, sorry. I'm so accustomed to her now, I forgot to warn you. She's not a monster. She's totally harmless. She's an elephant.'

'An elephant? What's an elephant?'

Humphrey gestured towards the stall.

'Where did you find such a creature?' said Elaine.

'She's from Africa.'

'Africa!' Elaine's face brightened. 'You've been to Africa? How wonderful. What's it like? Is it full of monsters? Will you tell me all about it on the ride?'

Humphrey shook his head, a little abashed. 'I've never been. I bought the elephant from a travelling circus that was visiting the castle.'

'Oh. But why did you buy an elephant?'

Humphrey smiled. 'You'll see. Don't worry. She's very friendly. Her name's Jemima. If you want her eternal loyalty, grab a carrot from that pile of vegetables and feed it to her. They're her favourites. Hold it out on your palm and she'll take it with her trunk.'

'Her trunk?'

'That long nose thing.'

'She eats with her nose?'

'Not exactly. Try it and see. Anyway, I shouldn't be too long. I just need to find my squire and get some things together for the trip. If anyone asks . . .'

'Oh, believe me, I've come up with a lie about what I'm doing in a stable before. I'll be fine.'

Elaine went back inside and shut the door behind her.

'Hello, Jemima,' Humphrey heard her say.

He grinned to himself and then went out past the stable block to the old barn to find Conrad. He had been moved there when he got too tall for the main castle, and although he complained continuously about the cold, Humphrey reckoned that he enjoyed the privacy. He was free to drink as much ale and smoke as much hemp as he wanted, and no doubt he would sneak in those local girls who were curious about being with a larger man. With Humphrey never leaving the castle, there was very little squiring on the agenda. It seemed like a decent enough life to Humphrey. It never occurred to him that Conrad might actually want to work.

He opened the barn door without knocking. Conrad was sprawled face down on the huge pallet that served as his bed, alone, mercifully, and wearing his (very) long underwear, also mercifully – Humphrey had no desire to see his squire's hirsute backside. The floor of the barn was strewn with discarded clothes, empty bottles, half-eaten plates of food, a couple of books, at least one of which had tawdry illustrations, bits of armour, and various other forms of detritus that Humphrey would rather not identify.

'Time to get up!' said Humphrey.

Conrad opened his eyes, closed them again, and groaned. 'It's the middle of the night,' he said.

'I know,' said Humphrey.

'Go away,' said Conrad, mostly into his pillow.

'No. We're going on a quest.'

'Not funny.'

'Really.'

After a moment or two, Conrad turned his head towards Humphrey, revealing the volcanic spots that covered his face.

'Really really?'

'Yep.'

'We don't go on quests. You don't go on quests.'

'We do now.'

Conrad sat up. 'It's Pentecost. I was just out with the squires. How can we . . . We're going on the Pentecost quest?'

'Get my armour and pack us both a bag.'

'Did everybody else die?'

'Of course everybody didn't die, Conrad.'

'Well then, why are they letting you go?'

'They aren't letting me. They don't know.'

'But –'

Humphrey sighed and leaned against the barn door.

'We were having the feast as usual,' he said. 'By which I mean getting hungry, waiting for the quest. This king type – not a real king, I hasten to add – turns up, looking for his wife who's gone missing. Everybody assumes that's the Pentecost quest, obviously . . .'

'Who got it?'

'Dorian.'

Conrad pulled a face. Then he said, 'Silas will be pleased, at least.' Silas was Sir Dorian's squire, and was a lot more popular than his master. 'If the quest goes well, he might be made a knight himself. Lucky bastard.'

'Yes, well, he can forget about that,' said Humphrey. 'Because I don't think it's the real Pentecost quest. I was still in the hall after everyone else had gone . . .' Humphrey left out the part about sitting at the Round Table. 'And a damsel comes in.'

'In distress?'

'In distress.'

Conrad took this in. 'Damsel trumps king,' he said. 'Always.'

'Exactly.'

'And you didn't go and get Arthur? Or one of the real knights?'

Humphrey bristled. 'No, I thought we could handle this one by ourselves.'

'But we've never been on a quest.'

'I've been on plenty of quests.'

'*I've* never been on a quest.' There was a hint of nervousness in Conrad's voice.

'Why does that matter?' said Humphrey. 'Don't you want to go on a quest?'

'Of course I do,' said Conrad. 'Just . . . why, suddenly, this one?'

'She asked me to help her. I've taken vows, Conrad.'

'That's never mattered to you before.' Conrad peered at his master's face. 'Is she pretty?' he said.

'She's getting married, Conrad, that's the whole point of the quest. We'll need my armour, a tent, no, two tents, saddle-bags . . .'

Conrad grinned. His teeth were a lot bigger than Edwin's. 'Very pretty?' he said.

Humphrey picked up an empty saddlebag and chucked it at his squire. 'Don't forget my sword,' he said.

Four

When they got back to the stable, Jemima and Elaine were both asleep. Jemima was lying on her side with the girl curled up next to her, her head resting on the elephant's belly, seemingly unconcerned by the fragrant balls of elephant dung that peppered the straw, or the risk of being crushed by a rolling pachyderm.

Humphrey cleared his throat.

Elaine opened her eyes. 'Ready to go?' she said. Then her eyes widened. 'Oh,' she said.

She had never seen a giant before. She was a little disappointed. She'd expected them to be taller. Broad of build, Conrad stood with awkwardly rounded shoulders and a self-conscious stoop, so that he somewhat resembled a roughly hewn canoe with a curved prow.

'Conrad, Lady Elaine du Mont, of Tuft,' said Humphrey. 'Lady Elaine, Conrad, my squire.'

'So that's why you needed the elephant,' said Elaine. 'Pleased to meet you, Conrad.'

'You're not going to run and scream?' Conrad sounded crestfallen.

Elaine felt bad for him that she'd missed the chance to look afraid. 'The elephant's got my back,' she said. Jemima let out a soft elephant snore. 'When I wake her up, she'll have my back,' Elaine corrected herself.

'Where did you leave your horse?' said Humphrey.

'I tethered him at the front of the castle.'

'They let you do that?'

'There was nobody there.'

'No guards?'

'No.'

'I suppose that's what happens when all of your knights are spending Pentecost in the same room, getting pissed,' said Humphrey. 'I'm surprised Camelot doesn't get robbed every year. Well, at least that means we'll get out without . . . Without a long, tedious goodbye. The Round Table guys can be so emotional.'

He glared at Conrad, trying to convey: *She doesn't know I'm not Round Table.* Conrad rolled his eyes: *It never even crossed my mind that you'd be honest with her about that.*

'Conrad,' said Humphrey, 'you load up Jemima, and I'll get Spencer.'

'Spencer isn't a lion or anything, is he?' said Elaine.

'He's just a normal horse,' Humphrey assured her.

Conrad went over to Jemima and woke her with a gentle rub of her brow. Jemima shook her head in protest, but was soothed when Conrad fed her a carrot. He started fixing bags to her back.

'Aren't you going to put on your armour?' said Elaine to Humphrey.

'Not until I need it,' said Humphrey. 'If you travel looking like a knight, the attention never stops. Every maiden's got a quest, every man wants to challenge you to a duel.' This was true, and it was tiresome, although more to the point was that Humphrey didn't want word getting back to Camelot of where he had gone, if he could possibly avoid it.

'So we're going incognito,' said Elaine. 'With a terrifying giant riding a monster.'

Conrad grinned at the 'terrifying'.

'He's nobody's idea of a typical squire,' said Humphrey. 'People will think we're travelling players.'

Conrad's grin dropped. He knew squires didn't usually look like him, but he didn't like to be reminded.

'If that's what you think is best,' Elaine said to Humphrey. 'You're the knight.'

'Except . . .'

'You're not the knight, for the purposes of this trip.'

'Correct.'

Elaine got up and brushed the straw from her cloak.

'Just one question,' she said. 'Where are we actually going?'

'To your home, of course,' said Humphrey. 'Always start at the scene of the crime.'

Elaine's face fell. 'Do we have to?'

'I need to find out about the joust and what happened there.'

And I need to find out a bit about you, he thought, but did not say.

'Please,' said Elaine. 'Anywhere else but there.'

'I'm sorry,' said Humphrey. 'There's no other place we can start.'

Elaine smiled bleakly. 'Well,' she said. 'If we must. But don't say you weren't warned.'

Five

They rode through the night, slowed down by the fact that elephants don't gallop, or even trot for that matter, and it was past dawn by the time they reached the border with Tuft. The customs post consisted of a wooden stool by the side of the road, occupied by a dwarf with a clipboard and such bushy eyebrows, moustache and beard that he appeared to be entirely fashioned from hair.

Elaine dismounted from her grey gelding, Juniper, ate one of her bread rolls, and gave the other to Conrad and Humphrey to share. Neither of them had thought to bring any food. While Conrad tried to persuade the customs official to allow an unlicensed monster over the border, Humphrey went behind a tree to change into his full knight's regalia in preparation for meeting Elaine's parents. His armour was dated, and so tight he could hardly mount his horse, but there wasn't a speck of rust on it. His coat of arms, a pair of silver antlers on a green background, was neatly painted onto his shield, and embroidered onto his tabard and pennant in a painstaking but wobbly stitch.

'Have you been polishing?' Humphrey said to Conrad as he emerged, buckling his breastplate. 'And sewing?'

'That is what squires do,' said Conrad.

'This giant's your squire?' said the customs official to Humphrey.

'Didn't he tell you that?' said Humphrey.

'I didn't believe him.' The dwarf gave Conrad a long, reappraising stare. Then he turned back to Humphrey. 'You're Round Table, are you?'

'From Camelot,' said Humphrey, letting a lift in his voice imply that he was agreeing.

'Never thought I'd see the day,' said the dwarf, shaking his head. 'A giant as a squire. I thought he'd be burning down villages, raping, looting and the like. Thought it'd be more than my job's worth with King Leo, letting a giant in. Even a small one. I feel quite ashamed of myself, making assumptions like that. Believe me, I know what it's like. People see me, they think trickster, con artist, thief. Never imagine that I might be a government official. People think with their eyes, not with their minds, that's the problem. Well, well. A giant squire. Good luck to you, Sir.'

'Thank you,' said Conrad, straightening his shoulders for once.

'And this maiden is with you too?'

'I'm a damsel in distress,' said Elaine, proudly. 'We're on a quest.'

'Very good, very good,' said the dwarf. 'A quest. That's made my week, that has. Anything to declare?'

Humphrey showed his sword and his bow and arrows, and Conrad his axe.

'Oh well, you'll be needing those, on a quest,' said the customs official. 'What about fruit or vegetables?'

'I took a carrot for Jemima,' said Elaine.

'Sorry,' said the dwarf, in a genuinely apologetic tone, 'I can't let any alien fruit or vegetables over the border without a permit. Them's the rules. I don't make them.'

'Well, that's easily solved,' said Elaine, and she fed the carrot to an appreciative Jemima.

'Excellent,' said the customs official. 'Very resourceful. And I tell you what, I'll turn a blind eye to your monster. I'll put her down as "deformed horse". Every little helps, eh? Have a nice stay. Good luck with your quest!'

'Thank you,' said Humphrey with a bow, which the dwarf was delighted by, and they were on their way.

Six

Elaine's home village, close to the Tuft border, had seen better days, although even in those better days it probably still looked as if it had been put together using an avalanche and some string. Her family's castle squatted at the top of a small incline like a fat, grey, constipated sheep. As far as Humphrey could tell, it occupied a position of no strategic importance whatsoever. The castle was separated from the rest of the hamlet by a moat, which was now dry, and in which a group of dusty children were kicking around the desiccated, severed head of a fox.

Under the crumbling walls of the forgotten castle, even Humphrey in his unfashionable armour and faded tabard gave off a bright, alluring glamour, the promise of something fresh and exciting from outside this miserable place. The kids looked up as they approached, allowing the most enterprising of them to boot the fox's skull hard against the side of the moat. 'Goal!' she crowed, as the others groaned.

Conrad took one look at the rotting drawbridge and shook his head.

'No way,' he said. 'Jemima will go straight through.'

At that moment, the kid who had scored the goal called out, 'Why's your horse got such a big nose?'

'She's not a horse, she's an elephant,' said Conrad.

'Ele-pants,' said the kid. The other kids laughed, not pleasantly. 'You're a bit short for a giant, aren't you?' said another kid.

'Short-arse!' shouted the first kid.

'Dwarf!' yelled a third.

They all started chanting, 'Dwarf! Dwarf! Dwarf!'

Then the first one threw a stone. It bounced off Jemima's rear flank. She responded with a low, grumbling sound.

'On second thoughts, I'll take my chances with the drawbridge,' said Conrad.

'Home, sweet home,' muttered Elaine.

A Moorish guard in mismatched armour stood by the portcullis, playing a cup and ball game. Every time he jerked the ball up on its string to try to catch it in the cup, the visor of his helmet slammed down and he had to stop playing to open it again. Even so, as they reined in beside him, the guard was visibly annoyed at having to put the toy down.

'What now?' he said.

'Is that you, Samir?' said Elaine.

'Might be.'

'It's me. Lady Elaine. Of here.'

Samir pulled his visor up and squinted at Elaine. Satisfied, he dropped it down again. 'And this lot?' he said.

'They're with me.'

'All right,' said Samir, nodding. The visor of his helmet clanged.

'Were you here the day of the tourney?' Humphrey asked him. 'The day Sir Alistair Gilbert was kidnapped?'

'Still working in the kitchens then. Frank was on the gate.'

'And where's Frank?'

'Ran off, didn't he?'

Humphrey turned to Elaine. 'The guard ran off? So he's our prime suspect.'

Elaine shook her head. 'This didn't have anything to do with Frank,' she said.

'Because guards are so notoriously incorruptible,' said Humphrey.

'Oi, watch who you call corrupt, mate,' said Samir.

'He can call whoever he wants corrupt, and you can call him Sir,' said Conrad.

'Cool your boots, half-pint,' said Samir. 'That's a bleeding ugly horse you've got there.'

'She is an elephant and she could kill you with one kick.'

'With a nose like that, I reckon I could kill her with a cold,' said Samir.

'Would you please let us through?' said Elaine. 'I need to speak with my parents as a matter of urgency.'

'I'm not the one who's causing trouble,' said Samir, but he hauled up the portcullis all the same.

'What about this Frank?' Humphrey said to Elaine as they rode through the gate. 'What makes you so sure he had nothing to do with Sir Alistair's disappearance?'

'He's a good head taller than the Knight in Black,' said Elaine. 'Anyway, Frank had another reason for running away. He got a maiden pregnant.'

'Is that all?'

'It's not a very tolerant castle,' said Elaine. 'As you will see.'

The cobbles of the stable yard were cracked, with moss and weeds growing through them. The stables themselves outnumbered the horses by about five to one. There was a stench of stale horse piss and dried shit. Even the chickens scrabbling around in the dirt looked depressed.

'Reminds me of your bedroom, Conrad,' said Humphrey.

'Reminds me of your love life,' Conrad replied.

They dismounted and waited for someone to take charge of Jemima and the horses. After a while, Samir sauntered up.

'I double as stable hand,' he explained.

'Who's guarding the gate?' said Elaine.

'I gave one of the kids a coin,' said Samir.

'He's probably sharpening it to throw at us even as we speak,' said Conrad.

They all held out the reins of their mounts to Samir.

'I'm not taking that one,' Samir said, looking up at Jemima.

'Fine. Jemima, stay,' commanded Conrad, looking his elephant in the eye.

Jemima deposited a heap of dung pointedly near Samir's feet, then found a patch of early morning sun and lay down. Samir took the rest of the horses to the stables.

Elaine led Humphrey and Conrad along a pathway of cracked and sinking flagstones to a side door into the castle.

'I can see why you're in a hurry to get married,' said Humphrey.

'It's that or the convent,' said Elaine, 'or being burned as a witch.'

As they climbed the stairs to the main hall, they heard feet scurrying behind them and Samir appeared again, slightly out of breath and carrying a rusty bugle.

'I'm also the herald,' he said. 'What's your name?'

Thus it was that their entry into the throne room was preceded by a tuneless fanfare and the listless announcement of 'Sir Herbert Divvol and his squire. And your daughter.'

Lord and Lady du Mont looked at Humphrey as if their cat had brought in half a chewed ferret and then regurgitated the other half on their shoes.

'Did you find him yet?' asked Lord du Mont while Humphrey was still mid-bow.

Humphrey straightened. 'No,' he said.

Lord du Mont sucked unhappily on whatever was left of his teeth.

The couple were seated in tall wooden chairs on either side of a huge fireplace, under enormous matching fur rugs that were just claws and teeth away from being entire bears. The rugs were necessary because the hugeness of the fireplace was not matched by the hugeness of the fire. Instead a pitiful pile of twigs and fir cones crackled as merrily as anything could under the lord's disdainful glare. It was so damp in the room that the walls trickled with water, and so cold – far colder indoors than it was out – that it wouldn't have taken much more for that water to turn to icicles. At least icicles wouldn't stink of mould, thought Humphrey. He breathed through his mouth to avoid the smell, and watched his exhalation turn to sad little clouds. He was surprised they didn't immediately start raining.

'Elaine,' said Lord du Mont, as if he had been trying to remember who she was.

Elaine curtseyed to her father.

Lady du Mont screwed up her face. Humphrey took an instinctive step back before deciding that no, it was unlikely that she was preparing to spit. Elaine stepped up to her mother, placed a hand on her bony shoulder and deposited what for want of any other word he would have to call a kiss on her powdery white cheek.

Lord du Mont squinted at Conrad, who was slouching to avoid grazing his head against the ceiling.

'Are you supposed to be a giant of some kind?' he said.

'I'm still growing,' said Conrad.

'Couldn't you afford to get a full-sized one?' Lord du Mont asked Humphrey.

'Conrad is an excellent squire,' said Humphrey. This wasn't true, exactly, but Humphrey was damned if he was going to watch the kid be insulted by this pair of old prunes.

'*Conrad is an excellent squire*,' repeated Lord du Mont. 'What about you? Are you an excellent knight?' His tone of voice answered his own question.

'Father, please be nice. He's here to help me,' said Elaine.

'If you hadn't been so careless, you wouldn't need his help,' said Lord du Mont.

'It wasn't my fault,' said Elaine. 'You can hardly have expected me to fight off Sir Alistair's kidnapper with my bare hands.'

'If you were a better prize, your fiancé might have made more effort to fight the kidnapper himself.'

'Please could you all keep your voices down,' said Lady du

Mont, holding skeletal fingers to her temples. 'My humours are out of alignment.'

'I'll need a list of everyone who attended the tourney,' said Humphrey, 'including a breakdown of those who did not go through the melee into the joust round, and what injuries they sustained.'

'Sir Herbert Divoll,' said Lord du Mont, as if he hadn't heard him. 'I don't know of a Knight of the Round Table by that name.'

'That's not his name,' said Elaine.

Conrad reached out a hand to stop her from talking, but it was too late.

'What is your name, then?' said Lord du Mont.

Humphrey paused. 'Sir Humphrey du Val,' he said.

Lady du Mont gasped. 'Of Castle Maudit?'

'Not *of* Castle Maudit,' said Humphrey, 'but yes, I am the man you are thinking of.'

Lord du Mont began to laugh.

'Congratulations, Elaine,' he said. 'You've hired yourself the ladykiller.'

Elaine's brow creased with the beginning of recognition. Conrad took a step towards Lord du Mont, his hand reaching for his axe.

'Don't,' said Humphrey.

Conrad stopped.

'I'm sure you're mistaken,' said Elaine to her father.

'He murdered his own wife,' said Lord du Mont.

Elaine shook her head in disbelief.

'He's not even a Knight of the Round Table, are you, Humphrey?' Lord du Mont continued.

'Sir Humphrey,' said Conrad.

'I am a Knight of the Court of King Arthur,' said Humphrey.

'And where do you sit, exactly?' said Lord du Mont.

Humphrey hesitated, but there was no point lying. 'At the Table of Less Valued Knights.'

Humphrey felt his heart sink as Elaine's disappointed eyes turned towards him, but refused to betray himself with a reaction.

'Does that even exist?' said Lady du Mont. 'I thought it was just a myth.'

'Oh, it exists,' said her husband. 'It's Camelot's dirty little secret. They're the knights spotless King Arthur would rather you didn't know about. Well done, Elaine. Of all the champions in Camelot, you bring me this one. I'd expect nothing less of you. Good luck trying to find that fiancé of yours now.'

Elaine, white-faced, said nothing.

'Samir,' said Lord du Mont, 'fetch Sir Humphrey his list, and then they'll be on their way. And Elaine?'

'Yes, Father?'

'You're going with him. And if you don't find Sir Alistair, you needn't bother coming home.'

Seven

Humphrey chose a road almost at random, a deep lane heavily shaded by tall elms, which curved south-eastward away from Elaine's village and further into Tuft. For a long time the only sound was the steady beat of horses' hooves and elephant's feet. They were exhausted from riding all night, but Humphrey wasn't ready to stop yet; not until the rutted land of their quest had somehow been made smooth again.

'You know the story?' he said eventually.

'I didn't know it was you,' said Elaine. She knew without asking what he was referring to, having thought about little else since leaving her parents' castle.

'It's different from what you've heard. She tried to kill me first.'

'You don't have to tell me if you don't want to,' said Elaine.

'She left me,' Humphrey persisted anyway. 'But she made it look as though it were a kidnap. I traced her supposed kidnapper to Castle Maudit. He was a giant. His name was – well, it doesn't really matter what his name was, does it? It was Ulrich, anyway. A group of us assailed the castle. But it was a trap. I wasn't in the vanguard because it was decided – I decided – that the other knights would disarm the guards while I searched for my wife – who I thought was imprisoned, of course. Her name was . . .' Humphrey's voice cracked.

'Cecily,' said Conrad, from high above them on Jemima's back.

'Her name was Cecily,' said Humphrey, forcing himself to

carry on. 'Ulrich's forces killed all my companions. All my fellow knights. While I was down in the dungeons. Where Cecily was getting ready to cut my head off with the giant's sword. It was as big as she was. It was a terrible misjudgement on her part – she was always arrogant. Out of the corner of my eye I saw the blade flash. I was trained to react fast, I was a knight. I thought the swordsman was her captor, and I struck. Just one blow. It was enough.'

Elaine shook her head, struggling to take it all in.

'How long ago did this happen?' she said.

'How old are you, Conrad?' said Humphrey.

'Fifteen,' said Conrad.

'Fifteen years,' said Humphrey.

'So Conrad is . . .'

'Ulrich's son,' said Humphrey. 'He was the only survivor. He and I were the only survivors. I took him back with me to Camelot.'

'You raised him?' said Elaine.

'He was a baby. I couldn't leave him there. I couldn't kill him.'

'Though I think some people would have,' said Conrad.

'You raised your enemy's baby,' said Elaine.

Humphrey allowed himself to glance at her. She was looking at him with intense curiosity, but equally intense sympathy.

'There's no such thing as an enemy baby,' he said, looking ahead again, feeling his shoulders start to unstiffen.

'But you could have given him to someone else to bring up,' said Elaine. 'To a woman.'

'Are you saying that a man can't look after a child?'

'I'm saying that most men don't want to.'

'I suppose not.'

They rode in silence for a short while, Elaine allowing her understanding of Humphrey to rearrange itself.

'So what makes you different?' she asked. 'That you would choose to bring up a child by yourself, a child not your own?'

'Maybe it's me,' said Conrad. 'Maybe it's because I'm irresistible.'

Humphrey grinned for a moment. Then his smiled faded as the memories crowded back in.

'It wasn't as easy as just leaving,' he told Elaine. 'After I . . . after Cecily . . . I mean, afterwards. I had to fight my way through what remained of Ulrich's guards. I managed to defeat them all, but I was injured very badly. Then, as I was crawling to my horse, I heard crying. I followed the sound, and there was this baby. This very big baby.'

'Me,' said Conrad, unnecessarily.

'I don't remember how we got back to Camelot. But they tell me that when I arrived, I was fallen forward on my horse, close to death, and I was clutching Conrad and wouldn't let him go. So they let me take him to my room. And I kept him with me while I recovered. At first I wouldn't speak to anyone other than the baby. After a while, Arthur was so worried he sent Quentin in to see me.'

'Who's Quentin?' said Elaine.

'Oh God,' said Humphrey, 'Quentin is this cousin of Merlin's. The King keeps him at court to counsel knights who've been on bad quests. Arthur is a big believer in the healing power of conversation, as if drinking and wenches hadn't been doing a perfectly good job of obliterating painful memories for centuries without help from the likes of Quentin.'

'Quentin wears clothes that he makes himself,' said Conrad, as if that said it all.

'Yes,' said Humphrey. 'He says learning a craft is good for a man, focuses the spirit, calms the mind. That's the kind of horse-shit thing he's always saying when he's not trying to get you to tell him how you feel about things. Every morning for months he'd plonk himself down at the foot of my bed and say, "Hello, Sir Humphrey, how are you feeling today?"'

'How he was feeling was sick of the sight of Quentin,' said Conrad.

Elaine laughed.

'Anyway,' said Humphrey, 'Quentin thought that looking after the baby gave me a sense of purpose. That I'd bonded with him because we'd been through the same trauma.'

'And had you bonded with him?' said Elaine.

Humphrey shrugged. 'I don't know. He's all right.' He winked at Conrad. 'And Arthur agreed that when he was old enough he could be my page, and then my squire. So here he is.'

Conrad bowed, and Jemima lifted her trunk in salute.

'And the Table of Less Valued Knights?' said Elaine.

'It was supposed to be a temporary recuperative measure,' said Humphrey. 'That's what Arthur said, anyway. But I think the truth is that nobody wanted me at the Round Table any more, not when so many of our brothers had died on my behalf. Some of them thought the massacre was my fault. I don't entirely disagree.' He shook his head, not wishing to dwell on this. 'Anyway, time passed. I was busy with Conrad. And the long and the short of it is that Castle Maudit is the last quest I ever went on.'

'Until this one,' said Elaine.

'Yes.'

'For me.'

'Yes.'

'Thank you,' she said.

Humphrey watched his horse's brown head bob in front of him, the green of the trees above, and beyond that the sky, the washed-out grey of old linen, veiling the weak glow of the sun.

'The problem we have is that your kidnapper knight was in black,' he said.

'I'm sorry?' said Elaine, who had been lost in her own thoughts.

'You know the story of Gawain and the Green Knight, don't you?'

'Of course.'

'Tell it to me.'

'Why?'

'Just tell it to me.'

'One Christmas,' said Elaine hesitantly, repeating the story she'd heard from travelling storytellers from Camelot, 'a green knight came to the court of King Arthur. The knight offered his neck to whoever was willing to axe it, on condition that he returned to the Green Knight a year later to have his own head axed in turn. Gawain hewed the Green Knight's head from his body, but the knight did not die. Instead he picked up his head and rode away.'

'I wish I'd been there to see that,' said Conrad.

Humphrey laughed. 'It was my first Christmas at the Round Table. Everyone thought it was hilarious. When Gawain realised he was going to have to go and get his head cut off in return, he turned as green as the knight himself. Poor lad barely touched his goose. Anyway, carry on.'

'A year later, Gawain left on his quest. He searched high and low for the Green Knight,' Elaine said, 'but nobody had heard of such a man. He –'

'Stop right there,' Humphrey interrupted her. 'Do you see?'

'No. Not really.'

'*Nobody had heard of a green knight.* That's actually helpful. Find your Green Knight, and you know you've got your man. Knights in black, though, are two a penny. Every lowlife, every would-be renegade, gets himself a suit of black armour. They think it looks dangerous.'

'In fact it usually just looks tatty,' said Conrad. 'Black armour scuffs up really badly. Shows every scratch. Take it from someone who polishes the stuff for a living.'

'Not this suit,' said Elaine. 'It was shiny as the back of a beetle.'

'Is that right?' said Humphrey. He grinned. 'Well, there we go. That's our way in.'

'I don't understand,' said Elaine.

'You will.'

'Tell me.'

Humphrey's eyes twinkled but he would not be drawn.

'You remember what happened to Gawain, of course,' said Elaine. 'He refused to be seduced by the wife of a lord who had shown him hospitality. Even so, the wife insisted on giving Gawain what she said was a magic girdle to protect him from the Green Knight. Actually it had no power at all. It was Gawain's honesty that saved him. The Green Knight was the lord, her husband, in disguise, and he had sent his wife to test Gawain. Knowing Gawain to be virtuous, he chose not to cut off his head. The moral of the story is that you should be honest with me, and tell me why it matters that the armour was shiny.'

'The moral of the story,' countered Humphrey, 'is that if you are being honest with me, then we won't have any difficulty completing this quest. Are you being honest with me, Elaine?' The question had an edge that he'd only half intended.

'Of course I am,' said Elaine, but she suddenly found the road ahead of huge interest, and she wouldn't meet his eye.

Eight

The next hamlet they came to, on the far side of a low, broad hill, was a tiny place, even more deprived than Elaine's village had been. Humphrey had seen houses of cards more robust.

'Nobody sneeze,' he said. 'Especially not you, Jemima.'

A few tumbledown shacks sloped around a desultory green. In front of one of them a man in rags sat in the dirt, drinking ale from a cracked clay pot.

'All right, mate?' said Humphrey as they approached. 'Don't suppose you know where I could get my horse shod round here?'

The man blinked a couple of times at the sight of Conrad on his elephant. Then he shook his head. Alcohol had made him see stranger things than that. 'Baker's,' he said to Humphrey.

'They shoe horses at the bakery?' said Humphrey.

'No.' The man wiped his mouth with the back of his hand. 'At the smith's.' He looked at Humphrey as if he were an idiot. 'The smith's name is Baker, Jim Baker.' He pointed with his ale-streaked hand. 'Just outside the village, beyond those trees there.'

'My parents gather their taxes from these villages,' said Elaine once they were out of earshot. 'They're always complaining how little the villagers pay. But look at them! They've got nothing to give. King Leo takes the crown's share first, and this is all he leaves them with.'

The smithy was in no better repair than the other houses in

the village, except that it had a tall stone chimney that didn't seem in too imminent risk of collapse, and an anvil in the yard with bent horseshoe nails clustered in the dust around it. Hammering came from within the forge.

Humphrey dismounted and knocked at the door. After a few seconds, the hammering stopped and the door opened to reveal a barrel-chested, red-bearded man wiping his hands on a dull green apron. He nodded to Humphrey, and then his eye moved on to take in Elaine – not without appreciation – and finally Conrad and Jemima. He considered Jemima's enormous feet for several long moments. Then he spat.

'I'm not putting shoes on that one without chaining her up first,' he said. 'I'm not having a monster kicking the place down, I'm not insured for that.'

'I'm actually here for information,' said Humphrey.

'I'm not insured for having the shit kicked out of me for spilling other men's secrets neither.'

'Perhaps we can discuss this inside.'

The blacksmith looked up at Conrad.

'I'm not having your heavy indoors,' he said. 'I don't like threats. You may think you're clever, bringing a giant, but my sister's boy's nearly as big as he is. He can lift that anvil one-handed.'

'I juggle anvils,' said Conrad, untruthfully.

'I quite understand,' said Humphrey to the blacksmith. 'I don't suppose you have any objection to me bringing the maiden in?'

'Maidens are always welcome,' said the smith, managing to give the impression of looking down Elaine's dress even though she was sitting on her horse above him.

'I'd just as soon wait . . .' she said. Humphrey gave her a look. 'I mean, I'd be delighted to join you.'

She dismounted, handed her reins up to Conrad, and followed Humphrey into the forge.

It was a low, dark, airless place, hot and smoky, with heavy tools and pieces of mutilated metal everywhere. The smith cleared some unidentifiable items off a grimy wooden block and indicated it to Elaine with a flourish.

Elaine sat down reluctantly, glad that she was wearing a riding dress that was already smeared with mud, rainwater, and something which she refused to concede was horse shit.

'Now, what do you think I can do for you?' said the smith.

'I'd like to know who you've been making black armour for,' said Humphrey.

'I don't do black armour,' said the smith with a show of horror. 'This is a respectable forge.'

Humphrey's gaze slid towards a distinctly black-looking helm hanging beside the fire, then back to the smith. The smith maintained his look of outraged innocence.

'Lady Elaine,' said Humphrey.

Elaine frowned. Humphrey rubbed his thumb and forefinger together. Of course. She was the one running the quest, she was the one with the money. What little there was of it.

She drew out her small yellow velvet purse and tried to identify the least valuable coin in it by touch alone. There was one so thin it felt bendable. She withdrew it and tossed it to the smith. He caught it and pocketed it in one movement.

'Now that I think of it,' said the smith, 'I suppose that, in some lights, some of the armour I have made could be said to have a dusky hue. Perhaps, with the proper encouragement, I –'

'Let me stop you there,' interrupted Humphrey. 'We both know how this works. I'm going to bribe you to tell me who you've made black armour for, then you're going to tell me who you've made black armour for. I can't stand all this coy toing and froing, it gets right on my wick. Name your price.'

'Twenty coins,' said the smith.

'No.'

'Nineteen.'

'No.'

'You're not going to suggest a counter-offer?'

'No. I can't be bothered. You're just going to carry on until I've had enough.'

The smith sighed. 'Three?' he said.

Humphrey nodded at Elaine. She dug three more coins out of her purse, shuddering when her fingers brushed against the smith's greasy palm as she handed them over.

'Anything within the last couple of months,' said Humphrey.

'There's a man called Tony the Outlaw. Really he's the cooper's son, only there's not a lot of call for barrels at the moment. Not a lot of call for anything, round here. So he got himself some black armour, and now he's robbing the rich.'

'To feed the poor?' said Elaine.

'To feed himself,' said the smith. 'And to feed me, now I think of it. He still hasn't paid the armour off. Why are you looking for men in black armour, anyway? Need a dodgy job doing?'

Humphrey shook his head. 'We're looking for suspects in the kidnapping at the du Mont tourney last week.'

'Is that right?' said the smith. 'I heard he did it himself after meeting the in-laws.'

'Shall we go find this Tony before he hears we're coming and runs away?' said Elaine to Humphrey.

'You're Lady Elaine, aren't you?' said the smith. He didn't wait for a reply. 'You're as pretty as they say, but I'm surprised they managed to find two men willing to fight for your dirty hand.'

Humphrey reached for his sword, only to find that he'd left it with Conrad alongside the rest of his armour. The smith laughed.

'Let's go,' said Elaine.

She grabbed Humphrey's arm and dragged him back outside.

'My family aren't popular in these parts,' she said to him as the door closed behind them. 'You get used to people saying things like that. It doesn't matter.'

'What happened?' said Conrad as he handed them the reins of their horses.

'The man in there didn't take kindly to being bribed,' said Humphrey. 'I think he was unhappy with the price we agreed. He gave us a few choice remarks about Elaine and her family along with our information.'

Conrad looked furious, but Elaine said, 'Just leave it. Please.'

Conrad nodded. Humphrey and Elaine mounted up and they all started back towards the village green.

'Are we allowed to bribe people?' said Conrad. 'It doesn't sound very knightly.'

'When did you become so puritanical?' said Humphrey. 'There isn't actually a prohibition against it in the Knights' Code. In fact, the Knights' Code relies a lot on interpretation. Lots of stuff about goodness, honour, faith and truth. Not so many specifics. And I'm not a Knight of the Round Table anyway. There's a reason the Less Valued Knights are less valued. It seems like a waste not to take advantage of it. Unless you have any better ideas?'

'Goodwill?' said Elaine.

Humphrey gave that one space so that everyone could admire it.

'Anyway,' he said, 'you wanted to know why it mattered that the kidnapper's armour was shiny. It was obviously brand new. So we'll find out who's been commissioning black armour lately, via bribes or "goodwill", cross-reference it against the list of knights that we know were participating in the tourney and therefore have an alibi, and that should narrow things down a bit. This Tony "the Outlaw" Cooper is, astonishingly, not on the list.'

'That's a shame because he sounds like a real catch,' said Elaine.

'So we'd better go and pay him a visit,' concluded Humphrey.

'Are you going to joust him?' said Conrad. 'Not another bribe?'

'Yes, Conrad, I'm going to joust him.'

'Hurray!' said Conrad. 'A bit of action at last!'

Nine

They stopped by a copse of oak trees on the way back to the village, so that Humphrey could squeeze back into his armour and Conrad could cut him down a jousting lance. Oak wasn't the ideal wood, especially green, but beggars could not be choosers, and nor could Less Valued Knights in a hurry.

'When was the last time you fought a duel?' asked Elaine, as Conrad tightened Humphrey's straps and tucked patches of goatskin under the bits of armour that chafed the most.

'How old are you, Conrad?' said Humphrey.

'You know how old I am,' said Conrad.

'You mean, not since Maudit? Not even in tournaments?' said Elaine.

'I've had enough men trying to kill me in my line of work without inviting more of them to do it for fun. Bloody hell, I swear this armour's shrunk. You didn't leave it out in the rain, did you, Conrad?'

'That must be it,' said Conrad.

'Are you going to be all right?' said Elaine.

Humphrey smiled at her. 'Are you worried about me?' he said.

'I don't want you to get hurt. Not because of me.'

Humphrey laughed. 'Don't worry. Really. I think I can handle Tony, the Outlaw of – what is this village called again?'

'It's too small to have a name,' said Conrad.

'But that's exactly the kind of thing that you would say in a story, just before we find out that Tony the Outlaw of Too Small To Have A Name is really good at jousting,' said Elaine.

'Do you know why stories are stories?' said Humphrey.

'Why?'

'Because unusual things happen in them.'

'That's what you'd say in the story too!'

'Honestly, there is no reason to be concerned. They train us pretty well at Camelot. Better than they do in Too Small To Have A Name. Isn't that right, Conrad?'

'Fifteen years is a long time,' said Conrad.

Humphrey shook his head, as much as he could in the tight neck guard.

'I spent five years as a Knight of the Round Table, and that doesn't count for nothing,' he said. 'Squire and page before that. So shut up the pair of you, before you start making me nervous as well.'

Elaine kept quiet while Humphrey checked his greaves. Then she said, 'But what if this Tony's the kidnapper?'

'Then we'll be damn lucky. Because your quest will be over in about half an hour's time.'

They made their way back to the village green where the man who'd been drinking ale from a cracked pot was still sitting, still drinking ale.

'Hello again,' said Humphrey. 'Don't suppose you know where Tony, the cooper's son, lives?'

'Tony the Outlaw?' said the drinker. 'That house right there.' He pointed.

'Thanks,' said Humphrey.

'Why would you go to all the trouble of wearing black armour if everyone already knows who you are?' said Elaine.

'Why bother being an outlaw if you don't get to wear the outfit?' said Conrad, who secretly thought black armour looked cool.

'Everyone in the village may know who he is,' said

Humphrey, 'but you need to wear something intimidating when you're robbing strangers otherwise they'll think you're an amateur and refuse to give you their money. People judge by appearances.'

Elaine nodded. She knew all about that.

Tony the Outlaw's house was one of the most decrepit in a very decrepit selection. The front door – a few planks of unpainted wood, roughly hewn, with a rope latch – had fallen from the frame and was leaning against the side of the building. Through the doorway, a young man with a light haze of stubble on his chin could be seen, standing at a table in his long under-wear, mixing a pot of whitewash and whistling.

Humphrey dismounted and passed the reins of his horse to Conrad.

'You stay back this time,' he said to Elaine. 'He might be dangerous.'

Humphrey adjusted his armour so that it wasn't cutting off the circulation to his legs, made sure his shield was in place, and then, in the absence of a door, knocked on the door frame.

Tony the Outlaw looked up.

'Oh crap,' he said.

'You might want to think about changing your name, mate,' said Humphrey.

'I didn't think I'd need to. We're a long way from Camelot here. Though not far enough, apparently.' Tony let go of the stick he'd been stirring the paint with and wiped his hands on a rag. 'What brings you here?' he asked. 'You can't possibly be looking for me. I'm strictly local. Surely King Arthur's got bigger fish to fry?'

'Quest,' said Humphrey. He indicated Elaine with his head. Tony squinted out the door and waved at Elaine, and Elaine, despite herself, waved back. When Tony saw the giant on elephant-back beside her, he did a double take. 'We're after something very specific,' Humphrey continued, 'so chances are you've got nothing to worry about. Where were you on the day of the tourney at the du Mont castle?'

Tony dragged his attention away from Jemima. 'Let me think . . .' he said.

Humphrey put his hand on his sword. 'Would you like me to jog your memory?'

Tony sighed. 'Bollocks,' he said. 'Right. This isn't going to look good. Tuft knights were all busy with the joust, local noblemen were all out watching. I took the opportunity to do a little bit of, ah, break and enter.'

'And take and leave?' said Humphrey.

'That too,' said Tony.

'You didn't go near the tournament itself?' said Humphrey.

'No, I hate the things. Never been a jousty kind of bloke. Although, I'm guessing . . .' He eyed Humphrey's armour.

'Yup,' said Humphrey. 'Sorry.'

'Can I at least put my armour on first?'

'Course. But where I can see you.'

'Back room, then,' said Tony.

Humphrey turned to the others. 'Conrad, if you hear me call out, you know what to do.'

Conrad cracked his enormous knuckles.

'That's quite a squire you've got,' said Tony as he led the way into the back of the house.

'He's just standing by in case you've got an ambush waiting for me back there,' said Humphrey. 'I've been caught out before.'

'Fair enough,' said Tony.

There was nobody in the back room, though, just a dusty sea of worn clothing and unwashed bedclothes, the incriminating black armour in a heap on the floor by the window.

'Sorry about the mess,' said Tony. 'I'm doing a few home repairs at the moment. It's something I do on the side. Though it's not going that well otherwise they might call me Tony the Builder.' Tony was pulling on his black cuisses and greaves. 'So how did you find me?' he went on. 'Bigwigs been complaining to Arthur?'

'Actually, we're not even looking for you. We're looking for the person who kidnapped the winner of the tourney. You didn't hear anything about that, did you?'

'Well, obviously I heard that it happened – we were all laughing about it down the Cock and Bottle, a knight being snatched like a screaming virgin. But nobody's got a clue who did it.'

'No rumours, even?'

'Nothing much. Nobody likes the du Monts, they were pleased to see them get egg on their faces. I think if it was someone we knew who'd done it, they'd have been boasting about it.'

'Lady Elaine's unpopular too?'

'The daughter? Was that her outside?'

'Yes.'

'She looks like a nice maid. Does it matter what people say?' Tony held up his arms. 'Can you help me buckle this breastplate?'

Humphrey yanked at the straps.

'It'll definitely be a joust, then?' said Tony. He looked rather dashing in his black armour.

'Sorry,' said Humphrey. 'I have to fight you, for the glory of God and King Arthur. Believe me, I'd rather not. But you've got to give the people what they want.'

By the time Tony had saddled up his horse, a skinny, mangy creature which spent most of its life tethered to a post in his back garden, and he and Humphrey had made their way to the village green, quite a crowd had gathered to watch. The villagers were excited to have a real knight on their patch, taking on their very own outlaw. Still more thrilling was the news of a giant riding a monster, which attracted a throng of children, all desperate to have a turn on Jemima's back.

'Nobody's frightened of me,' said Conrad, lifting a six-year-old girl up onto the elephant, and walking Jemima around in a circle. 'Why is nobody ever frightened of me?'

To give the villagers a proper spectacle, Humphrey and Tony the Outlaw feigned a series of near misses and light clashes of shields before Humphrey finally tipped Tony – a poor sportsman at best – off his horse and into the churned-up grass, to a chorus of oohs and aahs from the assembled throng. Even though the result was a foregone conclusion, Elaine was relieved when it was over, with no more damage done than a dent to Tony's black armour.

Afterwards, Tony swore fealty to Humphrey, as was traditional, and vowed to devote his life to the good of humanity from then on. Humphrey embraced him, then sent him on his way, to whitewash his house and no doubt to plot further crimes.

'Which will now all be committed in my name,' Humphrey muttered to his squire.

'It's not a perfect system,' said Conrad.

'And we're no closer to finding who kidnapped Sir Alistair,' said Elaine.

'On the contrary, we're one man down,' said Humphrey. He didn't speculate as to how many men they had to go.

Ten

They pitched their tents in a meadow close to Too Small To Have A Name, relieved to be sleeping off the long journey at last. Elaine had a tent to herself, within screaming distance, as Conrad put it, of Humphrey and his squire's – 'That's not exactly reassuring, Conrad,' she said. Jemima slept in front of Elaine's tent flap, though, which made her feel less vulnerable. Conrad and Humphrey shared a tent – 'Within snoring distance,' Elaine retorted later. (She assumed the giant-sized snorts she'd heard coming from their tent were from Conrad's epic nose, but in fact they emanated from Humphrey, while Conrad snoozed as quietly as a baby lamb.)

Conrad got up early the next day and went to buy them a meat pie for their breakfast, from a stall in the village that Tony the Outlaw had recommended. On the way back he passed a reasonably sanitary-looking midden and pinched a handful of vegetable scraps for Jemima. By the time he got back to camp, Elaine had emerged from her tent and was rubbing herbs on her teeth to clean them. There was no sign of Humphrey. Conrad went over to the tent and held the flap open so that sunlight shone directly into his master's face. Humphrey dragged his head out of the glare and opened his eyes.

'Good morning!' said Conrad.

'Morning? Since when do we get up in the morning?'

Conrad lifted the tent flap further up, so that Humphrey's face was in the sunbeam again. After a moment or two,

Humphrey gave in and pushed himself up to a seated position. 'It's a long time since I've slept on a bedroll,' he said. 'Are you sure I didn't lose that joust yesterday? Bloody hell.'

He hauled himself out from under the blankets, feeling a familiar stab of pain in his right knee, which no longer pointed in the same direction as his left thanks to a Saracen with a long lance and a short temper who'd knocked him off his horse many years ago. That was only to be expected. What had started to bother him lately were the other, newer pains which had never troubled him as a younger man. His feet felt uneven on the ground and his shins protested as he walked. His back seemed to be made of one resisting piece that refused on any account to bend. He was sure that one of his shoulders had lodged itself inches higher than the other. And why did the joints of his fingers hurt? That didn't even make sense.

He splashed some water onto his face in an effort to make himself presentable, pulled on his leggings and shirt, and went outside into the unexpectedly warm caress of the day. Despite himself, he smiled. He'd forgotten how much he liked being out of doors.

In the space beside the tents, Elaine was sitting on her saddlebag, holding a pewter plate with a slice of pie on it, which she was looking at with a marked lack of enthusiasm.

'What's the matter? Isn't it good?' asked Conrad, who had taken half the pie for himself. He tended to lean towards quantity rather than quality when it came to food.

'It's delicious, thank you,' said Elaine. There was no evidence to suggest that she'd actually tasted the pie. 'Good morning, Sir Humphrey.'

'Morning,' said Humphrey, wondering what he'd done to be busted back to 'Sir'. 'Is everything all right?'

'Absolutely,' said Elaine. 'It's just . . .' She paused, then carried on in a rush. 'Excuse me if I'm speaking out of turn,' she said. 'Obviously, I'm not a knight. And you're the one running the quest. But it seems to me, I'm not sure how efficient it is, to be going one by one to all the blacksmiths in Tuft, bribing them to tell us who they've made black armour for recently. If every village has a forge, it could take months to visit them all, and goodness knows what will have happened to Sir Alistair by the time we find him. If we find him. We don't even know that the kidnapper used a forge to get the armour made. He might have a private armourer, a lot of the good families do. And there might be secret armourers who only service the criminal fraternity and aren't to be found shoeing horses in little Tuft villages.'

Humphrey and Conrad stared at her.

'Did you sleep well?' said Humphrey.

'Not really,' said Elaine.

Humphrey took his slice of pie and sat down on the grass, which was still damp from dew.

'I'm sorry that you're not happy with my strategy,' he said carefully. 'Is there another approach that you'd like to suggest?'

'Well, I don't want to tread on any toes,' said Elaine, 'but I would imagine that the kidnapper targeted Sir Alistair either as an attack on my family, or as an attack on Sir Alistair or his family. Or, possibly, it has something to do with him being one of King Leo's knights. Those are the main theories I'm working with. I think we've probably ruled out it being anything to do with my family, otherwise we'd have received a ransom demand, or a message of triumph at the very least. So, if it were my quest, which it sort of is, I would head either to King Leo's castle, or to Sir Alistair's family seat, to find out whether there is any kind of motive for the crime. But I don't really know what I'm talking about.'

Humphrey nodded slowly, chewing on his pie. There wasn't a lot to chew, but it gave his mouth something to do while his brain worked. Conrad watched Humphrey's face, trying and failing to read his mood.

'Thank you for your thoughts,' Humphrey said at last. 'Given your concerns, what I propose is that we plot a course in the direction of Sir Alistair's home town, but we continue to stop at the forges we pass on the way, in case they have any information that may be useful to us. If that's acceptable to you?'

Elaine nodded, but after a couple of nods her head started to go into a shake. 'It's just, I'm in an awful hurry to find him,' she said.

'I'm aware of that,' said Humphrey.

'We're supposed to be getting married in less than a fortnight.'

'I'm sure, under the circumstances, that the priest won't mind postponing.'

'And I don't have unlimited funds. If you spend all our money on bribes, we're not going to have any left for food.'

'We can hunt for food,' said Humphrey. 'I brought my bow and arrows.'

'If you're sure . . .' said Elaine reluctantly.

'Trust me,' said Humphrey.

'Very well.' But Elaine didn't look happy. She handed her plate to Conrad and stood up. 'You can have mine if you like,' she said. 'I'm not very hungry. I'm going to . . .' She struggled to find an elegant turn of phrase. 'Perform my ablutions. Please don't come behind the tent.'

'She's not wrong, is she?' said Conrad to Humphrey, as Elaine disappeared around the side of her tent.

'No,' said Humphrey, his eyes on the space where she had been a moment ago. 'She's not.'

Eleven

Despite Elaine's misgivings, they continued to stop at all the forges along the road towards Sir Alistair's home, which was located at the far end of Tuft. Apart from checking on the buyers of black armour, Humphrey knew that smiths had loud voices – not only in that they had to shout above the tumult of the forge, but also in the sense that with so many travellers stopping to have their horses seen to, news travelled fast from smithy to smithy. If there were any rumours about the identity of the Knight in Black, a forge would be a good place to pick them up. Unfortunately, what happened was that word of their quest preceded them on the forge grapevine, making the smiths more recalcitrant and forcing the cost of bribes up.

They all hated visiting the forges, Humphrey included. Forges were stuffy, noisy and cramped, clouded with thick smoke that choked their eyes and throats and left their skin smeared with soot. But the more restless Conrad and Elaine became, the more Humphrey insisted on stopping at each and every forge, refusing to be in the wrong. Humphrey thought it was a bit rich for the two of them to complain; they weren't the ones who had to fight duels with every black-armour-wearing miscreant in Tuft, sometimes several in a day. When Conrad moaned that he was getting blisters from having to chop down so many trees to make lances, Humphrey stripped to his britches to show them both the huge yellow and purple bruises he was covered in from having been knocked off his horse so many times. Whatever he might claim, fifteen years without a quest made even the best of knights quite rusty when it came to jousting.

Meanwhile, although they still tried to ride incognito, they could hardly camouflage the individual who – to his vast irritation – was becoming known as Sir Humphrey's monster-riding jester. They were assailed at every turn by people who wanted to see Jemima for themselves, or who had heard that touching her thick grey hide would cure any ailment. Others, knowing that there was a knight travelling with the famous monster, chased after the group with quests of their own, which they hoped to entice Humphrey to take on.

'This,' Humphrey told Elaine, 'is why I don't travel in armour. A knight's work is never done. Rescuing damsels, fighting sorceresses, getting cats out of trees, opening tight jars. And all for honour, God's least fungible reward.'

And yet he was in no hurry to finish this quest. Back at Camelot, he'd got up late, eaten, drunk, gambled, caroused, got bored, got fat. That was his life. He hadn't realised how much he'd missed this: being on his horse, out in the world, with a sense of purpose for once. Even the fights were becoming exhilarating, as the more practice he got, the more often he won. As for having Elaine riding beside him – beautiful, funny, smart Elaine, who not only sang along with Conrad's dirty travelling songs but made up extra verses – who wouldn't want that to carry on for as long as possible? Of course, he reminded himself, she was betrothed. But perhaps, if it took him a long time to complete the quest . . . long enough for the kidnapper to tire of Sir Alistair . . . *What, and so the kidnapper kills him? That's your happy ending?* He tried again. What if he never found Sir Alistair . . . *So he stays locked up for ever, while you deflower his bride?* There was no satisfactory answer. But for as long as he didn't find Sir Alistair while still being able to demonstrate that he was looking, he felt that could enjoy being with Elaine without guilt.

Elaine, however, was growing more desperate with every passing day. Finally, on the morning of the day that should have been her wedding, she stared into her breakfast bowl, nauseated by the congealed beans therein, as tears brimmed in her eyes.

'We're never going to find him,' she said.

'You need to be patient. These things take time,' said Humphrey, aware of how lame he sounded.

'Sir Alistair and I should be getting married right now.' Her throat was cramped with the effort of not crying in front of them. 'Instead I'm cold and damp and I haven't slept properly for two weeks, and I'm in dirty clothes, sitting in a field with a disgraced ex-knight and a miniature giant, and we're no closer to finding out what happened to the man who is supposed to be my husband, and if we don't find him soon I may as well die.'

She got up from the fireside and went into her tent, pulling the flap shut behind her. It wasn't as effective as slamming a door, but the message was clear.

She barely said another word all day. When Humphrey fought his duel, against a woman this time, who had hair cropped short and a surprisingly deft way with a lance, Elaine didn't even watch, but chose that moment to go and refill their water skins at a nearby well. Humphrey, distracted by her absence, lost concentration, allowing the female outlaw to knock him from his horse, much to the delight of Conrad and the gathered crowd.

That night, Elaine went to bed without any supper. Humphrey decided to turn in early too, after enduring a seemingly endless meal of uninspiring food – breakfast's beans reheated, which were in turn last night's beans reheated – and relentless mockery from his squire.

Several hours later, however, he surfaced queasily from the depths of sleep to find himself being shaken by a determined hand.

'Careful,' he groaned, as the hand was gripping the very spot on his shoulder where the lady miscreant's lance had hit.

'Shh,' whispered the voice of his awakener.

Humphrey blinked in the darkness. The owner of the hand was Elaine.

'What are you –'

'Shh,' she whispered again. 'I think I heard something. Men. Near my tent.'

Humphrey nodded. He emerged swiftly from his bedroll, pulled on his boots and a tunic over his long underwear, and buckled a sword over the top.

They crept outside. There was no moon, but the stars were bright. Elaine's long white nightgown, unlaced at the throat, stood out against the darkness.

'Do you see anything?' she said.

'Not yet,' said Humphrey, who had seen nothing other than Elaine.

'It was coming from down the slope, near the river. I thought I heard voices.'

Humphrey set off towards the riverbank. Elaine followed him, catching up and slipping her hand into the crook of his arm. He felt the heat of it like a burn.

'Over here?' he whispered, his voice a little shaky.

'I think so,' Elaine replied, moving even closer to him as they approached the river, its water glinting under the constellations. Humphrey caught the scent from her hair. She appeared to be wearing perfume, which was strange for the middle of the night. His heart beat hard in his chest and he tried to keep his mind on the brigands who might lie in wait.

'I'm so glad you're here,' Elaine said to him. 'I feel safe with you.'

This stopped Humphrey for the slightest moment. There was something about the way Elaine said it that didn't quite ring true. Then he decided he was being ridiculous. Why shouldn't she feel safe with him? He was a knight. She was a damsel. That was the way things worked.

'I'm sure there's nothing to worry about,' he said, 'and if there is, I'll deal with it.'

Elaine responded with a squeeze of his arm. Humphrey scanned the darkness, looking for any sign of movement. Nothing. He crept forward. The slope became steeper close to the river-bank, and as Humphrey picked his way down he felt the sudden loss of Elaine's hand, as she slipped and fell with a shriek.

'Are you all right?' said Humphrey, dropping down beside her.

'It's my ankle,' said Elaine, wincing. 'I turned on it as I went down. I hope it's not broken.'

She lifted her nightgown to rub her ankle, her breath coming in ragged gasps. Humphrey tried not to let his eyes stray towards the revealed skin. Then she said, 'I think it may just be sprained. Do you mind checking?'

He hesitated.

'I'm sure you've handled plenty of broken bones before,' said Elaine.

Humphrey laughed nervously. 'My own, as often as not.'

He took hold of her ankle, telling himself there was nothing strange about this. He had done it for plenty of friends. He and Elaine were friends, weren't they? Her leg was delicately boned and pale, her skin impossibly smooth. To his annoyance, his hands were trembling a little, and he hoped that she wouldn't notice. Gently, he turned her bare foot first one way, then the other. It moved easily. He placed her foot back on the grass, taking just a moment too long to let it go.

He worked hard to keep his voice steady. 'It's probably a sprain. How does it feel?'

'A bit better,' said Elaine. 'It was probably just the shock of the fall. I'm sure the pain will pass. But do you mind if we wait here until I'm ready to walk on it again? I'm afraid to be alone in the dark.'

Humphrey remembered how she had ridden all the way from Tuft to Camelot alone in the dark. 'Take your time,' he said.

'Thank you. You're very kind.'

She leaned towards him slightly, so that their arms were almost touching. Somehow it felt more intimate than a touch itself. He felt his mouth go dry.

Maidens used to do this when he was young. Before he was dishonoured. Feign injury, feign catastrophe, feign anything to get close to him. But it didn't seem like the kind of thing that Elaine would do. She was so preoccupied with finding her fiancé, she'd been mute with misery all day. Of course, she didn't love Sir Alistair. He knew that. Was it possible . . . ? He felt flustered, as if she were the knight and he were the maiden. He didn't know what to do next.

'I think they're gone,' he said, sticking to the script they had agreed on.

'Who?' said Elaine.

'The men you heard?'

'Oh yes,' said Elaine vaguely. 'They must have run away when they heard us coming.'

There had been women in his life, of course. Plenty before Cecily and plenty since. Serving maids these days mostly, though there was nothing wrong with that, they were as sensible and good-humoured as any other girl, indeed more so than some ladies he could think of. When he'd sat at the Round Table, the bored wives of other Round Table knights, or the ambitious wives of Errant Companions, sometimes made it clear that his attentions would be welcomed. He'd try to avoid them, disliking their lack of sincerity and not wanting to risk his companionship with his brethren. Of course, once he got demoted to Less

Valued, he was suddenly invisible to those very same ladies who'd so admired him the day before. So he was no naïf. He could tell what Elaine wanted him to do, and he knew he wanted the same thing. But something about this situation was paralysing him.

'The stars are beautiful tonight, aren't they?' said Elaine. She wasn't looking at the stars, though, she was looking at him. He was almost sure he could see the invitation in her eyes. He cast his misgivings aside.

'I couldn't care less about the stars,' he said, and he leaned over and kissed her.

Sometimes a kiss can hit you harder than a lance with the force of a galloping horse behind it. This was one of those times. But suddenly Elaine pushed him away.

'I'm sorry,' she said, almost yelping in distress. 'I can't do this.'

And he realised that this was her true voice, and that everything else she had said since waking him up had come from a place of falseness. A hole opened up in his soul and his heart fell through it.

'Lady Elaine,' he said, looking away, across the water. 'Surely you know that I will follow this quest through to the end, no matter what? You don't have to repay me in this way.'

'It's not that,' said Elaine, in a voice of anguish. 'I wanted to . . . I mean, I felt . . . I truly felt . . . But my intention was base. Please forgive me.'

'Of course I forgive you,' said Humphrey. 'There is nothing to forgive.'

'I wish I could explain,' said Elaine. 'I'm so sorry.' She reached towards him for a moment, then drew her hand back without touching him. 'But I can't. I can't. I'm sorry.'

'I understand. You are betrothed to Sir Alistair,' said Humphrey.

'It's not that,' Elaine said again.

'Then what is it?'

Elaine shook her head. She wiped tears from her eyes. Then she got up and ran back to her tent, on her ankle which was not at all injured, leaving Humphrey alone under those stars which were indeed beautiful, but so cold.

Twelve

The next day, Elaine rose for breakfast early. By the time Humphrey emerged from his tent she had finished her meal and returned to her own tent to pack up for the day's ride. Conrad was still chattering about the woman who had unhorsed Humphrey, because in his world that had happened the day before, and not a lifetime ago. Both Humphrey and Elaine took extra care over the grooming and saddling of their horses that morning, thoroughly brushing manes and tails, closely examining hooves for mud and stones, ensuring the perfect alignment of bridle straps. If they didn't speak to each other it was perfectly normal because they were preoccupied with the journey ahead.

The road took them along the riverbank that had been the setting for the scene of the night before. By daylight the river seemed innocuous enough, the water twinkling prettily under the sun, the road lined with chestnut trees which provided welcome shade. It should have been a pleasant ride. But the silence between Humphrey and Elaine grew until it was a fourth companion which even Conrad couldn't ignore. First he stopped teasing Humphrey, put off by the lack of response, and started to sing instead. Then, when Elaine didn't join in, he stopped that too. A heavy sleeper, he had no idea that his master had been woken by Elaine in the night, or what had passed between them. All he knew was that both Humphrey and Elaine had gone to bed angry and that they appeared to have got up even angrier. He fretted that he had done something wrong. Was it the food?

Was it just him, causing annoyance merely by being himself? He placed one of his hands palm down on Jemima's warm neck, trying to take comfort in her steadfastness, but it wasn't enough for the elephant to like him. He needed his companions to like him too. Meanwhile, for Humphrey and Elaine, enormous, anxious Conrad on his waddling elephant had no more presence than a cloud.

Shortly before noon they reached a point where the river diverted into a wood which grew so thick that Conrad and Jemima would not be able to pass without uprooting dozens of trees. Humphrey stopped, and the other two drew up alongside. Conrad looked down at him, awaiting instruction. Elaine gazed straight ahead.

'I'm sure we can skirt around it,' said Humphrey, in a light voice that sounded unnatural to him. 'It doesn't look that big a forest.'

'Whatever you say,' said Conrad.

Elaine only nodded.

So Humphrey led the way across the heath that bordered the wood. As he rode, he tried to think of the words he might say to Elaine that would make everything normal again. It was only a kiss. How many maidens had he kissed? He had thought her willing. He could simply apologise. But she had leaned into him, had responded, he was sure of it. Then why had she pushed him away? This was the path that his thoughts had been following all day, and it circled back on itself, over and over. There was only one other direction his thoughts were inclined to go, which was to remind himself of what he knew, that women were not to be trusted, and what happened when you followed your heart instead of your head; but that was a road he had fifteen years' practice in ignoring, and he was able to turn away from it now.

As his thoughts started around the circle yet again, a horrifying scream came from the direction of the trees. Before he had fully registered that a man was galloping directly towards him brandishing a huge black sword, blows were already raining down on him. Just in time he managed to draw his sword. As he fought for his life he realised that it was the man who was screaming, that he was, in fact, barely more than a boy, and that, even as he hacked at Humphrey with his sword, he had his eyes screwed tightly shut.

PART TWO

Thirteen

A week before Pentecost, the morning of her father's death, Martha had been awoken by the sound of bells. This was wrong. Generally Martha woke up and rang a bell, and her maid Deborah came. Having been woken up, she did ring her bell to find out what was going on, but the delicate sound was drowned out by the clang of the louder bells outside, and nobody answered.

Growing tired of waiting, she pushed back her bed curtains and got out of bed. It was still dark in her room, and no one had been in yet to light the fire, so it must have been unfathomably early. She wrapped herself in a long, moss-green cashmere dressing gown, opened up a pair of shutters blinkering a window, and peered out into the icy morning. In the pre-dawn light she could see a few figures hurrying from one place to another, but no sign of an army, mob or fire. Nothing important, then. She yawned. Pulling the shutters to, she shuffled back towards her bed.

Just then, the door to her bedchamber burst open and Deborah flew in and prostrated herself on the floor. This was also wrong. Deborah usually strolled in chatting, as if she and Martha were already mid-conversation. There was never any prostrating.

'Deborah, what –' began Martha, but Deborah interrupted her.

'The King is dead, long live the Queen!' she said.

Martha sank down on the edge of her bed, while Deborah alternated bowing, curtseying, trying to make her mistress drink a cup of hot brandy, and saying 'The King is dead, long live the Queen,' over and over. Martha waited for grief to come, but it too was drowned out by the incessant ringing of the bells.

The death of her father should have come as no surprise. He had been ill for many years, a feebleness of the mind that had taken hold not long after her brother, Jasper, had died. At first, the court had taken his confusion and mood swings for grief. By the time the King could no longer tell the difference between Martha and her dead brother, calling her Jasper and enquiring about her exploits at the Round Table, it was impossible to hide the severity of his condition, and a Regency Council had been established to take on the day-to-day business of ruling.

As far as Martha was concerned, it was pretty easy to tell the difference between her and Jasper, for reasons quite aside from him being male and dead. Jasper had been tall and muscular and handsome, witty and intelligent and accomplished. He had been a Knight of the Round Table in Camelot, with all the goodness and bravery that implied. He had travelled all over the land on quests, having experiences and gaining wisdom and meeting people, one of whom was a Pict he was supposed to be civilising in Scotland, who hadn't wanted to be civilised and who had cut off Jasper's head. But if that hadn't happened, he would have had all the attributes which would have made him a wonderful king.

Martha, on the other hand – even Martha didn't know what Martha was. She presided over jousts, opened country fairs, exclaimed at the beauty of babies and judged vegetables. She shook hands. She sat at banquets next to foreign dignitaries who talked across her to other foreign dignitaries or lectured her on their own achievements. She bestowed favours upon and accepted love poetry from knights and the sons of lords who had never actually spoken to her. She wore stiff dresses and uncomfortable shoes. She smiled.

But after her brother died, she woke sometimes in the middle of the night, with her heart pounding and her mouth dry. She would think *I am going to be queen one day*, but she had no idea what qualities she would bring to the role. Would she be a fair queen or a cruel one? She didn't know if she was cruel or fair. She didn't know how she was going to exude authority and actually rule, because unlike her brother, who was born to be the King, she was a nothing person with nothing to offer except that she existed. And now her father had died and she was the Queen and the one thing that she did know was that she wasn't ready yet.

There was a knock at the door.

'Come in,' she said.

Sir John Penrith, the Chancellor and head of the Regency Council, bounced into the room and gave a jaunty little bow. Deborah curtseyed. This was her day for curtseying to everyone.

'The King is dead, long live the Queen,' said Sir John in cheery greeting. He was a skinny man with a pot belly and long white eyebrows that grew like a peacock's tail feathers.

'Good morning, Sir John,' said Martha.

She didn't know Sir John particularly well. Mainly she saw him in chapel, where she noticed he had the habit of sticking his tongue in the Communion wine.

'Everybody's waiting,' he said, raising one of those eyebrows at the sight of her robe. 'I think it would make a better impression if you were dressed.'

'Waiting?'

'For you, my Queen. Deborah, would you fetch an appropriate dress for Her Majesty?'

'Yes, sir,' said Deborah. She bobbed a curtsey at Sir John, then one at Martha, realised that the one for Martha had not been lower than the one for Sir John, curtseyed again lower to Martha, felt that was uneven somehow, gave Sir John another curtsey but made sure it was a smaller one this time, bowed to Martha, and backed out of the room.

'It's just a short meeting,' said Sir John, 'nothing to frighten the horses. Would you mind if I sat down?'

Without waiting for an answer, he hitched up his leggings and sat on Martha's favourite armchair by the fireplace, leaning back with a contented sigh and crossing his legs at the ankle.

'I must say,' he said, 'I'm rather looking forward to retirement. I'm thinking of France. The weather's lovely in the south.'

'Retirement?' said Martha.

'The French can be a little stand-offish, it's true,' Sir John continued, 'but the cuisine! Richer than Midas, but the sauces are exquisite.'

'You're stepping down?'

'I might take up boules. I've always fancied it. My parents forced me into book-learning, but I have the soul of an athlete.'

'But who's going to be my chancellor?'

'Why, my dear, anyone you like. You're the Queen now.'

The door opened again and in came Deborah, curtseying elaborately with every step. She had some black fabric draped over one arm, around which a few moths drifted.

'I'll leave you ladies to it,' said Sir John. 'I'll wait right outside the door until you're ready to go downstairs. *Le Roi est mort, vive la Reine*, as they say in France.'

After Sir John went out, Deborah held up the fabric, which turned out to be a somewhat old-fashioned dress.

'This was your mother's, from the plague era,' she said. 'She was never out of mourning then. Well, until the plague got her.' She gave the garment a suspicious glance, then brightened. 'It's been in the attic a good long while. I'm sure there's nothing to worry about.'

Martha removed her dressing gown and nightgown and stood in her underwear, her arms raised as Deborah slipped the dress over her head. The garment was cold and damp against her skin and smelt of mould.

'There we go!' said Deborah. 'Oh, wait.' She reached out and pulled something away from Martha's armpit. 'Spider! What a big one! Hairy, too.'

Deborah ejected the arachnid out of the window.

'Perfect,' she said, turning back to Martha. 'You look exactly like your father just died.'

Fourteen

Once Deborah had pinned up her heavy red hair, Martha joined Sir John outside her bedchamber and he led her to the throne room, which had been co-opted by the Regency Council as a meeting space during her father's illness.

Most of the room was taken up with a long wooden table piled high with papers, along both sides of which were seated richly dressed elderly men, whom Martha recognised from around the castle. So many of the men had ear trumpets they looked like a brass band.

'The King is dead! Long live the Queen!' the men chorused.

'Good morning, gentlemen,' said Martha.

There were two empty seats at the table. Sir John made his way towards one of them, so Martha headed towards the other.

'Not there, Your Majesty,' said Sir John. 'There.'

He pointed to the dais at the far end of the room. Of course. There was the throne, ornate in gold leaf and red velvet. This was where she belonged now. Stacked up next to it, and detracting from its grandeur in a way that, at that moment, Martha found reassuring, was a teetering pile of papers and scrolls. Next to it was another pile of papers, and next to that, another one. Next to that one was another pile of papers, and next to that pile of papers was a pile of papers.

Martha picked her way up the steps to the dais and looked at the throne. *Am I really going to sit here?* She turned and sat down. There was a huge puff of dust. She arranged the folds of her mother's dress, which swamped her skinny frame, and surveyed the room. There were a lot of bald pates.

'Are we waiting for someone?' she said, looking at the vacant seat.

'Pardon me?' said Sir John. 'Oh, no. That chair belongs to the Crone.'

'Where is she?'

'To be honest, we're not sure. She hasn't been to a meeting since Christmas. We're keeping her chair free in case she decides to come back. She never contributed much anyway, we just felt we needed a woman, for balance. But we have a new woman now, don't we?' He raised his voice. 'A very warm welcome to Queen Martha on behalf of all the members of the Regency Council!'

'Speech!' cried one of the men.

The others took up the call. 'Speech! Speech! Speech!'

Martha cleared her throat.

'It is an honour –' she began.

'Sir John!' interrupted the first man.

'Sir John! Sir John! Sir John!' chorused the others.

'Oh, well, if you insist,' said Sir John. He climbed up onto his chair. 'Your Majesty, my lords, bishops, gentlemen, and, *in absentia*, the Crone. It is the dawning of a new era for our nation. We have new hands on the reins. New boots urging the Horse of State on, from walk to trot to canter to gallop. It is a good horse. A noble horse. Glossy of coat and frisky of tail. A hacker. A jumper. Strong enough for a warrior, gentle enough for a child. Perky ears. Excellent teeth. Huge brown eyes. And a foaming, stinking lather of honest sweat. A great horse can make a great rider of any man, or, to a lesser extent, woman, if he, or if necessary she, trusts in the horse. But the rider must also guide the horse, guide it with wisdom, empathy, compassion, and the occasional application of spurs. One beloved rider has fallen at the fence of life today, but another has risen from the paddock.

Queen Martha, we entrust you with this sacred saddle. Good luck, and giddy up.'

The men whooped and cheered, banging their fists on the table, aside from one fellow at the end of the table closest to Martha, so lined and wrinkled that he looked like a crumpled handkerchief recently pulled out of the bottom of a boot. He said loudly to his neighbour over the applause, 'I didn't catch any of that. What was the part about the ears?'

'Thank you all,' said Martha. 'I will endeavour to ride this horse as best I can and –'

'Three cheers for Queen Martha!' said Sir John. 'Hip hip!'

'Hooray!' chorused the men.

'Hip hip!'

'Hooray!'

'Hip hip!'

'Hooray!'

'Now, where to begin?' said Sir John, climbing back down off his chair. 'There's so much to get through before we leave you to it.'

'Leave me to it?'

'Of course. The King is dead.'

'Long live the Queen!' said the men.

'You are the monarch now, and in full possession of your faculties. There is no need for a Regency any more. Of course, I would suggest that you appoint some advisers to assist you with your decision-making, particularly in areas that are inappropriate for a female – the archbishopric, for example. But the men of this chamber are advanced in years, and ready to pass the burden, and gift, of power on to the next generation.'

'Not me!' called a voice.

'No, of course, not Ludovic, he's quite the spring chicken.'

'I'm seventy-two!' said Ludovic.

'He'll carry on as Master of the Rolls, if it pleases Your Majesty.'

Ludovic pushed himself to his feet and bowed.

'But for the rest of us,' said Sir John, 'once the funeral, the coronation and the wedding are out of the way, we'll be bidding you a fond, though not entirely regretful, au revoir.'

'The wedding?' said Martha.

'I suppose, if you deem it necessary, a few of us could stay on perhaps another week, two at most, to ensure the smooth handover of power. But then we really must be on our way.'

'What wedding?'

'And of course once Your Majesty is settled with a husband, he can take over much of the decision-making, as is natural.'

'I have no intention of getting married,' said Martha.

Sir John gave her a patronising smile. 'Your Majesty does not need reminding that it is against our constitution for a woman to rule without a husband,' he said. 'But there's no need to concern yourself. Your parents arranged it all when you were born. We've already sent a pigeon across the border, and Prince Edwin should be here by nightfall. The wedding will take place in the morning.'

Martha's hands gripped the arms of the throne so tightly that they almost snapped off. 'I'm meeting him tonight and you expect me to marry him tomorrow?'

'By no means,' said Sir John. 'It's unlucky for a groom to see the bride the night before the wedding. You will, as tradition dictates, spend the eve of your wedding locked in a tower and meet Prince Edwin at the altar. Unless you wish the first act of your reign to be one of iconoclasm?'

'I wish no such thing. But –'

'Then rejoice! By all accounts he's a handsome fellow, looks terrific in a crown, and the trade and military alliance will be a great boon for the kingdom. Or should I say queendom? Ha ha.'

The men all laughed too.

'No, of course not,' said Sir John, 'that's not even a word. But we'll make sure you have a nice dress for the ceremony, so there's nothing to worry about. I'm sure there'll be time for a fitting once we've worked through a bit of this legislative backlog –' he indicated one of the piles of papers, '– and we've done a few hours in court –' indicating another, '– and a few other bits and pieces. And then, once you're married – remind me, Diary Secretary? I can't keep track.'

One of the old men consulted a scroll. 'King's funeral the day after tomorrow, and coronation the day after that.'

'Bumper week for you, Archbishop,' said Sir John to a short fellow with tufty ears and a large gold cross around his neck, who simpered in return. 'Sir Thomas, are preparations for the banquets under way?' he continued.

'I've got teams of village children slaughtering and plucking herons around the clock,' answered Sir Thomas, a man surprisingly scrawny for a head cook.

At the far end of the table, three gentlemen began an argument with the Archbishop over which was the best banquet food. The Archbishop favoured duckottapin – a duck stuffed with an otter stuffed with a terrapin – and put up a particularly spirited fight.

'As Master of Hounds, may I put a claim in now for leftovers?' said a dome-headed man sitting close to Sir John. 'Before they all go as alms. It's good for the dogs to vary their diet, and the villagers are quite happy with root vegetables year-round.'

Silence. All the heads in the room turned to look at Martha.

'What say you, Your Majesty?' said Sir John.

'Oh. I suppose so, yes,' said Martha, who was still preoccupied by the thought of her wedding.

Half the men at the table smiled and nodded, and the other half glowered.

Was that it? My first ruling as queen?

'Right then,' said Sir John, 'so let's see. Apart from the wedding, funeral and coronation to arrange, you need to go over this year's taxes and budget, check on the grain reserves, inspect the troops, cast your eye over the newest engineering projects (you're going to love our plans for the dam, though we do have a rebellion in the valley to stem – never mind, they'll be a lot quieter after we've flooded them), make your maiden speech to your loving subjects, arrange a state visit to Camelot, assert your authority over the running of the castle and surrounding villages, sit in the civil court, sit in the criminal court, burn some deviants at the stake, and feed the dogs, as you just decreed . . . Shall we get started?'

Fifteen

By the time of the dress fitting that evening, Martha was so exhausted she could barely stand, but she teetered in front of the mirror in the tower room where she was to be incarcerated all the same. She looked at herself from the side, and then from the front. Then from behind, peering over her shoulder, and then from the front again. It was undeniable: she looked terrible.

'Perhaps with more corsetry?' suggested Deborah. 'And some padding? Around the tits area, Your Majesty?'

'I'm already so corseted that I can't sit down, or breathe, or eat, and we're having an eighteen-course wedding banquet.'

'Maybe if I shorten the sleeves,' said Deborah. 'Make a feature of your forearms.'

'Or maybe if my wedding dress wasn't black, or I actually wanted to get married, or my father hadn't just died.'

'I'll try the sleeves,' said Deborah.

Martha held her arms out as Deborah jabbed her with pins.

'Thank you, Deborah.'

There was silence as Deborah considered the results.

'The shorter sleeves aren't working. That was a terrible idea,' she said. 'I'll take them down again. But I'll put some more frills on the bodice, bulk up the bust, that should help a bit. And the veil will cover your freckles.'

'Perfect.'

'By the time he finds out what you actually look like, it'll be too late.'

'That's very comforting.'

Encouraged by this, Deborah began stuffing handfuls of itchy lace into Martha's cleavage.

At that moment there was a knock at the door. Although she knew it would only be a temporary reprieve, Martha was relieved. 'Who is it?' she said.

'It's . . . Mistress . . . Smedley . . .' came the reply. Martha could barely make out the words, as the woman in question was panting so hard from the effort of climbing the stairs.

'Mistress Smedley?' she said. 'Why on earth? Deborah, let her in.'

Deborah opened the door. Mistress Smedley, Martha's former governess, half stood, half knelt on the stone threshold, scarlet-faced and bent double. She was not built for speed. Under one arm was a large, leather-bound book.

'Your . . . Majesty . . .' she gasped.

'It is always a pleasure to see you, but what are you doing here?' said Martha.

'The King . . . is dead . . .' wheezed Mistress Smedley.

'Yes, I know. That's not what you came here to tell me, is it?'

Mistress Smedley shook her head and tried to continue.

'Long . . . live . . .'

'Glass of wine?' suggested Martha.

'. . . The . . . don't mind if I do . . . Queen . . .'

Deborah hooked an arm around the erstwhile governess and dragged her over to a damask-covered chair by the fireside. Mistress Smedley managed two glasses of wine in the time it took to get her breath back.

'I'm sorry to burst in on you like this,' she said at last. 'Is that your wedding dress? I think it could do with some padding at the top.'

'That's what I told her,' said Deborah.

'My bodice is so full of stuffing I'm beginning to know how the duckottapin feels,' said Martha.

'Speaking of stuffing,' said Mistress Smedley. 'Oh, my dear. I have allowed a terrible, terrible lacuna in your education. An ellipsis. You know what an ellipsis is, don't you, dear?'

'Of course.'

'A little absence. Nothing important. Or so I thought. You were always so sweet and so innocent. I didn't want to . . . Well. And then this morning I realised that if I didn't tell you now . . . Oh my poor, sweet, motherless child.'

Mistress Smedley loosened her grip on the leather-bound book she had been clutching to her ample bosom. She slid it along her knees towards Martha.

'I think you'd better take a look,' she said.

'*An Illustrated Guide to Married Life*?' read Martha from the gold lettering on the cover.

'Oh Lordy,' said Deborah.

'Open it, dear,' said Mistress Smedley.

'Very well,' said Martha. 'Deborah, are we done?'

'I think I should loosen you up,' said Deborah. 'We don't want you fainting.'

'Fainting?' said Martha, but she allowed Deborah to unlace her corset. Then she took the book from Mistress Smedley's lap and opened it on her dressing table.

'Oh,' she said. 'Well. That's fine. I already know what I look like, in the state of nature.' She went to close the book.

'Turn the page,' said Mistress Smedley.

Martha did.

'Ah. I see that, beneath his britches, the human male is no different from the animals of the field. Very interesting, thank you, Mistress Smedley.'

She was about to close the book once more, when Mistress Smedley again said, 'Turn the page.'

Martha sighed and turned the page. There was another silence. Martha went so pale that even her freckles began to fade.

'On reflection, maybe waiting until the night before the

wedding to tell her was a mistake,' whispered Mistress Smedley to Deborah.

'You can't . . . you can't possibly . . . think that I . . . would . . . with a complete stranger?' Martha managed to say.

'I think you'd best give the Queen a glass of wine,' Mistress Smedley told Deborah.

'I don't need wine. I need for this not to be happening.' Martha turned another page. 'Oh, saints alive, no.'

'It's not as bad as it looks,' said Deborah, peering over her shoulder.

'You know about this, Deborah?' said Martha. 'Who else knows?'

'It is an essential part of married life,' said Mistress Smedley.

'Essential? You mean everybody does this?'

'If you want to have children, it is required.'

'If I want to have children? I have to have children, because I'm the Queen. My wishes on the matter do not come into it.'

'It is your duty.'

Martha straightened, eyes narrowing. 'Don't talk to me about my duty. I know my duty. I do nothing except my duty. I spent half an hour this morning discussing hazelnut production with the deputy head kitchen gardener. That was my duty, as I understood it. Nobody said that this –' Martha jabbed a finger at the book '– was part of my duty too.'

'I'm sorry,' said Mistress Smedley, 'but it is the burden of womanhood.'

'It's really not that much of a burden,' said Deborah.

Martha turned another page.

'Jesus Lord of all, he puts that there as well? Is there no end to this?'

Mistress Smedley craned her neck to look at the drawing.

'That one is not strictly necessary for the procurement of children.'

'Then why do it?'

'Men like it.'

'And women?'

There was a pause. 'It can be quite pleasurable,' said Deborah at last.

'You're not even married!' said Martha.

Deborah looked off to the side. 'I mean, I've heard it can be,' she mumbled.

'I'm sure the Prince will be gentle with you,' said Mistress Smedley.

'Gentle? Gentle like breaking a horse? Gentle like when we force-feed the geese to make pâté? This –' Martha pointed at the latest elaborately wrought illustration '– doesn't look very gentle.'

'There's nothing wrong with giving it a bit of oomph,' said Deborah.

Martha went to turn the page.

'I'd advise that you skip the next one,' said Mistress Smedley.

'How much worse can it get?'

Martha turned the page.

'Oh, that's a good one,' said Deborah.

'I won't do it,' said Martha.

'Sweetheart, you must,' said Mistress Smedley.

'I refuse. I'm the Queen.'

'All the more reason that you must. There are some responsibilities that are greater even than that of a queen to her country, and those include the duty of a wife to her husband.'

'Well then, I'm not getting married.' Martha slammed the book shut with a triumphant expression.

But outside, the bugles were already heralding the arrival of Prince Edwin.

Sixteen

Edwin hadn't ridden all the way to Puddock Castle. He'd been driven in a coach with eight horses that were replaced whenever they started to tire. It was his unbiased opinion that the horses got slower, fatter and lazier after they'd crossed the border from Tuft. But there was no way he was going to arrive at the castle in a carriage like some pathetic girl, so a little way down the road he'd got out and mounted his horse, Storm, also transported to Puddock by carriage. First impressions were very important. So a black stallion it was, ridden just far enough to work up a sweat and a bit of masculine odour. The horse, not him.

He reined in Storm just inside the front gate and surveyed his new castle. Loyalty to Tuft insisted that it wasn't as good as the castle back home, but rivalry with his older brother, Leo, who had claimed that castle for himself, demanded that this one be better. It was undeniably bigger, which was a start. Perhaps once he'd made some improvements – knocked a few walls down, added some wings – he could assert its superiority and take the credit for himself, not Puddock.

He got down from Storm and handed the reins to a stable hand. Lined up by the main entrance to the castle were trumpet players or something, dressed in the red livery of the castle. Edwin didn't care much for music, it seemed a pointless waste of noise, but he liked a fanfare when he arrived in a place, so that was fine. They could stand around and play whenever he came and went, unless he was sneaking out to visit some wench's bed. Kings didn't have to sneak, of course, but Edwin liked sneaking. It added thrill to the chase. The livery he'd get changed to his colours. What were his colours? He didn't need to have the same ones as Leo any more, crappy yellow and blue. He'd have black. That was dangerous. That said King. *Prince Consort*, he heard in his head, in Leo's smug-boy voice. *Fuck off, Leo.*

He looked around, hoping to catch sight of his wife-to-be. He was going to have to beget some sprogs with her so he hoped she was at least vaguely shaggable. But there was no sign of her. Never mind; the servants were where the real action was, sextacularly speaking. Leo always got the best ones, back home, but here Edwin should have first dibs. He'd take a tour of the kitchens later, there were bound to be decent tits in there, and failing that, he'd get some in from the village. Did they have *droit de seigneur* in this godforsaken kingdom? If they didn't, he'd institute it. He was going to be king, after all. *Prince Consort.* King.

A group of what appeared to be beggars were clustered in the courtyard, but as he was preparing to sweep past them, one broke away from the others and bowed.

'The people of Puddock welcome Prince Edwin of Tuft!' said the beggar.

'Oh. Thanks,' said Edwin, wondering if this decrepit old man was going to ask him for money.

'I am Sir John Penrith, Chancellor of the Puddock Regency Council,' the beggar declared. He gestured to the scrappy old men gathered behind him, and they bowed as best they could. *Christ,* thought Edwin, *this place is worse than I thought.*

'So it's the wedding, tomorrow, eh?' he said. 'I hope there's a banquet, I could eat a horse. Not Storm. He's a stallion, you know. I mean, I could eat a stallion, if I wanted to, but Storm's my stallion and I don't want to eat him. What I mean is, I've got a big appetite. Not just at table! I mean in bed. But in that case, not for horses.'

Sir John stared at him for several seconds. Just as Edwin was about to conclude that the man was a halfwit, and explain the joke more slowly, Sir John gathered himself with a visible effort and said, 'I trust you had a good journey.'

'You trust right,' said Edwin. 'Though the real ride's happening tomorrow night, if you know what I'm saying.'

This time Sir John only needed to blink once or twice before continuing. 'Allow me to show you to your chambers,' he said. He turned to go inside.

'I'm not talking about horse riding,' said Edwin, following him.

'Indeed,' said Sir John, climbing the front steps.

'I'm talking about sex.'

Sir John didn't reply. Edwin assumed he hadn't heard, but he wasn't repeating himself for this deaf old coot. He squared his shoulders and marched, no, swept into the castle. Unless marching was better.

If he looked up at the window of the tallest tower, he didn't see anything there.

Seventeen

In the room at the top of the tower where she and Martha were now locked, Deborah was standing on a stool and leaning as far out of the window as she could, which is to say that she had her left cheek pressed up to the bars, with her nose and eyelashes protruding just far enough to be considered free of incarceration.

'He doesn't look too bad,' she said.

Martha was sitting leaning against the wall, eating candied fruit in as disconsolate a way as she could, given that she really liked candied fruit.

'He's quite good-looking, really,' said Deborah. 'For a prince.'

'Excuse me?' said Martha through a sugary mouthful of satsuma peel.

'I mean, a prince of Tuft. They're all inbred there. No chins. But he's got a chin, quite a big one, actually.'

'Please don't talk about his chin.' Some of the drawings she had seen had involved chins in places where chins should not be.

'Come and have a look at him,' said Deborah. 'He's honestly not that bad. He's still got most of his hair.'

Martha shook her head. 'No point.'

'You're going to have to marry someone,' said Deborah. 'If you want to rule. And you have to rule, you're the Queen. And you know they're not going to let you choose.'

Martha didn't want to admit it, but Deborah was right.

'There'll be a list,' Deborah went on. 'You say no to this one, they'll just go to the next one. You could do worse. I've heard things about Prince Cuthbert of Brack, on the servant grapevine. He makes the pictures in that book look tame.'

'Don't talk about that book,' said Martha.

'May I borrow it?' said Deborah. 'If you're done with it?'

Martha shuddered. 'By all means.'

'Mistress Smedley says the pictures were done by monks,' Deborah mused. 'I wonder how they do their research?'

'I dread to think.' Martha chewed on a sliver of lime. 'So what does the servant grapevine say about Prince Edwin?'

'They say he's not as bad as his brother, Leo.'

'And what do they say about Leo?'

'They say he's a cock, Your Majesty.'

Martha swallowed her lime. 'Let's have a look at this Edwin, then.'

Deborah climbed off the stool and helped Martha up onto it. She pressed her face up to the bars and observed the scene in the castle courtyard. Prince Edwin was standing to one side, talking to Sir John. Deborah was right – there was nothing in particular to object to in his body or his face.

'I suppose he is no better and no worse than anybody else,' said Martha.

She turned back to the room and caught sight of her black wedding dress, hanging limp by the mirror.

Eighteen

As Martha appeared at the back of the chapel on the arm of Sir John Penrith, the organist, a converted Saracen who was so short he had to sit on two cushions, struck up a funereal tune, as if the music for today's wedding and tomorrow's interment had got confused. The lugubrious minor chords added to Martha's sense of encroaching doom. At the entrance to the chapel was an honour guard of soldiers, supposedly there for her protection, but, Martha suspected, really posted to ensure that she wouldn't run away. She walked down the nave, the eyes of the gathered dignitaries fixed upon her, and Sir John's arm felt less like a means of support and more like a shackle binding her to the prison of marriage.

They reached the front of the chapel where Prince Edwin was waiting. Sir John let go of her and stepped to one side, and all at once Martha missed that restrictive but familiar arm. She wondered if Edwin was dreading this as much as she was. She, at least, had had a glance at his face the night before; whereas in her ludicrous dress, with a heavy black veil wound around her head, his bride must look to him like a cross between a beekeeper and a very fancy ottoman. She drew back her veil with trembling hands and looked up at her husband-to-be. Edwin grimaced, unable to conceal his disappointment. Martha blinked rapidly to stop the tears that had sprung to her eyes. *It is your duty*, she reminded herself, echoing Mistress Smedley's words of the night before, and with a sickening lurch remembered the other duty that awaited her later.

The Archbishop stepped forward, and Edwin replaced his scowl with a smile. Martha gasped. Surely teeth of that magnitude could not exist in nature? There was a ripple of shocked laughter in the chapel, and Martha turned. She spotted Mistress Smedley and Deborah, sitting together close to the back. 'Help,' she mouthed. But there was nothing they could do.

A layer of icy sweat slathered Martha's skin under that infernal dress. She felt utterly trapped. Images from the book kept appearing, unbidden, in her mind. She tried to focus her thoughts on Edwin, tried to ask herself whether he'd be intelligent, kind, a demon at cards, but all she could think about was that thing between his legs and what he was going to do with it. Although he hadn't been married before – maybe he didn't know what was required? Was it up to her to inform him? Perhaps she'd pretend she didn't know either, and they could adopt a baby from some peasant girl who'd got herself pregnant by mistake – Good Lord – how could such a thing happen by mistake? It's not as if you wouldn't notice. And even if Prince Edwin did know, and wanted to, *I'm the Queen. I can just refuse.* But there was that unfortunate vow she'd be making in a few tiny minutes: to love, honour and OBEY. Oh, she could see why they put that in, now.

The music of the organ pounded loud and discordant in her ears. She tried to keep her eyes on Edwin's face – nice face, nice face, nothing to be scared of – yet she couldn't help but glance at the fateful bulge between his legs. It was quite big, but squidgy-looking, not at all like in the drawings. Oh praise God, maybe his didn't work properly! She looked back up again, into his dark brown eyes, and felt the beginning of hope – he was surely just a normal young man, maybe he was frightened, maybe he didn't want to marry a stranger either, maybe he'd be happy to wait before consummating the marriage (wait, perhaps, for the rest of their lives) – and then he smiled again, and all she could see was those enormous, awful, extraordinary teeth clamped on one of her nipples (as per illustration page twelve) and she fought the urge to gag.

There had to be a way out. She could – she could – break one of the stained-glass windows – push the lectern to the wall – climb up and jump out? Or grab the sceptre off the Archbishop and fight her way past all those soldiers? Frantically she looked around the congregation, desperate to find someone who might rescue her. But they were all sitting placidly watching her go to her miserable fate. Was nobody prepared to get themselves killed to release her from this marriage?

It was too late, anyway. The Archbishop had already started. 'Dearly beloved, we are gathered here today . . .'

Dearly beloved? What did love have to do with any of this?

Nineteen

By the end of the wedding banquet, the ring on Martha's finger was tighter than her corset and heavier than the wedding cake. She sat beside her new husband at the centre of the high table, perched on a dais overlooking the guests. Or they would have been overlooking the guests, except that blocking their view was an enormous marzipan sculpture of Puddock's national bird, the hoopoe. The marzipan was slightly sweaty, which made her feel nauseous. Or maybe it was the man she was sitting next to who was making her feel sick.

'This banquet is rubbish. Back in Tuft, we'd have had fifty courses at least,' Edwin was saying, pellets of semi-chewed food flying from his mouth. 'For my birthday we had spit-roasted foox – that's the head of a fox attached to the body of an ox.'

Please don't say spit again, thought Martha. *Better still, please don't say ANYTHING.*

'I had the foox's drumstick,' continued Edwin, with a shower of masticated porcupine goulash. 'It was massive and I ate it all. Speaking of big bones, who does a man have to bone to get a goblet of wine in this place?'

Martha leaned around the marzipan hoopoe and gestured to a servant, who fetched two more cups of wine from the fountain in the centre of the room. It had been fashioned from the body of a small whale, so that the wine emerged from its blowhole and cascaded back into its mouth. The whale had begun to slump so that red wine dribbled out of the sides of its mouth, and the wine itself had an aftertaste of brine. Still, at least it got you drunk. Martha held her breath and knocked back half her cup in one swallow. She wondered whether her lips were stained as dark as Edwin's. They made his teeth stand out like tombstones. Soon she'd be buried under those teeth.

'It was my birthday,' Edwin continued, 'so I said Leo should have the parson's nose. But foxes don't have parson's noses, did you know that? Neither do oxes.'

'Neither do oxen,' said Martha.

'Is that the head of an ox and the body of a hen? But then it would have a parson's nose. Golly, you are stupid.'

Martha's eyes fell on a long knife, lying next to the ribcage of a suckling goat. If she killed him, what would happen? The penalty for murdering your husband was being burned at the stake, but Sir John might be merciful and have her head taken off with a sword instead.

'Don't look so forlorn,' said Edwin. 'Being stupid is good in a wife. And now that I'm the King, I can make all the difficult decisions, so you don't need to worry about anything.'

'Prince Consort,' said Martha.

Edwin choked and spat out a tangle of gristle.

If I ask really nicely, Sir John might be merciful and have my head taken off with a sword even if I don't kill Edwin.

'You're so lucky your brother got killed,' said Edwin.

'Yes, what glorious good fortune,' said Martha.

'I wish mine would die. Then I'd be King of Tuft instead of here.'

'You're not King of here. You will never be King of here.'

Edwin opened his mouth to remonstrate, but on the far side of her, Sir John had got to his feet.

'Perhaps now would be a good moment for a toast,' he said. He tapped the side of his goblet with a knife to get the room's attention. 'To the bride and groom!'

'The bride and groom,' chorused the guests, and everyone drank.

'And to the bride's beloved father, departed but yesterday,' said Sir John.

'And to my dear brother, and my mother,' said Martha quietly, before she raised her cup.

'Oh, I've got a good one,' called out Edwin. 'Here's to the King. What king? Fuc-king!'

The guests laughed, some genuinely, but most nervously.

'And now, to the bedchamber!' said Sir John.

To the bedchamber? That seemed like a strange toast. But before Martha had a chance to drink, Edwin leapt up, grabbed her, threw her over his shoulder and started to run for the door.

'Put me down. Put me down!' Martha battered her fists against Edwin's back. 'I'm the Queen!'

'That's the spirit!' said Edwin, slapping her on the bottom.

The rest of the guests had got up and were chasing after them.

'Where is the damn bedchamber?' yelled Edwin.

'I'm not telling you,' said Martha into his flank. With every step his shoulder jabbed into her stomach, and she was at serious risk of regurgitating the entire banquet down his back.

'Up the grand stairs and across to the east wing,' called Sir John. 'Follow the rose petals!'

'Rose petals, see?' said Edwin. 'Because you're going to get deflowered.'

The pun was the first sign that Edwin had any intelligence at all, but being carried upside down up the stairs followed by a mass of baying subjects, Martha was not in the best position to appreciate it.

Twenty

As Edwin lugged Martha up the stairs and prepared to take what had damn well better be her virginity, he reflected that there was a silver lining to every cloud. She was far too skinny to be a decent lay, but at least she didn't weigh much. Dropping her in front of everybody would be bloody embarrassing.

He had been to plenty of weddings before, and he'd always looked forward to the moment when the guests chased the bride and groom into the bedroom and ripped off the bride's clothes. He was thrilled that it was his turn now, but Martha didn't seem to be as excited about it as he was. She was kicking and squirming on his back, almost as if she wanted to be dropped. Edwin clutched her tightly and ran along the trail of rose petals, swerving back and forth to avoid the grabbing hands.

Reaching the bedchamber, he hauled Martha inside, followed immediately by the drunken, shrieking mob. He chucked Martha onto the bed.

'Go on then,' he said to the mob, 'and hurry up.'

He stood aside.

Martha lay in a ball on the bed, her knees pulled up and her arms wrapped tightly around herself. *I hate you all*, she thought, as her subjects crowded around her, yelling and cheering as they ripped strips off her wedding dress. She recognised several members of the Regency Council, some of whom were wearing party hats. The throng were laughing, singing, clapping, comparing prizes ('I got a sleeve!'), behaving as if it was a cross between Christmas morning and a fox hunt. Somebody actually shouted, 'Tally-ho!' On it went, for what felt like hours: grabbing, grabbing, grabbing.

These were the people who were supposed to obey her, respect her, love her? These were the people for whom she would spend the rest of her life in servitude, fighting their wars, administering their laws, leading them, protecting them, anticipating and providing for their every need? These gannets?

For them she had married that, that, *thing* she could not bring herself to call a man, who was standing to one side and yawning while his bride was torn to pieces before his eyes? Who was merely waiting his turn to ravage her in ways unimaginably worse than this rabble's greedy, grasping fingers? Whose daughter she might bear, for her to be thrown to the mob in turn?

And all because of an accident of birth, and the accident of death that had taken her brother away – a brother who would never have been treated in this way on his wedding night. Nobody had touched so much as a thread of Edwin's clothing, she noticed.

She gritted her teeth and refused to cry.

I hate each and every one of you. Why would I want to be your queen?

Despite everything, a few tears squeezed through and dripped hotly onto her nose and cheeks. She could feel the fingernails of her subjects clawing at her very flesh.

Suddenly, Edwin's voice cut through the shrieking of the crowd.

'That's enough! Everybody go! Now!'

The hands stopped tearing, and Martha felt a pathetic relief and gratitude to her husband, which was swiftly replaced by a new and different terror. This was it. Every horror in that book was about to befall her. She began to shudder, backing into a corner of the bed like a wounded animal. But Edwin just staggered over to the bedside, muttered, 'Long day,' collapsed face first onto the mattress and began to snore.

This might be her only chance.

Twenty-One

Edwin appeared to be a deep sleeper; that was lucky. Martha packed as quickly and silently as she could while he snored, stuffing a few essentials into a set of saddlebags she found in the stables. There were plenty of leftovers from the wedding banquet and she wrapped a selection of the most appealing dishes to tide her over, reasoning that she could buy more on the road. Though money was a problem. She had never used it, had no idea what anything cost, so she didn't know how much she'd need. She didn't want to weigh down her horse, but nor did she want to run out. Ideally, she'd take enough to last her for the rest of her life, as she couldn't imagine how she was going to get more, but this seemed a little unrealistic. In the end she took several handfuls of gold from the treasury, which, unbelievably, was left locked but unguarded at night. She had seen where the treasurer kept the key when he'd taken her on the tour. If she'd been carrying on as queen, she'd have done something about that, but she wasn't carrying on as queen. By the time the sun came up she'd be gone. Let Edwin run the country and see how he liked it. She felt a stab of disquiet at this thought – he might like it, but she doubted that the country would – but she ignored it.

Deborah slept in a small chamber near Martha's room in case she was needed in an emergency, which this most certainly was. Martha slipped inside, leaving the door slightly ajar to allow in light from the candles in the corridor. She shook Deborah awake, explained in the briefest terms that she was leaving, and whispered a few hasty instructions. Deborah wasn't the most discreet person in the world, but that couldn't be helped.

'And you're never coming back?' said Deborah.

'Never,' said Martha.

Deborah started to weep. She flung her arms around Martha and held her tight, sobbing into her hair. 'You were always a good mistress. I'll miss you, I really will.'

Martha was startled. She tried to remember the last time someone had hugged her, and came up with nothing.

'Don't cry,' she said, awkwardly patting Deborah's back. 'I'll send for you as soon as I get to –'

'Don't tell me where you're going,' interrupted Deborah. 'You know I can't keep a secret.'

That doesn't bode well, thought Martha.

'Are you sure you'll be all right on your own?' asked Deborah.

'I'm certain,' said Martha, who wasn't. 'Don't worry about me.'

'I won't,' said Deborah, who would, and she wept a fresh slew of tears.

'Goodbye, dearest Deborah,' Martha said, feeling a surge of warmth for her loyal maid, and she kissed her on the forehead. Deborah appreciated the kiss, but she might also have liked one of the gold coins in Martha's bags. Martha didn't even think of it.

She returned to the stables, saddled her horse, Silver, and rode the sleepy and reluctant beast to the Crone's cottage, a stone shack surrounded by pines on the edge of the castle estate. She knocked on the door, first gently with her knuckles, then, when that drew no response, thumping hard with her fists. Eventually, the door creaked open to reveal a small girl, around twelve years old, with huge brown eyes. She was wearing a nightgown and wrapped up against the cold in a rough woollen blanket.

'Who are you?' said Martha.

'I'm the Acting Crone,' said the girl.

'I need to see the real Crone,' said Martha. 'It's an emergency.'

'She isn't here.' The girl looked terrified. 'Aren't you the Queen?'

'Yes. Let me in.'

The girl stood to one side, and attempted a curtsey as Martha passed her. It didn't really work with the blanket. Then she closed the door.

The cottage was tiny. Was this how all commoners lived? There was just the one room, smaller than Martha's bedroom. At one end was what Martha supposed was the kitchen bit, a large fireplace with a spit and a heavy wooden table on which was some fruit and a knife. There was another, smaller fireplace at the other end of the room with a couple of settles pulled up to it. On either side of that fireplace were alcoves, curtained with heavily patched drapes. Sleeping areas, Martha supposed – she couldn't see a bed. The window by the door had a good view of the castle. Martha peered out of it to make sure she hadn't been followed, then closed the shutters and turned back to the girl.

'Tell me where the real Crone is,' she said.

'I don't know,' said the girl. She was so frightened she was shaking. 'She drank too much scrumpy last Christmas and made herself disappear. I haven't seen her since. I didn't tell anyone because I thought she might come back, and I didn't want to get her into trouble, or me thrown out of the castle. I've been the Acting Crone since then, but I'm just an apprentice really. My name's Nancy.'

'Can you do magic?' said Martha.

'Some,' said Nancy.

'Good. I need you to turn me into a boy.'

Nancy's eyes widened.

'Or a man, I suppose,' said Martha. 'It's up to you. But I've got to get away from here. I don't want to be queen, and even if I did, I can't stay here and be married to that, that . . . to that. I can't let him – well, anyway. I can't. But the whole country will be looking for me so I need to be in disguise as somebody that no one will ever imagine is me. I need to be a man. Or a boy. Male. Can you do it?'

Nancy took a deep breath. 'No, Your Majesty.'

'*No?*' This was not a word Martha was accustomed to hearing. 'Why not?'

Nancy paused. 'May I speak freely?'

'Please,' said Martha, thinking, *well, freely-ish*.

'I'm only a beginner.' Nancy's voice didn't sound free. If anything it was so constrained that she could barely get the words out. 'Magic is quite hard,' she added miserably.

'Don't you just think about it and it happens?'

Nancy hesitated, then cleared her throat. 'May I show you something, Your Majesty?'

'If you must. But be quick about it. I'm in a hurry.'

Nancy led Martha over to the kitchen area, where three apples were sitting on a chopping block.

'I made those with magic,' she said.

'Congratulations,' said Martha, wondering why she was looking at apples.

'Pick up the one on the far left. I mean, please. If it please Your Majesty.'

Martha tried to do so but she couldn't get hold of it. It seemed to disappear in her hand.

'What's wrong with it?' she said.

'It's only what an apple looks like. I didn't realise I had to make it solid.'

Martha picked up the apple next to it.

'This one seems fine,' she said. She bit into it and immediately spat into her hand. 'That's . . . that's . . .' She took another tiny bite, and this time chewed and swallowed. She pulled a face. 'There's something about this that's not right at all.'

'I know. I forgot to give it any texture.'

Martha put the textureless apple down, and handed Nancy

the chewed-up morsel. Nancy discreetly dropped it in a composting bucket. Martha picked up the last apple on the board.

'And this one?' she said.

'Try it, Your Majesty.'

Martha took a bite.

'Nice crunch,' she said. 'Juicy. Sweet. Well done. This is a very good apple.'

'Until you cut it in half,' said Nancy.

Martha looked at her with surprise and then sliced the apple in two.

'Oh, I see,' she said. 'No core. But you know, that's actually an improvement. When they serve apples at the castle, I have one of the cooks cut the cores out for me. And the peel, and any bruises or worms.'

'Even so, I forgot to put one in. So it's not exactly like a real apple. I also don't know if it is nourishing, or if you could eat a thousand of those and starve to death.'

Martha put the knife down.

'So what you're saying, if I understand correctly, is if you turn me into a boy, I might be like one of those apples. Not quite right.'

'Yes, Your Majesty.'

'I'll take that risk,' said Martha.

Nancy curtseyed again, but she still looked worried. 'Your Majesty is always right, of course. But . . . but with your permission, I still think it's best if I just make you look like a boy, rather than . . . trying to . . . make all the bits right. It's just that . . . I haven't . . . seen everything myself.' The girl was blushing now. 'So I'd have to guess.'

Martha thought of the book.

'On consideration, perhaps that's wise,' she said.

'And also, before I start, there's something I should give you.'

Nancy delved into a cupboard and emerged with a tiny, corked opaque glass bottle, which she handed to Martha.

'The Crone was working on a universal panacea before she made herself disappear,' she said. 'This is the only dose that's left. It should restore you to your right form.'

Martha held the bottle up to the light. She could see something viscous inside.

'Should?' she said.

'I haven't tried it,' admitted Nancy, 'and the Crone was very secretive about it, so I don't know if it works.'

'So if it doesn't work, I may never be able to change back?'

Nancy shrugged helplessly. 'Hopefully, it works.'

Martha nodded and put the bottle in the pocket of her cloak. 'All right,' she said. 'I'm ready.'

Nancy looked petrified, almost as scared as Martha felt. She went over to an alcove and came back with some socks, a pair of scissors, and a rather tarnished mirror, which she propped up against one of the settles. She was shaking so much she nearly dropped it.

'Let's start with your hair,' she said. 'No magic required.'

Martha wasn't delighted at the thought of Nancy putting a pair of scissors to her head when her hand was trembling to such an extent, but all the same she positioned herself in front of the mirror. She unpinned her hair and let the thick tresses fall down her back. She'd always been vain about her hair. It was one of the few womanly things about her. She ran her hand through it for the last time, feeling the silk of it in her fingers. Then Nancy took hold of it all in a bunch and sliced it away at the neckline. Martha felt a surge of – what was it? Panic? No, not panic exactly . . .

'Now for the beard,' said Nancy. 'I'm not sure how this will feel so I'm sorry if it hurts.'

She stood beside the mirror and stared intently at Martha. Martha kept her eyes on her reflection. After a few seconds, her chin started to itch, at first just a little, but it quickly became almost insufferable.

'What are you –'

'I need you to keep your face still. Sorry.'

Martha clenched her fists to stop herself from scratching. Then just as she was about to protest again, a huge red beard erupted from her face and spilled down the front of her tunic. She looked like a ginger waterfall. She gasped in astonishment and started to laugh. It wasn't panic she was feeling. It was excitement.

'I think there's a little bit too much,' she said. 'Can you make it go back in?'

'I don't think that's a good idea. It might sort of fill up your head. I'll cut it with the scissors.'

After Nancy had snipped away for a while, she stood back so that they could admire her handiwork. In silence they contemplated the flowing moustache and beard Nancy had left her with.

'It's a bit . . . Viking,' said Martha.

'Oh,' said Nancy, hurt.

'Maybe you could trim it a tiny bit more?'

Nancy had another go. This time, when she stood back, the moustache and beard had been replaced by patchy outcroppings of hair, not unlike the remaining traces of grass on a field after a vigorous joust. Martha looked like a young boy who had only recently started shaving and was a long way from getting the hang of it.

'Perfect,' she said. It was far from perfect, but there wasn't much that could be done about it now, short of starting again from scratch, literally, which Martha was loath to do. 'But I still have the form of a woman,' she continued. 'Can you change my shape a little, to resemble that of a man?'

Nancy winced. 'I'm afraid it might be very painful.'

'But necessary,' said Martha. She removed her cloak. Underneath she was wearing men's clothes, stolen from Edwin. She stripped down to her undershirt.

Nancy swallowed and nodded her head. 'Hold still.'

The young crone reached out a hand and placed it on Martha's sternum. After a few moments, Martha felt a terrible dragging in her shoulders as they pulled away from one another, getting broader. Then, with a sound like a cork popping, an Adam's apple bulged out of her neck. Her breasts began to feel hot, then got hotter, to the point of burning.

'That hurts. Quite a lot,' she said.

'Sorry. I'm being as quick as I can.'

Martha felt a tightening, as if she was holding her breath and couldn't exhale. In the mirror, she watched as her breasts flattened and disappeared. Her stomach churned.

'I've changed my mind!' she yelled before she could stop herself.

But her breasts were already gone, and Nancy staggered back from the effort of it.

'I hate it,' said Martha, a sob entering her voice. But as she pulled her tunic over her head she caught sight of herself in the mirror again. She truly did look like a boy. She turned slowly, regarding herself from all angles. 'My apologies,' she said. 'You have done an excellent job.'

'The last part is the easiest,' said Nancy.

She handed over the pair of socks. Martha looked at her quizzically.

'For . . .' But Nancy was too embarrassed to finish her sentence, and instead waved in the general vicinity of Martha's britches.

Martha blushed. 'I'll . . . apply them later,' she said.

'One final thing,' said Nancy. 'I think I should make myself forget that this ever happened, so that I can't tell anybody about your disguise, even if I'm tortured.'

'Surely nobody would torture a child?' said Martha.

Nancy looked at her oddly. 'Your soldiers do it all the time,' she said. 'Anyway, I will cast a spell of forgetfulness on myself, so that your secret will be forever safe.'

'Thank you, Nancy,' said Martha. 'I will always remember your help and generosity, and –'

Nancy closed her eyes and began to mutter to herself.

'Wait, you're doing it right now?' said Martha. 'I don't think that's a good . . .'

Nancy opened her eyes. When she caught sight of Martha, she screamed.

'Man! Strange man! Strange-looking man in my house!'

She snatched up the scissors and waved them at Martha. Martha grabbed her cloak and ran.

Twenty-Two

It was a bloody boring funeral, even for a funeral. They shouldn't call it a funeral, thought Edwin, but a dulleral. He laughed at his own joke and had to cover his mouth with a handkerchief to pretend that he was crying, though why he'd cry over the death of some senile old king he'd never met was beyond him. Next to him, Martha was stiff and silent, as she'd been all day, from the moment he'd woken up to find her sitting in the armchair in the corner of the room, already in her mourning clothes and the impenetrable black veil she'd worn for the wedding. Opening his eyes and seeing Martha in her weeds, his cock had given a twitch – he owned her now, and a man wanted to make his mark. But before he could do anything about it, there had been a knock at the door and in had come that man from the Regency Council to tell them that the funeral was about to begin, so he'd had to dress in a hurry and run. And actually perhaps it was more gentlemanly to wait until his wife's father was buried before boffing her. More kingly.

Not that Edwin thought he'd be able to get it up after all this tedium. (That was just an exaggeration for comic effect, he re-assured himself. Of course he could get it up, he could always get it up. No problems in that department. None at all.) But Sweet Lord, couldn't they just dig a hole, bung the old King in the hole, fill up the hole? A prayer or two, yes, for decorum's sake. But did there have to be all this endless talking? It wasn't enough that the Archbishop appeared determined to read out the entire Bible from cover to cover. But Jesus, Mary and all the Saints, was there a competition going on for the world's longest sermon? At least Martha was wearing a veil and could fall asleep if she wanted to, nobody would notice. It wasn't fair, being a man and having a face everybody could see. Maybe if his eyebrows got longer with age he could comb them down over his eyes and nobody would be able to tell if they were shut. If this funeral lasted much longer he'd be able to try it out.

I could start a new fashion. Call it the Edwin. Edwin tugged one of his eyebrows downwards and tried to figure out how long it was. It was useless. Barely made it to the top of his eyeball. Maybe he could get some kind of eyebrow wig crafted out of horsehair? Or, forget the eyebrows, perhaps men could start wearing veils, like women? No, that was ridiculous.

'Those boyhood days,' the Archbishop was saying. 'I remember them well. The boy who would be archbishop and the boy who would be king. Playing together, like ordinary boys, though only one of us had divine right. As the Bible says, *All your children shall be taught by the Lord, and great shall be the peace of your children.* Isaiah 54:13. Although we were taught by Master Kenwood, or was it Ken Wood? Can you believe it, I don't recall! But he had a frightful temper and just the one eye, and the only peace we knew was pudding. By which I mean pease pudding. A pun, you know? A ha. A ha ha. Ah, me. Those boyhood days. We never did actually eat pease pudding.'

In a minute, thought Edwin, *even the corpse is going to be so bored it'll get up out of the casket and walk off in its winding sheet.*

'As we grew into young men,' the Archbishop droned on, 'I became accustomed to living in Peter's glorious shadow, or rather the shadow of his glory, a shadow, by definition, not being glorious. Although, of course, all things of the King are covered in glory, and therefore his shadow was, indeed, glorious. Peter had all of the women – the girls who would be queen – and I less so, which prompted Peter, immortally, if that isn't a tactless word to use under the circumstances, although he lives on in the immortality of God, glory be to God, to say, "Have you ever thought about making a virtue of necessity and taking a vow of chastity?" And thus began my path to the priesthood. I owe him so much. Oh, those young manhood days.'

My God, will this funeral never end?

Edwin missed home. He missed his own young manhood days. He even missed Leo, in a way. Leo's purpose in life was to make Edwin feel small. But that meant Edwin's purpose in life was to prove himself to Leo, and without Leo there to watch him, everything he did felt a bit pointless. So, for example, if Leo had met Martha, he'd have been all, 'I don't fancy yours much,' and Edwin would have been, like, 'She may not be all that to look at, but she goes like a mule,' and Leo would have been, 'Have you shagged a lot of mules then?' and Edwin would have been, like, 'Get lost, Leo.' Where was he going to get that sort of quality banter round here? He wondered what Leo was doing right now. He wouldn't be at a bloody not-very-fun-eral, that's for sure. He'd be giving a wench a good seeing to, probably, or down in the dungeon tormenting the man in the iron mask.

Maybe there was a man in an iron mask at this castle he could torment? That would pass the time.

'Martha,' he whispered, 'do you have a man in an iron mask in your dungeon?'

But Martha didn't respond. Lord, she was nearly as dull as this funeral. Though nothing was as dull. Nothing!

At least the Archbishop was finally winding up. 'And now he has once again beaten me, this time to the grave. But I'm sure I will see him again in Heaven, where, perhaps, I will finally be in charge. Thanks be to God. Now I'd like to invite the dear departed King's daughter Martha to say a few words.'

Martha jumped in her seat as if she had been bitten by a rat. Maybe she'd been asleep, or maybe she'd actually been bitten by a rat! That would liven things up.

'Martha?' said the Archbishop.

Martha shook her head vigorously.

Sir John, who was sitting on the other side of her, leaned in and said quietly, 'Your Majesty, as Queen, and the daughter of the deceased, it behoves you to . . .'

At this, Martha got up and ran from the chapel.

Brilliant, thought Edwin, *why didn't I think of that? Oh, hang on –*

'I must see to my wife,' he said, and ran out of the chapel after her.

She was fast. It took Edwin a while to catch up with her. She'd only slowed down for a moment by the servants' staircase, pausing before heading up the main stairs and into their bedchamber. When Edwin arrived, she was sitting on the bed with her arms wrapped around herself, shaking.

'Good idea, running out like that,' he said. 'That funeral was deathly. I mean, obviously it was. What I actually mean is deathly as a metaphor for boring.'

Martha didn't say anything. Maybe she was upset. Fantastic! Now he could comfort her.

He sat down on the bed beside her.

'Don't be sad,' he said. 'If your father wasn't dead, you wouldn't be queen, and we wouldn't be married.'

She still didn't say anything. He put an arm around her. *This is it*, he thought. *This is the perfect time for us to bonk. Because I will be doing it in a caring way, and she will be grateful, and maybe let me do more.* He reached to pull her veil off.

'Stop!' she said, in a strange voice.

'I love you,' he said, which was the sort of thing husbands said, and went on tugging at the veil. She pushed his hands away.

'I'm not her,' she said. 'I'm not Martha.'

She took the veil off herself. It was Martha's servant, the skinny one – well, obviously. Edwin felt panic pouring into him. Where was his wife? What was this bitch doing in her clothes?

One thing was certain, he had to get rid of her before anybody else found out. He grabbed the girl around the neck and started to squeeze. She struggled against him, clawing at his hands to try to make him let go.

'She made me do it!' the girl hissed with all the air she had left. 'She made me dress in her clothes and told me to be silent so that she'd get a head start before you found out!'

That stopped him. 'Found out what?' he said. The girl was turning blue so he loosened his grip slightly.

'That she ran away.'

'She ran away?'

Edwin let go of the girl and she fell back on the bed, gasping. It was probably a bad idea to kill her, he'd have to get rid of the body and he didn't know the castle well enough yet to hide a corpse. And this place was so insular and parochial that people might notice if a servant was missing.

'Where did she go?' Edwin asked.

'I don't know.' The girl started to cry. 'If I knew I would tell you. It's true. She knows I can't keep my mouth shut, that's why she didn't tell me.'

'Listen to me,' said Edwin. 'She didn't run away. She was kidnapped. And if you tell anybody that she wasn't, I will kill you. You will tell everyone that it was her captors who made you impersonate her. If you say otherwise, I will accuse you of conspiring with them and you will be burned at the stake, a death so agonising you will wish I had strangled you.'

The girl nodded frantically. 'Yes, sir.'

'Yes, Your Majesty,' Edwin corrected her.

But he wasn't Your Majesty, not yet. He hadn't been crowned. And if anyone found out that the marriage hadn't been consummated, he'd have no legitimacy at all.

He thought fast, as fast as he was capable of. He had to get Martha back and a crown on his head or there'd be pretenders to the throne coming out of the woodwork faster than termites.

That he'd be consummating the marriage went without saying. Even if he didn't need to do it for legitimacy, he was determined to teach her a lesson about what happens to girls who misbehave. Besides, he needed an heir. But as soon as she had a child, his child, she was disposable. Find her, sprog her up, then kill her. That was the plan.

But how was he going to find her? He'd send the army on her trail, but they were loyal to Puddock, not to him, and if push came to shove, he was the one who would get shoved. He'd have to call in assistance from elsewhere. But where? Turning to Leo was out of the question. If he found out that Edwin's wife had run away from him, Edwin would never live it down.

There was only one place he could go to for help: Camelot.

Twenty-Three

Martha decided to ride south as far as she could, then board a boat to France. Once there she could take the universal panacea and resume her life as a woman. She'd be far enough away that nobody would know her for the missing Queen of Puddock, or even if they did, they wouldn't care. Sir John had made France sound nice. She had never been, had never even seen the sea before, although she spoke fluent French, alongside Latin, Greek and Castilian. These were some of the pointless accomplishments of being a princess.

It took her a while to get used to riding like a man, with one leg on either side of the horse, but once she'd got the hang of it she found it much better than side-saddle. It didn't hurt her back, for starters, now she didn't have to twist around to see forward. Having the sock between her legs was maybe the strangest part, but the way the movement of the horse made it rub against her was far more pleasant than the closest equivalent she could think of, which was the chafing of a new boot on her heel. No, it was definitely nicer than that. The unexpectedly exciting feeling of the sock added to the thrill of being out in the open, the wind in what was left of her hair, alone (most of the time)! Free (almost)! And with each passing day, heading away from the castle, and Edwin, and responsibility (definitely)!

The money thing turned out to be easier than she'd antici-pated. It seemed a gold coin would pay for most things, although some of the tradesmen looked at it strangely before accepting it. A few even gave her some money in return, which made very little sense, but she didn't want to show herself up by querying this. Maybe they felt sorry for her because she looked so young and lost.

The innkeepers certainly didn't feel sorry for her, though; she rather wished that they did. She was appalled to discover that not only did most inns have no such thing as a private room, they had no such thing as a private bed. She had never so much as shared a room with another person before, let alone got into bed with a smelly, snorting, flea-ridden member of the general public. Side by side on a lumpy mattress with a hairy, flatulent stranger – and this stranger would be a man, as often as not – she would lie, sleepless, staring at the ceiling and wondering how long it would be before she was murdered, and how often they washed the sheets. She wasn't sure which train of thought led to the more horrifying destination. The only advantage of the situation was that whenever an innkeeper crept up to her bed to try to rob her, as they so often did, she was invariably awake and able to chase him off. She didn't know why the innkeepers always seemed to target her. Every one of the people in the room must have been travelling with their own bag of gold, so why couldn't they try to steal someone else's money once in a while?

Daytime was better. She hadn't realised how different life was for men. They looked her straight in the eye when they spoke, asking her questions and listening to her answers, treating her with the easy, casual respect of equals. She liked it, but she was thrown by the expectation that she would have something to contribute to conversation. The frustration that she had felt as a girl her entire life – that nobody believed her to be competent at anything – was replaced by the terror that her competence was now assumed. Either way, her actual abilities didn't seem to come into it.

She found herself walking differently, taking wider steps

in her comfortable britches and boots, standing up straighter now that she no longer had to bow her head to avoid accidentally making eye contact with anyone. And whether because she was now a man or because she was now a commoner, nobody guarded their speech or conduct around her. Despite what she had been told, men gossiped just as much as women. In the inns where she slept and taverns where she ate, the big rumour was that La Beale Isoud had been spotted bathing in her chemise in the Cornish sea. Did this mean that love was restored between her and Tristan, and if so was this a good thing? (General opinion: true love will out, and they'd give her one themselves if they had the chance.) The other story, inevitably, was that the Queen of Puddock had been kidnapped (not run away, Martha noted), and that the King (ha! Was that how he was styling himself now?) was heading to Camelot to enlist the Round Table in a quest to find her. When people asked her opinion of that, she just shrugged.

In fact she shrugged as much as possible when asked about anything, because, like the apple without the core, Martha discovered that she and Nancy (mainly Nancy) had forgotten something important: she still had a woman's voice. She worried that her feminine intonation would alert everyone to the fact that she wasn't the man she was pretending to be. But after a while she realised that her high voice, combined with her slight build and dubious facial hair, served to reinforce the perception that she was very young. Given her evident naivity, this was in fact to her benefit.

So on the whole her escape plan appeared to be working. Indeed, when from time to time she forgot entirely that she was meant to be male and said things like, 'What lovely earrings, are those amethysts?' to some barmaid or other, rather than taking her for the impostor she was, the ladies fairly melted. Even though she had no interest in soliciting the attentions of women, she felt flattered and a little smug. It seemed that, in some ways, she was better at being a man than men were themselves.

Twenty-Four

Then, as things are frustratingly accustomed to do, everything changed.

She had stopped for lunch in a pleasant spot by the shores of a millpond, at the bottom of a gentle slope, surrounded by a copse of trees. Before unpacking the pheasant pie she had bought from the inn where she had stayed the night before, she led Silver down to the shores of the pond to drink. She left the horse at the edge of the water, then took a few paces back, because the ground was boggy and she didn't want to get her feet wet. She looked up at the clouds and wondered whether it was going to rain later.

'Martha,' said a voice.

'Yes?' said Martha, without thinking. And then – too late – 'I mean, no. Sorry. I thought you said – something else.'

'Martha,' said the voice again. It was a woman's voice, sonorous and clear, and it appeared to be coming from across the pond. Martha tugged at Silver's reins to try to drag him away, but he refused to lift his head out of the water.

In the middle of the pond there was a ripple, which grew into a small wave flowing outward in all directions, as first a sword, then a hand holding the sword, and then an entire woman, with arm outstretched, emerged from the water. The woman was wearing a blue gown and had long black hair flowing loosely down her back. She was completely dry and looked normal in every way apart from the fact that she was standing on the surface of the pond and holding a massive sword.

'I am the Lady of the Lake,' she said.

'What? It's not a lake. It's a millpond.'

'It's a Lake.'

'The mill is right there!'

The Lady of the Lake or Pond declined to look at the mill.

'You are Martha Penrose?' she said. 'Queen of the tiny realm of Puddock?'

'Look, it's not my fault it's a pond. There's no need to insult the realm.'

'I have a message for you, Martha.'

'I'm not Martha,' said Martha.

'You're not?'

'No.'

'You said "yes" a minute ago.'

'Well, I'm not.'

'Oh. Sorry.' The Lady lowered the sword and scratched her foot with it. 'It's true, you don't look much like a Martha. I probably should have noticed that.'

'Don't worry about it.'

'Well, this is embarrassing. I'm so sorry. I must have made a mistake with my paperwork. I haven't quite got the hang of it all yet. I'm not really the Lady of the Lake, you see. I'm just the locum. Nimue, the usual Lady of the Lake, has run off with Merlin and they needed somebody to cover. Usually I'm the Woman by the Well, and I started off as the Child at the Crossroads. Anyway, I had it in my schedule that I should appear now . . .' The Locum of the Lake or Pond peered up at the sun. 'Yes, and that Martha would be here, with a grey horse – the horse is here, at any rate – running away from her destiny, and that I should give her this sword and tell her that her brother is still alive.'

'My brother is still alive?'

'No. Not your brother. Martha's brother.'

'How can my – can Martha's brother still be alive? He was killed by Picts years ago.'

'I'm sorry, but if you're not Martha I can't tell you that.'

The Locum of whatever it was began to descend back into the water.

'What's the sword for?' said Martha quickly.

It was a beautiful sword, made of obsidian, black and gleaming, with two huge emeralds in the hilt. Martha felt something inside her ache to hold it.

'This? It's a magic sword. Its entire purpose is to protect Martha and help her get her brother back. That's why I was supposed to give it to her. Oh well. I've totally cocked that up, now. I may as well just chuck it back in the Lake.'

The Locum of the Lake/Pond swung her arm back as if to throw.

'Don't do that!' cried Martha.

'You're right. It's dangerous, throwing swords in lakes. You never know what might be under the surface. Or who. You'd think I'd know that, being of the Lake. I'll carry it down with me.'

The Locum of the Lake/Pond resumed her disappearance into the water.

'Wait!' said Martha. 'What if you gave it to me and I gave it to her?'

The Locum of the Lake/Pond paused, about knee-deep. She peered at Martha with suspicion.

'You know Martha?' she said.

'Yes.'

'The same Martha?'

'Queen. Running away from the castle. Dead brother. I mean, not dead brother. Yes. She's my best friend.'

'How do I know you're not just saying that to trick me into giving you the sword?'

'Well . . . Ask me anything about her.'

The Locum of the Lake/Pond thought for a bit. 'What's her favourite colour?' she said.

'Brown,' said Martha.

'Wrong.'

'But it is brown.'

'Nobody's favourite colour is brown.'

'Yes it is!'

'No it isn't.'

'So what's her favourite colour, then?'

'How am I supposed to know?'

'But you just asked me!'

'Exactly. I wouldn't need to ask you if I knew the answer.'

Martha fought the urge to march over the surface of the water and throttle the Locum of the Lake/Pond.

'Can't you just trust me?' she said instead.

'Why should I?'

Martha tried to think of a reason and couldn't come up with anything.

'Forget it,' said the Locum. 'I'll sort out the paperwork and we'll get it to her another way. I just hope nobody kills her in the meantime, while she's unarmed. I'm still in my probationary period.'

'What if I told you . . .' said Martha. She looked around to make sure that nobody else was within earshot. 'That I am Martha.'

'You just said you weren't Martha. You don't look at all like a Martha.'

'I'm in disguise.'

'You're a boy.'

'I'm in disguise as a boy.'

'You've got a beard. Sort of.'

'I know.'

'I'm sure they'd have mentioned it, if Martha had a beard.'

'It's a magic beard.'

'Make it do something, then.'

'No. I mean the fact that I have it is magic.'

'So it doesn't do anything.'

'It grows out of my face. Isn't that enough?'

'Well, it's not much of an act. I wouldn't pay to see it.'

'I'm a girl with a beard. A *queen* with a beard.'

'Says you.'

'What can I do to prove it to you?'

'A minute ago you were trying to prove that Martha was a friend of yours, and you didn't do a very good job of that either.'

'That's because Martha isn't a friend of mine.'

'Aha!'

'I *am* Martha.'

'Oh.'

'I'm here when you said I would be, aren't I? I've got the right horse with me. I'm the right height, the right build, I know Martha's favourite colour –'

'I still don't believe that it's brown.'

'It's because it goes with her hair! My hair!'

'Still weird.'

'I have the voice of a woman.'

'That's true,' conceded the Locum of the Lake/Pond. 'But it might be that your voice hasn't broken yet.'

'Of course it would be broken – I've got a beard.'

'You just said it was a magic beard.'

Martha clenched her fists and tried not to scream.

'If I looked like a girl you wouldn't make me go through all this,' she said, with as much calmness as she could muster. 'What kind of proof were you going to ask for?'

'Well, none.'

'You were just going to give the sword to any old girl who walked past with a grey horse –'

'At precisely the right time.'

'At precisely the right time! And here I am!'

'Looking like a boy.'

'In disguise!'

The Locum of the Lake/Pond hesitated. 'Do you have some form of identification?'

Some form of identification. Martha could only think of one. She grabbed hold of the waistband of her britches and yanked them down, sock and all.

'Good enough for you?' she said.

The Locum of the Lake/Pond averted her eyes. Martha pulled her britches back up.

'I concede that you are female,' the Locum said primly. 'I will allow that you may therefore be Martha in disguise. Thus, I will give you this sword and a message.'

'What's the message?'

'Your brother is still alive.'

'I know. You already said that. What else?'

'Nothing. That's the message.'

'That's it? Where is he?'

'I can't tell you that. All I can do is give you this sword, and –'

'Why can't you tell me?'

'All I can do is give you this –'

'Tell me where he is!'

'I can't.'

'Why not?'

'It's a thing.'

'A thing?'

'A Lake thing.'

'It's a pond!'

'Secrecy is the cornerstone of the Sorcery industry. If you put your complaint in writing I will raise it at the next Lake board meeting, but until then, all I can do is give you this sword –'

'Fine. Give me the godforsaken sword.'

Neither of the women moved.

'You need to come and get it,' said the Locum of the Lake/Pond.

'In there? Not all of us can walk on water, you know.'

'There's a boat.'

The Locum indicated a small wooden boat tied to a rickety jetty.

'I'm not getting in that. I'm the Queen of a tiny realm, remember?'

'I don't recall that there's any prohibition on royalty and boats.'

'Can't you bring me the sword?'

'If you want to rescue your brother you must come and receive this sword from me. It's regulations.'

'Is there someone else I can talk to?'

'If you put your complaint in writing I'll raise it with the –'

'Forget it! I'll get in the damn boat!'

Martha picked her way over to the jetty. She climbed gingerly into the boat, untied it, sat down and picked up the algae-stained oars. 'This had better be worth it,' she said.

'It's a very good magic sword,' said the Locum of the Lake/Pond. Martha felt the pull of the sword again, though she was loath to admit it.

'And if I wield this sword,' she said, trying to figure out how to make the boat go in the direction of the Locum rather than round in a small circle, 'I'll rescue my brother?'

'Not definitely. Pull harder with the right.'

'Not definitely?'

'Good acts one way. How Evil responds is up to Evil. I know it's not ideal, but it took us years to negotiate that contract.'

'I am on the side of good, though?'

'I can't confirm it. Evil often thinks it's the good one and that Good is evil, and as for Sorcery, we're inscrutable. If you stick your oar in and push with it, you'll go in reverse.'

Martha concentrated on the boat for a while. Every time she lifted the oars out of the water, cold pond water dripped down from the blades and up her sleeves. Every so often the Locum of the Lake/Pond would make observations like 'Have you never been in a boat before?' and 'Could you get a move on, please, I have a Chalice of Chastity to deliver before my shift is up', which didn't help with Martha's mood at all.

'These oars are giving me splinters,' said Martha.

'Put on some gloves?'

'You're not helping.'

'I'm not here to help.'

'You don't say. Surely I'm close enough, now?'

'Not even almost.'

'What if I don't want to rescue my brother?'

'Martha,' said the Locum of the Lake/Pond, her voice suddenly serious. 'We have done a bit of research, you know. We don't give these swords to just anybody.'

Martha focused all of her will on moving the boat in the right direction, as the rain clouds she had spotted earlier began to deliver their load. Finally she drew up alongside the Locum, dropped the oars and wiped her sweaty forehead on the back of her wrist. She signed and dated the form the Locum gave her, and then, at long last, she took possession of the sword. As soon as she touched it a thrill ran up her arm. She closed her hand around the hilt and felt the perfect rightness of the way it filled her palm. She gave it an experimental swoosh. It was a good swoosh, though it made the boat rock alarmingly.

'I've got to give you this as well, or I won't get my bonus,' said the Locum, tossing a sword belt with a plain leather scabbard into the boat at Martha's feet.

'Thank you,' said Martha.

'You're welcome,' said the Locum, a little sulkily, as the murky water of the pond swallowed her.

Twenty-Five

Forgetting that she had planned to have lunch, Martha remounted Silver and guided him back towards the road. But she didn't know which way to turn. Jasper was still alive. How was it possible? His bones had been on display in a glass case in the castle chapel for the last six years. They were decoratively arranged around a sentimental watercolour of the boy in his prime, which had been framed with the precious stones that gave Jasper his name. Then again, she supposed the bones could have been anybody's. Jasper's squire had arranged for the flesh to be boiled off them before sending them home, so none of them had ever seen the body. But if they weren't Jasper's bones, whose were they? There was no way of asking the squire, because he, too, had been killed, not long after Jasper's death. Martha shook her head. Apparently there was no such thing as Jasper's death. So where was he? What had happened to him? And why had he never come home?

Martha tried to feel joy and relief in the fact that her brother was still alive, and of course she did feel those things. But she also felt a deep, terrible sense of disturbance. Death was not the worst fate that could befall a person, far from it. Her father was better off dead than alive in the state he had been in. And she remembered a story she had heard as a child, which had given her nightmares, about Elaine of Corbenic, the mother of Galahad. Until Lancelot rescued her, she was trapped by a sorceress's spell for years in a bath of boiling water, consumed in endless, hopeless agony. What if Jasper was in a similar predicament? Did she really have the ability to rescue him, even with a magic sword? She drew the sword again for a moment, looked at its beautiful, gleaming blade. She had no idea what to do with a sword, she had never even held one before. She had to hope that the sword knew what it was doing.

As for where to look for Jasper, she had no idea. He had been in the far north when he died – when he disappeared – or so she had been told. In reality he could have been anywhere. And that was six years ago. Who was to say that he hadn't moved since then? Curse that damned bitch in the pond! Why couldn't she have told her where to find him? Martha should have commanded her, as Queen –

Martha stopped. She wasn't Queen. If Jasper was alive, he was the King. She was just a princess, same as she had always been. When she found Jasper, he would take his rightful throne and she would . . . Go back to a life of putting rosettes on marrows? And of being married to Edwin? No. Martha would find him, she would rescue him, she would send him home, but she was not going back to that.

Which didn't solve the problem of where her brother was. Martha had nothing, no clues, no way to even begin tracking him down.

Except what had the pond woman said? That the purpose of the sword was to help Martha find her brother. Not just save him. Find him.

Martha dismounted from Silver and removed the sword from its scabbard. She placed it on a flat piece of ground, put her hand on the hilt, and then spun it as fast as it would turn. The direction in which the sword pointed when it stopped? That was the way she would go.

Twenty-Six

It turned out that you couldn't spin a sword on any old piece of ground, because clumps of grass or sticking-out stones tended to get in the way, so every time she came to a suitable piece of flat rock or earth, Martha stopped to check for directions. The sword appeared to be pretty keen on heading northwest, more or less back the way she'd come from, guiding Martha away from the crossing to France. Instead they travelled through Puddock and across the border into Tuft – a hefty amount of her gold being confiscated at the customs post on the way in.

At first it was an uneventful journey, though Martha had a feeling of disquiet, having no way of knowing whether the sword was taking her closer to her brother or just in random directions.

Then, late one night, she had gone to the dining room of an inn. The inn was slightly off the path designated by the sword, but it was pouring with rain, and if she'd carried on in the direction the sword had wanted her to travel she'd have been riding for at least another two hours before reaching shelter. She decided to pick up the path in the morning, and headed for the nearest village, a rather bleak place where the houses were still black with soot from the last time marauders had tried to burn it down, which, had they succeeded, would probably have been an improvement. The inn was called the Dipsomaniac Camel, and she supposed that the sign might have been of a camel, but she had never seen a camel, and neither, she was fairly certain, had the sign painter.

Despite the lateness of the hour, the inn's dining hall was still busy, perhaps because the sleeping quarters were outside up a flight of steps and nobody was ready to head out into the pouring rain.

Martha took a seat at the end of a long, thickly hewn wooden table, and the barmaid brought her a sour ale and a trencher of stale bread and rancid butter. A few seats down from her was a man dressed as a knight, surrounded by a circle of onlookers. Martha couldn't believe that he was a real knight; it seemed more likely that he had stolen his colours, possibly from a corpse. The flesh of his blotchy, purple face seemed to be melting away from the bone like bad tallow, his desultory pieces of armour were rusty and unmatched, his teeth outnumbered the hairs on his head, his eyes outnumbered his teeth, and he both looked and smelt as if he'd been rolling in a midden. To Martha's astonishment, the supposed knight's audience – which was considerable – was hanging on his every word.

'I've reason to believe that she's in the vicinity,' he told the group. 'Possibly being held in this very village.'

'What would the Queen of Puddock be doing in a cesspit like this?' called out a stocky man with a greasy cowlick of hair half obscuring one eye.

Martha's hand flew to her sword's hilt, and she'd half started out of her chair before she remembered that she was in disguise. She sat back down and took a deep breath to steady herself.

'Who is that?' she asked a scrubby-faced boy who was sitting across from her, and who didn't look old enough to be in a tavern, let alone making his way so steadily through the tankards of ale littered around his trencher.

'Sir Gordon Pencuddy. He's a knight. I'm his squire.'

'He really is a knight?'

'Of a sort. He is of the Table of Less Valued Knights.'

'And what is it he's saying about the Queen of Puddock?' Martha managed to choke out.

'That silly wench? Haven't you heard? She's gone and got herself kidnapped. This is why they shouldn't let women rule. Sir Gordon and I are trying to track her down.'

'Succeeding, thank you!' called Sir Gordon, while some people cheered and others hooted their derision. 'The reward is as good as mine.'

'I'm sure she'll give you a reward once you weasel her out!' shouted a lanky, lantern-jawed man at the far end of the table.

'That skinny piece? I'd sooner ride a weasel,' said Sir Gordon.

'He would and all!' said the man with the cowlick.

'Though there's no need to look at the mantelpiece when you're stoking the fire,' said the knight.

The gathered crowd laughed.

'There's a reward?' said Martha to the squire.

'Well, the new King with the giant teeth went up to see Arthur in Camelot,' said the squire.

'You mean the Prince Consort,' muttered Martha.

'Arthur gave him his very own Knight of the Round Table to go running around looking for his bitch. That Knight's reward will be virtue, of course. But Sir Gordon reckons if he finds her first, this King will have to give us a real reward. If he doesn't, he'll just refuse to hand her over. I'm sure he can find some use for her. It's not every Less Valued Knight who can boast of tupping a queen, even a minor and scrawny one.'

'She'd die first,' said Martha.

'Or during. Or after, I have no doubt,' said the squire. 'The King won't hold onto her for long, now she's been kidnapped and sullied. He'll keep her until she's spawned an heir, and then my guess is she'll meet with an unfortunate accident, leaving him to rule as Regent.'

Martha felt her insides heave. She knew he was right. If she'd ever considered heading home to Puddock – and on several miserable, sleepless nights, she had – this made her determined never to return.

'What makes you think she's here?' she asked Sir Gordon.

'I can't reveal my sources,' said the Knight, 'but they are very reliable.'

'Bullshit,' the squire told Martha. 'He's checking every village from here to Cornwall. She's got to be somewhere. It's basically a lucky dip.'

'I'd give her a lucky dip!' said the lanky wit from the crowd.

'Well,' said Martha, standing up, her heart pounding madly in her chest, 'it's been delightful meeting all of you fellow men, but I've got a long ride in the morning.'

'You know, you look a bit like the Queen,' said Sir Gordon, squinting at Martha. 'Are you sure you're not her brother?'

'Her brother is dead,' said Martha.

'Seriously, though.' The knight took a shiny, newly minted coin out of a pouch at his belt and held it up. 'Spitting image, apart from that caterpillar on your lip.'

'Very funny,' said Martha, forcing herself to laugh. 'I wish I had half her money. Goodnight, everyone.'

She forced herself not to run until she was out of the inn. Then she raced to the stables, mounted Silver, and rode away as fast as she could.

Twenty-Seven

From then on, Martha travelled with one hand on her sword, for reassurance. She tried to avoid people as much as possible, buying herself a bedroll so that, when the weather was good, she could sleep under trees rather than in inns. Instead of frequenting markets, she attempted to gather her food from the wild as much as possible, though that proved harder than story-books would have her believe. She was hungry all the time.

A few days after the encounter at the Dipsomaniac Camel, Martha was riding through a small wood bordering an area of heathland in the centre of Tuft. The wood was fairly dense but not particularly brambly, with minimal immediate threat of carnivores, bandits or stinging nettles, so she decided to stop to pick berries for breakfast. After what felt like hours, she had managed, triumphantly, to gather a small palmful of green wild strawberries, which, though she pretended to herself to find them delicious, were tongue-shrivellingly bitter. At least there probably weren't enough of them to give her the runs. Defecating, it turned out, was far from the highlight of this horseback adventure, especially as she hadn't thought to pack a spade, and the sword managed to shirk digging activities by developing a stubborn weight and unwieldiness when brought into proximity with dirt.

After she'd eaten her berries and remounted, she picked her way through the trees, trying, and mostly succeeding, not to let low branches smack her in the face. It was slow going, so she decided to cut across the heathland, even though there was more chance of running into other people on open ground.

She was just turning towards the heath when her sword erupted out of her scabbard and, with Martha clinging to the hilt, smacked her horse hard on the rump. Silver reared and bolted out of the woods. Martha screamed and tried to pull on the reins with her unsworded hand, while the sword itself led the charge, dragging Martha, horse and all, towards a group of travellers: a man, a woman, and what appeared to be a giant, riding on – if the drawings she'd seen in the castle library were to be believed – an elephant.

'Stop it, stop it, stop it, stop it, stop it!' begged Martha, as the sword swung at one of the travellers – she didn't know which, because she had her eyes shut, her arm juddered painfully as her blade clashed against what must be her opponent's sword with resounding metallic clangs.

I'm going to die, she suddenly thought, with perfect clarity. *What a ridiculous way to go.*

And then the fear took over once again.

PART THREE

Twenty-Eight

Humphrey knocked the boy from his horse and jumped down after him, fighting his way forward while the boy parried his blows surprisingly expertly for someone who had his eyes shut.

'Leave me alone!' shouted the boy, in a high, girlish voice. 'Stop hitting me!'

'I'm not hitting you,' said Humphrey, grunting with the effort of the fight. 'You don't "hit" with swords. And anyway, you tried to kill me. You're not in a position to make demands.'

'I didn't mean to!' wailed the boy.

'To me it looked a lot like you meant to.'

The boy was now staggering backwards under the weight of Humphrey's assault, the knight swinging his blade harder and faster to try to deal the mortal blow. Still, somehow, the boy managed to fend him off, even though he hadn't opened his eyes so much as a crack.

'Humphrey's going to kill him,' Elaine said to Conrad in a horrified voice. She had never seen anyone die, and had no wish to, especially not a terrified child.

'I expect so,' said Conrad, with an attempt at casualness. He had never seen anyone die either, but, as both a squire and a giant, he thought it was the kind of thing he should take in his stride. He didn't feel like he was taking it in his stride – in fact he felt a cold, sick terror, and an urgent desire to urinate – but maybe that came with practice.

'Can't you do something about it?' said Elaine.

'Why should I?' said Conrad. 'The boy started it!' Which was true enough. Quite apart from that, the last thing he wanted to do was climb down from the safety of Jemima's back and enter the fray.

'He's a child!' insisted Elaine.

'He must be as old as I am.'

'He's frightened!'

'Well then, he shouldn't have attacked a knight!'

This was undeniable. But Elaine couldn't sit doing nothing while this scared kid was hacked to pieces, even if he had started the fight.

'Humphrey, leave him alone!' she shouted.

'If I stop, he'll kill me,' Humphrey shouted back.

'No, I won't!' said the boy. But still his sword fought on, repelling Humphrey's every stroke.

Conrad and Elaine had both seen duels at tournaments, but this was different. It was ugly and brutal, devoid of the courtly flourishes knights added to entertain the crowd. It was a work-manlike, determined push towards death. Not knowing what else to do, Elaine jumped down off her horse and leapt onto Humphrey's back, putting her hands over his eyes.

'What are you doing?' yelled Humphrey. 'Do you want to get us both killed?'

He tried to shake her off, still waving his sword, now in-effectually, at his opponent. The boy, finally released from the onslaught, turned and began to run. But the blade of his sword got tangled in the undergrowth, and he tripped and went flying, dropping his sword as he fell. He lay winded in the grass, whimpering and trying to find the strength to crawl away.

'Get off me, Elaine!' said Humphrey. 'Let go, you insane woman! It's fine. I'm not going to kill him.'

Elaine let go, falling painfully to her knees. Humphrey sprang forward, rolled the boy onto his back, straddled him with a knee on each arm, and held his sword to his neck, so tightly that he broke the pale skin. The boy moaned with fear.

'I thought you said you weren't going to kill him!' Elaine was outraged.

'Well, I'm certainly not going to let him kill me,' said Humphrey, but he relaxed the sword slightly. A trickle of blood ran down the boy's throat. 'Who are you?' he demanded.

'My name's Mar – Marcus,' the boy replied. He had his eyes open, finally.

'What the hell were you doing, Marcus?'

'I don't know,' replied the boy.

Conrad snorted.

'I don't!' Marcus insisted, an indignant tone entering his voice. 'It wasn't me, it was the sword! It just jumped into my hand and attacked for no reason.' He glowered at the sword, which was lying peacefully on the grass as if butter wouldn't melt in its sheath. 'I thought you were supposed to be protecting me!' he snapped at it.

Humphrey glanced at the sword, which did not react to Marcus's admonition. 'Conrad,' he said, 'secure the sword.'

Conrad dismounted from Jemima and marched over to the sword, irritated by how frightened he felt of it and determined not to let it show. He put one of his heavy boots down on top of the blade. He tried not to imagine the sword rearing up and slicing his foot in half.

'Where did you get that elephant?' Marcus asked him.

'You know what it is?' said Elaine, surprised.

'The elephant is none of your fucking business,' Conrad growled at Marcus.

'Forget about the elephant. Where did you get that sword?' Humphrey asked.

'The sword is none of your . . .' Marcus began – but thought better of it as Humphrey's blade pressed against his throat again. 'It's a magic sword,' he said instead. 'The Lady of the Pond – of the Lake – gave it to me.'

'If it's a magic sword, what's its name?' said Humphrey.

'Its name?'

'Yes, all magic swords have a name.'

There was a brief pause. Then Marcus offered, 'Leila.'

'*Leila*?' said Humphrey.

'Leila's a name, isn't it?' said Marcus.

'Magic swords aren't called things like Leila,' said Conrad. 'They have names like Excalibur.'

'This one's called Leila,' said Marcus.

'Leila's a girl's name,' said Conrad.

'So?' said Marcus.

'Swords are male.'

'Why?' said Marcus.

'Why d'you think?' said Conrad.

Marcus shook his head in confusion.

'Look at it,' said Conrad.

Marcus looked at the sword for a moment, then blushed.

'And you claim that it's Leila who attacked me, not you,' said Humphrey.

Conrad rolled his eyes at Humphrey's use of the sword's supposed name.

'Yes!' said Marcus. 'I was just riding through the woods when she jumped out of her scabbard and into my hand. She hit Silver, my horse – if the little giant thinks Silver an acceptable name for a horse?'

Everyone looked at Conrad. He nodded irritably.

'Good,' said Marcus. He turned back to Humphrey. 'And then when Silver galloped towards you, Leila just started attacking you, I don't know why.'

'He was probably pissed off because you gave him a girl's name and now he's trying to get you killed,' said Conrad.

'It's a black sword,' noted Elaine.

'So what?' said Marcus.

'You've got quite an attitude for someone in your position,' said Humphrey, though he couldn't help but admire the boy's pluck.

'Do you think it's a coincidence that it's black?' Elaine said to Humphrey.

'Let's find out,' said Humphrey. 'Marcus, where were you on Saturday, a fortnight ago?'

Marcus blanched. 'I . . . I can't tell you,' he said.

'You think you're in a position to deny me?' said Humphrey. He slid the edge of his sword along Marcus's gullet, but the boy refused to speak. Humphrey couldn't push his sword any harder without cutting Marcus's throat, which would be counterproductive, so instead he pressed his knees heavily into the boy's skinny biceps.

'Very well!' cried Marcus. 'I was at the Queen's wedding! Queen Martha's wedding, in Puddock!'

'Oh right. You were at the Queen's wedding,' said Conrad. 'As guest of honour, I'm sure.'

'What makes you think we'll believe that?' said Humphrey.

'I work – worked there. At the castle. That's why I didn't want to tell you. I ran away. I don't want them to find me. I stole some money. And the horse. And . . . and the sword. It belongs to the Queen. I lied before.'

'So he isn't called Leila,' said Conrad.

'Yes she is,' insisted Marcus. 'Queen Martha called her Leila.'

'Then Queen Martha is an idiot.'

'She is not!'

'Enough,' said Humphrey. 'Marcus, can you prove that you worked at the castle?'

'I know everything about Queen Martha. I was one of her pages. Ask me anything.'

'What's her favourite colour?' said Conrad.

Marcus hesitated, almost as if he had fallen afoul of this question before. 'Blue,' he said.

'That doesn't count. Everyone's favourite colour is blue,' said Conrad.

'Describe her husband,' said Humphrey.

'Her husband? Why do you want to know about him?'

'You were at the wedding, weren't you?'

'Fine. His name's Edwin, he's next in line to the throne of Tuft. He's tall. Blond hair. Dark eyes. Sort of handsome, I suppose, until you see his teeth.'

'What's wrong with his teeth?' said Elaine.

'They're gigantic.' Marcus shuddered. 'And he's stupid, and a bully and a braggart. You know he's calling himself King of Puddock now, when he's only the Prince Consort? He's the kind of man who lies about his jousting record.'

'I don't know if you're the Queen's page or not, but you've definitely met Edwin,' said Humphrey. 'Do you own any black armour?'

'What? No, of course not. I don't own any armour. Even these clothes are stolen. If I had armour, I'd be wearing it. Why aren't you wearing armour, if you're a knight?'

'How do you know I'm a knight?'

'The little giant said so.'

'Would you stop calling me the little giant?' said Conrad, and was annoyed to see Humphrey stifle a laugh.

'The Knight was riding a black horse,' Elaine said. 'This boy's horse is grey.'

'People can change horses,' said Humphrey.

'I think you should kill him,' said Conrad.

'No!' yelped Marcus, his voice higher-pitched than ever.

'Please don't,' said Elaine, putting her hand on Humphrey's arm.

'I'm sorry but I've got to admit Conrad has a point,' Humphrey said to Marcus. 'You burst out of the woods and tried to take my head. Give me one good reason why I shouldn't take yours.'

'We've already established that it was the sword to blame, not me,' said Marcus.

'You'll forgive me if I don't find that entirely persuasive.' Humphrey's blade pressed against Marcus's throat once again.

Marcus lay silently for several moments, his breath coming fast, the blood draining from his already pale face.

'Well?' said Humphrey.

'I'm thinking,' said Marcus in a strangled tone. 'Surely you can spare me a few seconds to try to save my life.'

Humphrey nodded. Conrad let out a grunt of exasperation.

'I can help you find the Queen,' Marcus said at last.

'We're not looking for the Queen,' said Elaine. But Humphrey raised his eyebrows with an expression of interest.

'You're a knight, aren't you?' said Marcus, appealing directly to him. 'I thought all the knights were looking for the Queen. I met one in a tavern only a few days ago who said he had good information that she was nearby.'

'Sir Dorian Pendoggett?' said Humphrey.

'No. He was called, um . . . Sir Gregory? Sir Gordon. Pen-something else.'

'Gordy?' said Humphrey, astonished. 'But he's a Less Valued Knight. And not just slightly less. He got caught selling fake Holy Grails. What happened to Dorian?'

'I don't know anything about a Dorian,' said Martha. 'But Sir Gordon said he was trying to get to the Queen first, because there was a reward.'

'How big a reward?' said Humphrey.

'Knights don't do things for the reward,' Conrad reminded him peevishly.

'Yes, but it never hurts,' said Humphrey.

'It's a huge reward,' improvised Marcus. 'And the thing is, Sir Gordon thinks that she's been kidnapped, but I know she ran away.'

'How would you know something like that?' said Conrad. 'Don't tell me, the Queen confided it all in her beloved page.'

'Actually I overheard her talking to her lady-in-waiting. Whose name is Deborah, if you want to check. Martha ran away on her wedding night because she didn't want to be married to that idiot Edwin. The plan was for Deborah to dress as the Queen for her father's funeral the next day, with a heavy veil, so that Martha could get a head start before anyone found out she was gone. Anyway, she left so quickly that she abandoned most of her possessions, and that's when I took my chance, taking the sword and the money and the horse. I assumed everyone would think that Martha had taken them. And it would have been a good plan, except that Leila wants me to take her back to Martha.'

'And part of her plan was to attack me?' said Humphrey.

'His plan,' Conrad corrected.

'Well, it's worked, hasn't it?' said Marcus. 'I'm telling you about the sword now, and about how Martha ran away –'

'*Queen* Martha,' said Humphrey. 'You keep calling her Martha.'

'*Queen* Martha, and now you need to find her and give her the sword back, don't you? She might be in danger without it. And you're a Knight of the Round Table – you can't refuse.'

There was a lengthy silence as Humphrey pondered. At last he said, 'Well, it's certainly something that a Knight of the Round Table would do.'

'And something that a knight who wasn't of the Round Table would do to get back onto the Round Table,' muttered Conrad.

'Isn't it in your code?' said Marcus. 'To give all maidens succour?'

'You're not a maiden,' said Conrad.

'But the Queen is,' said Marcus.

Conrad narrowed his eyes at the boy.

'So where is she, then?' said Humphrey.

There was a split second of hesitation before Marcus replied, 'I don't know.'

'Kill him and let's get out of here,' said Conrad.

'But the sword knows where she is!' said Marcus quickly. 'If you spin the sword, it points towards the Queen, so you know which direction to ride.'

'Or it just spins and points in a random direction,' said Conrad.

'Let's test it,' Humphrey said. 'Conrad, put the sword on a patch of earth and scratch YES and NO into the dirt on either side.'

Conrad picked up Leila, holding her at arm's length. 'If it were up to me . . .' he said to Marcus, and he drew a line across his neck with his finger. Nevertheless, he prepared the ground, embarrassed by his ungainly writing.

'Right,' said Humphrey. 'Let's ask this sword some questions. Leila, is it daytime? Conrad, spin the sword.'

Conrad put his hand on the hilt of the sword and gave it a push. Nothing happened. He pushed harder, but the sword refused to budge. He pushed as hard as he could, but still the sword did not turn.

Fury in his voice, he said, 'It won't move.'

Humphrey looked at Elaine.

'Lady Elaine, would you be willing?' he said.

'If he can't do it, I don't see what I'll be able to do,' said Elaine. She didn't even want to go after this queen, but she wanted Marcus to die even less, so she obligingly tried to spin the sword. Again the sword would not move.

'Conrad, hold Marcus down,' said Humphrey. 'And don't break him.'

Conrad pinned the boy down with one huge hand while Humphrey went to try his luck with the sword.

'I could snap your neck like a toothpick,' Conrad hissed at Marcus.

'Not if you don't want to get in trouble with the boss,' replied Marcus.

Humphrey tried with all his might to spin the sword. Again, she refused to move.

'Maybe she'll only spin for me,' Marcus said.

'All right,' said Humphrey. 'I can see there's only one way to do this. Conrad, release him. Marcus, you get up and walk – slowly! – to the sword. When I ask the question, spin her gently, with your left hand.'

'Him,' muttered Conrad, reluctantly releasing his hold on the boy.

'And if you try anything funny, I will kill you, whether it's the magic sword's fault or not. Understood?'

'Understood,' said Marcus.

He went over to Leila and knelt down.

'Please don't do anything that will get me killed,' he begged the sword. The sword did not respond.

'Leila,' said Humphrey, 'is it daytime?'

Marcus put his left hand on the sword's hilt, feeling the familiar thrill beneath his fingers. He took a breath and spun the sword, which turned easily at his touch, coming to rest pointing at YES.

'Leila,' said Humphrey, 'is my name Humphrey?'

YES again.

'Leila,' said Humphrey, 'is Marcus telling the truth?'

The sword turned for a long time before finally coming to rest pointing at NO.

'Interesting,' said Conrad.

'Well?' said Humphrey.

'It's because Queen Martha's favourite colour is actually brown,' said Marcus.

'Nobody's favourite colour is brown,' said Conrad.

'Why would you lie about something like that?' said Humphrey.

'Because nobody ever believes me when I tell the truth!' said Marcus, looking pointedly at Conrad. 'Martha likes brown because it goes with her hair, and it reminds her of animal fur.'

'Martha sounds like a bore,' said Conrad.

'There's no right or wrong reason to like a colour,' said Elaine.

'Whose side are you on?' said Conrad.

Elaine held up her hands.

'What else are you lying about?' said Humphrey to Marcus, in an attempt to return to the point.

'Nothing, I swear!' said Marcus. 'Nothing important,' he added under his breath. Then, louder, he said, 'I was at the wedding, Martha did run away, and Leila does know where she is.'

'Leila, do you know where Queen Martha is right now?' Humphrey asked the sword.

This time it was a swift YES.

'Which direction?'

The sword came to the end of its spin pointing at Marcus.

'East,' said Humphrey.

'Oh, come on,' said Conrad.

Elaine took a step forward. 'I've got some questions for the sword.'

'By all means,' said Humphrey.

Elaine knelt on the ground beside the sword. 'Leila, did Marcus have anything to do with the disappearance of my fiancé, Sir Alistair Gilbert?'

Marcus spun the sword. The answer was NO.

'Leila,' said Elaine breathlessly, 'do you know where Sir Alistair is?'

Marcus spun the sword. Leila spun round and round so many times that they began to think she was never going to slow. But suddenly, abruptly, she stopped, at the exact midpoint between YES and NO. They all stared.

'I think she means *maybe*,' said Marcus eventually. 'Leila, can you help Lady Elaine find this Sir Alistair?'

He pushed on the hilt. The sword spun round. YES.

'Marcus can stay,' said Elaine, standing. 'The sword too.'

'Since when is it your decision?' said Conrad.

'It will save us lots of time,' said Elaine. She brushed dirt from her knees. 'Now when we find the knights in black armour,

Humphrey doesn't have to fight them. We can just ask Leila if they were involved.'

'So everybody's calling it Leila now?' said Conrad.

'Get back on your elephant and shut up,' said Humphrey. 'We're heading east.'

Twenty-Nine

Sir Humphrey took custody of Leila, and Martha felt the loss as if she had been wrenched away from a friend. She rode at the front with him, Silver's bridle roped to his horse's saddle, while Lady Elaine and the irritating little giant followed. She was only allowed to touch Leila when spinning her for directions. This Martha did with the cold blade of Humphrey's own sword at her throat, so there was no way that she could pick Leila up and attempt to fight her way out of her predicament. She would ask the sword, 'Leila, which way should we go?' knowing that asking Leila to direct them to the Queen would not only fail to get them to wherever Jasper was, but would also unmask her very quickly, assuming the others were smart and paying attention. The knight and the maiden seemed sharp enough, she supposed; less so the little giant. He probably used most of his brainpower getting commands to his distant hands and feet. Fortunately nobody seemed to pick up on Martha's duplicitous choice of words. Leila was sending them in a broadly south-easterly direction, yet again back the way Martha had come, though not with enough predictability to make either herself or Martha surplus to requirements. Why Leila had forced her to do a massive detour, with the sole result of getting her captured by Humphrey, Martha could only speculate. All she could think was that Jasper, himself, was on the move.

Meanwhile she was terrified that her secret identity was going to be revealed. It was one thing pretending to be a man for a few hours in a crowded and noisy tavern. It was something else entirely to pass as male for day after day after day.

The first test had come early on, when Humphrey had pulled up his horse and announced that it was time to shoot the yellow arrow, which turned out to have nothing to do with archery. Elaine headed for a bush. Martha nearly followed her before she realised that she was supposed to accompany Humphrey and Conrad to a nearby stand of trees.

What do I do, what do I do, what do I do? thought Martha, as she skirted round Jemima – the creature made her nervous. She cursed that young Crone's insistence that she couldn't turn her into an anatomically correct boy; how hard could it be? It was sheer laziness on her part. Humphrey and Conrad, clearly accustomed to companionable pissing, headed for the same tree, chatting as they went. Martha chose one a few paces away.

'Don't go running off, now,' said Humphrey.

'Wouldn't dream of it,' said Martha, whose only thought was of running off. Oh, and of relieving herself, because her bladder was full to exploding. She stared at the tree trunk in front of her. *Come on, think, think, THINK!*

'You're taking your time,' observed Humphrey.

'My buttons are snarled up,' said Martha.

There must be an answer. Distract them and squat as quick as I can? Wet myself? What?

The tree trunk, she noticed, was shedding bark. Some of the pieces flaking off it were quite big. As quietly and subtly as she could, and thanking the Lord that she'd picked a tree wide enough to hide what she was doing, she peeled a large slice of bark from the tree, pulled down her britches a few inches, put the bark in between her legs as a kind of sloping ledge and then pissed onto it, allowing the urine to slide down the bark and onto the ground in front of her. Success! Martha felt triumphant.

These practical problems seemed the hardest to solve, but in many ways they turned out to be the easiest. People saw what they expected to see. So if a man was hesitating before taking a piss behind a tree, it was more likely that he had a shy bladder than that he was a woman and constructing a piss-slope from bark.

Beyond these mechanical matters, though, Martha consistently said and did the wrong thing. On the first night they pitched their camp, Humphrey sent Martha and Conrad together to get firewood. Martha tried to snap the branches from trees while Conrad looked on in disbelief. At last he pointed out that green wood wouldn't burn, and there were plenty of fallen boughs to choose from.

'Do it yourself, then, if you're so clever,' said Martha.

'Talk to me like that again and I'll cuff you,' said Conrad.

Martha's jaw dropped. Nobody had ever threatened to cuff her before, not even when she was a baby.

She staggered back to camp bent double under the weight of the wood she was carrying, unable to see why Conrad, who was bigger and stronger and better suited intellectually to manual labour, couldn't carry it all himself. Humphrey, meanwhile, had dug a pit for the fire, so Martha plonked down all of her wood in the middle of it. Humphrey stared at her.

'Aren't you going to light it?' said Martha.

'You don't just pile the wood in a heap,' said Humphrey.

'Why not?' said Martha. 'It all burns, doesn't it?'

Humphrey knelt down and started painstakingly arranging the wood into a pyramid, which seemed completely pointless to Martha, as it would look exactly the same once it was ablaze.

Once the fire was lit, Humphrey, Conrad and Elaine began pitching the tents. Martha took the opportunity to dig through her saddlebags looking for a book to read.

'Aren't you going to help?' said Conrad.

'No,' said Martha.

'That wasn't a question,' said Conrad.

'Yes it was,' said Martha.

She sat down on a stump and opened her book. Seconds later,

she found herself picked up by Conrad, tucked under his arm, and carried towards Elaine, who was laying out her tent. He dropped her, sprawling, to the ground.

'She's a lady,' he said. 'Help her.'

Martha opened her mouth to protest, but she was in a bind. If she said that a lady was just as capable of pitching a tent as a man, then she had talked herself into helping, even if the others didn't realise it. If not, then it was her role as man to do the tent-pitching, and, worse, she had lost the argument with Conrad. She decided that the best solution was to supervise Elaine, offering useful advice, even though she had never pitched a tent before. It didn't look that hard. She could tell that Elaine was grateful for the input by the way she kept saying, 'Thank you, Marcus,' the strain in her voice no doubt due to the effort of hauling the canvas around.

After they had eaten their mediocre meal and it was time to sleep, Martha headed instinctively towards the women's tent. It was only when she saw Elaine's shocked expression that she realised she was supposed to sleep with Humphrey and Conrad. The tent wasn't really big enough for three, especially if one of those three was Conrad, but at least she had her own bedroll. Inside the tent, the two men stripped to their underwear and climbed beneath their blankets. Martha searched through her belongings until she found the little wads of cotton she had brought with her from the castle, then began carefully wiping rosewater onto her cheeks and forehead. Then she applied lemon juice to her freckles to lighten them. It was only when she was pulling a silk pillowcase out of her bag that she realised both men were gawping at her.

'What?' she said. 'It keeps your skin smooth. You should both get one.'

She was making mistakes, she knew, each mistake compounding the mistake before and making her look increasingly suspicious. *How do men behave?* she asked herself, but she only knew how men behaved when they were with a princess, not how they behaved when they were with one another. She needed to learn, and fast, and resolved to watch Humphrey and Conrad, as covertly as she could.

Thirty

Or rather, increasingly, she covertly watched Humphrey. She didn't know what to make of him. He was her captor. He could kill her at any time. Leila must have had her reasons for attacking him, even if Martha didn't know what they were. Somehow Humphrey must be involved in Jasper's disappearance, or be standing in the way of Martha finding him. Even if she hadn't been in fear of death at his hand, she wouldn't have been able to trust him.

And yet there was something appealing about him. She was drawn to his rugged looks and manner, so different from the wan courtiers she was used to in Puddock. The dry way he teased Conrad and even Elaine. Martha hated being teased, and yet she found herself wishing Humphrey would tease her too. She was mesmerised by his effortless confidence, the way he assumed the lead and everyone else just fell into line. If she'd had that kind of natural authority, maybe she could have been queen after all.

She felt a sort of agitation whenever he was near her. In their fight, when he had straddled her, forcing her arms down with his knees, he'd been close enough for her to smell his odour of salt and leather, and she'd felt a sudden, oddly pleasurable alertness. This feeling never went away so long as he was close by, and he was always close by. It gave her the same gnawing sense in her stomach as hunger, the same slight nausea. And even in that first moment, when she should have been concentrating on staying alive, she found that she wanted to impress him very much. It was a feeling that increased with the passing days.

They always rode in the same formation, Martha up front with Humphrey, then Elaine and Conrad behind. Martha and Humphrey rode in silence, while Elaine and Conrad chattered away to each other like two canaries. From time to time Humphrey would glance back at Elaine with an expression that Martha found all too easy to interpret. Elaine was lovely, her face fresh as a new sweep of snow. Martha wanted to slap her. Weren't queens the ones who were supposed to be effortlessly beautiful? She wondered if Humphrey would look at her that way if she still had the appearance of a woman. But no, even before her transformation, she'd looked like an underfed fourteen-year-old boy.

Humphrey never looked at her at all, and only addressed her to bark instructions. Apparently he was still bearing a grudge over Leila trying to kill him, even though Martha had made it clear that it had had nothing to do with her. He was obviously an unreasonable man. In her previous life as a princess, if anyone was displeased with her they knew to keep it to themselves, or at least to speak ill of her only when she was out of earshot. If there was sulking to be done, she was the one to do it. Her odd, heightened awareness of Humphrey made the way he was ignoring her all the more irritating. Why was it that the more objectionable he was, the more she craved his attention?

She had been determined not to speak first, to make him come to her and apologise. But she needed to know why Leila had attacked him, what it was that linked him to her quest to find Jasper. That was what mattered; she must put her dignity aside. So one morning as they were riding through a broad pasture, the grass still wet with dew, she abruptly said, 'Have you been at Camelot long?'

Humphrey turned to her, a look of surprise and amusement on his face.

'So you *can* speak,' he said.

She refused to reply.

'I'm not in Camelot, I'm in a field,' he said, infuriatingly.

Conrad, who was within earshot, sniggered.

'But you've been a knight a long time,' Martha persisted, feeling at once annoyed and superior for being the one making the effort. At least she was capable of behaving like an adult.

'Twenty years a knight,' conceded Humphrey. 'Five years before that as a squire, and five years before that a page. I've been there since I was eight years old.'

'So you were friends with Jasper?'

'You mean Prince Jasper of Puddock? You seem to be on awfully familiar terms with the Puddock royal family.'

'Sorry,' said Martha, cursing herself for yet another misstep. 'Yes, I mean Prince Jasper. I'm just asking because I remember him from when I was a little g- boy. Back at the castle. I was only . . .' Had Martha chosen an age for herself? She couldn't remember. 'Eight, I think? When he died.' She tried her best to keep her voice calm and natural, but she was wondering whether Humphrey, too, knew that Jasper wasn't really dead.

'I wouldn't call us friends exactly, but I liked him,' said Humphrey.

'Why weren't you friends?' asked Martha.

'Well,' said Humphrey. 'He was heir to a throne. I know that everyone thinks of Camelot as an egalitarian place, but there are still questions of status.' Humphrey hadn't mentioned to Martha that he was a Less Valued Knight and that Round Table knights didn't tend to fraternise with him.

'You were jealous of him?' said Martha.

'Watch it,' said Conrad, behind her.

'It's all right, Conrad,' said Humphrey. 'I'd rather talk than die of boredom, no matter how rude my interlocutor.' He turned his attention back to Martha. 'No, I wasn't jealous of him. I'd sooner eat my own arms than be king.'

'Really?' said Martha, thrilled at having found this common ground. 'I don't think that would help. They'd probably still make you do it, even without arms.'

'I was joking,' said Humphrey.

'So was I,' said Martha, 'though I think I'm right about the arms.' She allowed herself a smile. She couldn't remember the last time she'd smiled. To her delight, Humphrey laughed.

'And Jasper,' she continued, 'I mean Prince Jasper, do you think he wanted to be king?'

'I don't know,' said Humphrey.

'Do you think he would have been a good king?'

Humphrey pondered this. 'That's a difficult question,' he said at last.

'Why?' said Martha.

'You ask a lot of questions,' said Conrad.

'Calm down, Conrad, it's called a conversation,' said Humphrey. 'It's complicated,' he said to Martha. 'What makes a good king?'

'You're asking me?'

'Yes, I'm asking you.'

'Um, I suppose . . .' said Martha. 'Being honourable? And valiant?'

'Those are abstract terms,' said Humphrey. 'People don't just walk around being honourable and valiant. In fact, if you meet anyone who walks around making a show of being honourable and valiant, they're generally a prick. I mean, name someone who you think is honourable and valiant.'

Martha thought for a bit. 'Lancelot?' she said.

Humphrey burst out laughing and turned in his saddle. 'You hear that, Conrad?' he said. 'Marcus thinks Lancelot is honourable and valiant.'

Martha felt her face redden.

'I don't give a fuck what Marcus thinks,' said Conrad.

Humphrey rolled his eyes and turned back to Martha.

'Surely you know that Lancelot is screwing Guinevere?'

'What's screwing?' asked Martha.

'What's *screwing?*' said Humphrey. He stared at her incredulously.

'Leave him alone, he's just a kid,' said Elaine. She and Conrad had edged forward and were now riding close behind Humphrey and Martha, the better to join in the conversation.

'You know – the thing men and women do to make babies?' sneered Conrad.

'Oh,' said Martha. 'Yes, I do know. I've seen pictures.'

Conrad snorted so loudly that it might have been Jemima. Elaine had a fit of the giggles, while Humphrey just gazed at Martha with open-mouthed amazement.

'So they're doing that on purpose?' Martha pressed on, through her embarrassment.

'On . . . ? Yes, they are doing it on purpose,' said Humphrey. He turned to Conrad with a smirk, and Conrad couldn't help but grin back.

'The point,' said Humphrey to Martha, 'is that Lancelot may be the best knight in the world – truly, he actually may be – but he is far from perfect. Nobody's perfect. Well, Galahad might be pretty much perfect, but you just want to smack him in his smug chops, so that makes him not perfect. Lancelot is honourable on his horse, not honourable between the Queen's thighs. Valiant in battle, not valiant pretending to Arthur's face that he's his best friend. So would Lancelot be a good king?'

'No,' said Conrad, just as Elaine said, 'Yes.'

'The ladies love Lancelot,' said Humphrey. 'What do you think, Marcus?'

Martha hesitated. 'No?' she said.

'Why not?'

Because I'm not a lady.

'Because he's a hypocrite?'

'You see – that's what I'm saying. Everyone's a hypocrite. If you exclude all the hypocrites, nobody's going to be king.'

'Even Prince Jasper?'

'Yes. Even him.'

Martha felt herself wondering how much she really wanted to know about her brother. When she'd thought he was dead, the book was closed – he was perfect. But now that he was alive, she felt a vertiginous panic about what she might be about to learn.

She took a deep breath. 'In what way was he a hypocrite?'

Humphrey scrutinised her anxious face. 'You knew him at the castle?' he said.

'Yes,' she said. 'When I was little.'

'You hero-worshipped him a bit, maybe?'

With all of my heart. 'I barely remember him,' she said.

'All right,' Humphrey said, 'if you really want to know. He talked grand talk about the importance of brotherhood and knightly values, but he was a lazy sod. Never put himself forward for a quest he didn't have to go on. I realised a long time ago that you don't actually have to like going on quests, you just have to be willing to do what's necessary. I started feeling a lot better about myself when I figured that one out. Anyway, some of the knights had a problem with Jasper over that, but I didn't, not really. He did lord it over everyone a bit because he knew he was going to be King of Puddock one day. I already told you I wasn't grand enough to be his friend. So that was annoying, but it was understandable. On the other hand, he was nice to his squire.'

'That matters,' said Conrad.

'It really does,' agreed Humphrey. 'He bought his fair share of drinks. And, most importantly, when it came right down to it, you could trust him. He'd have been as good a king as anyone. I mean, he was a decent bloke, and that's all you can hope for, since who becomes king is essentially luck of the draw. Look at Arthur. He's made a fair fist of it for someone who got the crown by pulling a sword out of a rock. Sure, he's a sanctimonious bugger and a terrible bore if you're stuck next to him at dinner, but I doubt anybody could have done a much better job.'

'He's better than King Leo of Tuft,' said Elaine.

'Better than Edwin,' said Martha, with a twinge of guilt at having left him in charge of her nation.

'Better than any of us,' said Humphrey. 'Do you think you'd be a good king?'

'Me?' said Martha, appalled. She had only just begun to relax at the thought that Jasper had no real skeletons in his closet, and now she was being invited to open her own.

'Yes, you, if however many thousands of people died and it ended up as your turn. Could happen. Bad plague year.'

'No,' said Martha. 'I'd be a terrible king. I don't know how to do anything. You saw me with that magic sword, I didn't know what I was doing, I was terrified, I couldn't even keep my eyes open. I can't fight. I can't lead an army. I can't lead, full stop. I'm hopeless. I can sit politely at a banquet and laugh at people's bad jokes, and I can shake hands and admire people's pigs. That's it. Sum total of my qualifications. I would be a disaster as king.'

The others were silenced by this surprisingly passionate outburst.

'Pigs?' said Humphrey eventually.

'Yes,' said Martha. 'I was always accompanying Princess Martha to county fairs. Puddock is full of pigs. I am quite the expert.'

Humphrey raised his eyebrows. 'You're a pig expert,' he said. 'That I would not have guessed.'

Then Elaine spoke up. 'I'd be an amazing queen,' she announced.

'You would, would you?' said Humphrey.

'Yes. I would be beloved and gracious and wear a massive crown with so many jewels on it that nobody could look at it directly, like the sun. I would recline on satin pillows while naked men fed me raspberries with all the bugs picked out. Have you ever noticed how many bugs there are in raspberries?'

'Billions,' said Conrad solemnly.

'Yes. I hate bugs. They really spoil raspberries. Well, there'd be no bugs for Queen Elaine. And I would have ten – no – seventeen ladies-in-waiting just to do my braids. People would come from miles around to see them. I mean the braids. The ladies-in-waiting, of course, would have been chosen for their remarkable lack of beauty. I would have a table of knights that would be the envy of Camelot, and it would be triangular in shape. I would sit at the apex. My library would be three times the size of that of Constantinople, and I would have read every book. Twice. My wisdom would be renowned the world over. I would dance every night and bestow alms on the poor, not at the same time. I would bring peace to all humanity.'

'What about taxes?' said Martha.

'Taxes?' said Elaine.

'I've noticed that there are a lot of decisions to be made about taxes. Being king is a full-time administrative position, you have no idea what it's like. When my – when the last King of Puddock became ill and couldn't rule any more, an entire council of elders got together just to do his job. People think ruling's glamorous but it's a nightmare.'

'Do you have a sense of humour, Marcus?' said Conrad.

'There's nothing funny about taxes,' said Martha.

'Indeed,' said Elaine. 'Which is why I would abolish them.'

'A woman of the people,' said Humphrey.

'You'd be a much better queen than I would,' said Martha.

'Oh I don't know, shave your beard off, put you in a dress . . .' said Conrad.

The others laughed at this, but Martha's heart thumped in her chest.

Thirty-One

It took several days for Sir Dorian to prepare for the quest to find Martha. His squire, a plump, cheerful lad by name of Silas, was despatched to oil, sand and polish his second-best suit of armour, alongside his third best, in case the second best became damaged during the adventure ahead. (Sir Dorian was saving his best suit of armour for a special occasion, such as when he would return, triumphant, with Martha, and King Arthur would promote him to some position of prominence in his court.) His page, Keith, a quiet boy just shy of ten years, was charged with gathering provisions and packing, with great difficulty, Sir Dorian's pavilion, bed, folding table, chair, lamps and portable stove, all of which were loaded into a cart that would be driven by Keith and Silas at a careful distance from Sir Dorian, so as not to spoil the effect of the solitary knight errant on his lonesome quest. The fact that he was riding alongside Edwin did threaten to get in the way of this image, but that could not be helped. Edwin was the bearer of the Pentecost quest, and insisted on accompanying Dorian on the journey, no matter how often the knight assured him that he could stay behind and wait in the safety of Camelot.

Edwin, for his part, was sick with disappointment at the knight he'd been assigned. He'd been hoping for one of the famous ones, Lancelot or Galahad, or even one of the second-tier knights like Sir Bors. Who'd ever heard of Sir Dorian?

Though he would never have admitted as much, even to

himself, Edwin was jealous. Ever since boyhood, he had wanted to be a Knight of the Round Table. As a child, nothing excited him more than when Tuft Castle hosted tournaments, and all the knights would arrive on their huge stallions, gleaming in their elaborate armour, colourful pennants flying. They would bow to him (and Leo) before enacting the incredible feats of skill, courage and dexterity that were the jousts. (He wasn't such a fan of the melees, as the churning mud would spatter his best clothes.) His favourite childhood game was Knights. Usually he played with his brother, but Leo always made him lose, which wasn't fair, so sometimes he'd play with the son of a local lord, who liked dressing up as a princess. This boy – Edwin couldn't remember his name, just that in princess mode he liked to be called Gwendoline – would pretend to have been captured by a dragon or a giant or an evil uncle, and Edwin would fight his way past whatever dangers they imagined with his wooden sword and rescue him. Then, as he recalled it, one day Gwendoline was simply gone. There was no explanation, and his absence was never discussed, at least not in Edwin's presence. As children do, Edwin soon forgot about him, but looking back on it now, he wondered if the kid had been removed for his own protection. Tuft wasn't a place for boys who wore dresses.

Anyway, back when his father was still alive, Edwin had once confided in him his wish to be a Knight of the Round Table. When his father had stopped laughing, he'd said that being a knight required certain properties – intelligence, integrity, hand–eye coordination, the ability to sleep out of doors without freaking out about bats – none of which Edwin had. Besides, the King said, there was no way he was sending a son of his to Camelot when they had perfectly good knights at their own court. But Tuft knights didn't have a special table and they didn't go on quests. Being a knight in his father's castle was just a fancy way of being one of his dad's guards, or, later, one of Leo's, which was unthinkable. So Edwin had given up his dream. And now that he was finally on a quest, the knight was getting all of the glory, and he – the King! (*Prince Consort*, sniggered Leo in his mind) – was riding behind.

In order to find Martha, Sir Dorian had told Edwin that they would need the assistance of the Lady of the Lake, who had arcane supernatural knowledge which would help Edwin trace the Queen's whereabouts. (Although Sir Dorian hadn't said that she would 'help Edwin'. He had said she would 'help me', which Edwin found infuriating.) As plans went, this sounded straightforward enough. Except, as it turned out, there was no such thing as the Lake. There were lakes, in which the Lady might or might not be, as took her fancy. So, in fact, what they were doing was riding between bodies of water, hanging around for a bit until they were sure that no Lady was going to turn up, and then riding on.

Even this might have been tolerable if Sir Dorian hadn't been distracted by extra quests every five minutes. But once word got out that there was a knight errant about, it seemed like every Tom, Dick and Harry was waylaying them to ask for Sir Dorian's help, and when Edwin said Tom, Dick and Harry, what he meant was Thomasina, Dilys and Harriet.

Just hours after leaving Camelot, riding south towards Puddock to see if they could pick up Martha's trail, they passed a village churchyard where a young damsel in a golden dress lay on the ground beside a fresh grave, weeping piteously. Sir Dorian reined in his horse.

'Fair maiden,' he said, 'I am Sir Dorian of the Round Table. May I be of some assistance?'

The damsel scrambled to her feet, furiously wiping her eyes. She smoothed the creases of her dress and dropped a low curtsey, allowing both Sir Dorian and Edwin a good look down her bodice. It was a bodice worth looking down.

'Isadora Duquesne,' she said in a low, thrilling voice.

'I'm Edwin, King of Puddock,' said Edwin.

'Puddock doesn't have a king,' Isadora said. She turned her attentions to Sir Dorian. 'Good Sir Dorian, I need to be avenged on behalf of my beloved, taken from me by a fellow named Barnabas, an unworthy type living in a village not three miles from here. If only you could help me!'

'Fear not,' said Sir Dorian, 'I will give you all the help that is within my power to give. Pray lead me to this villain.'

Isadora curtseyed again, then began wending her way along a narrow path in quite the wrong direction from where they'd intended to go. Sir Dorian followed, seemingly forgetting about Edwin.

'But aren't we supposed to be going to Puddock?' Edwin complained as he scrambled to catch up with the knight.

'All in good time,' said Sir Dorian without turning round.

'No use protesting,' called Silas from the cart, which he and Keith were struggling to manoeuvre along the tiny path. 'This is the way it always is.'

When they reached Barnabas's home – a decent-sized place, if you weren't used to castles – Sir Dorian lowered the visor on his helmet, took a lance from his squire, and smashed down the door. A young man with thick brown hair ran out. He had obviously been having a meal, and when he heard his front door explode he had forgotten to put down his half-eaten bread roll. Apart from the breadcrumbs in his beard, he was a well-turned-out individual, and Edwin felt both excited and slightly sad that Sir Dorian was going to kill him.

'Miscreant!' said Sir Dorian, drawing his sword. 'You have dishonoured this lady!'

'Which lady?' Barnabas spotted Isadora. 'Oh, it's you. I might have known.'

'You have slain the lover of this good maid,' said Sir Dorian, 'and so I must –'

'What? Wait, wait,' said Barnabas, white-faced. He turned to Isadora. 'Simon's dead?'

Isadora flushed. 'I never said he was dead.'

'But the knight . . .' said Barnabas.

Isadora shook her head. Barnabas suddenly realised that he was still holding the bread roll, looked around for somewhere to put it down, couldn't see anywhere, was unwilling to toss it to the ground, so, with a slightly foolish look of resignation, hung onto it.

'You were weeping on a grave,' said Sir Dorian to Isadora.

'Not on Simon's grave,' said Isadora, a little defensively. 'It was just a comfortable place to lie.'

'Was it the graveyard on the road from Camelot, by any chance?' said Barnabas. 'You and your obsession with knights!'

'You said that this gentleman had taken your lover away,' Sir Dorian said sternly to Isadora.

'He did!' said Isadora. 'And he's no gentleman.'

'Is this true?' said Sir Dorian to Barnabas.

'I am a gentleman,' Barnabas bristled. 'But as for the rest of it, I suppose, in the loosest possible sense, one could say that I took him away. Simon had got dull as swill, spending all his time mooning after Dora, and all I did was persuade him to come out and get a drink or two –'

'Or three,' said Isadora.

'– down at the tavern, and she's got her petticoat in a twist about it.'

'So he's not dead,' said Sir Dorian.

'He's not even hurt,' said Barnabas. 'Nothing worse than a hangover, anyway.'

'We were supposed to be spending the evening with my mother,' said Isadora.

From Edwin's point of view, it was pretty embarrassing that Sir Dorian had made a detour off an important quest for a king (*prince consort*) for such a trifling matter, but Sir Dorian laughed.

'Joust to make it worth my while?' he said.

'Oh all right,' said Barnabas, 'but don't get me in the stomach, I've only just eaten.'

Barnabas, who seemed an amiable, slightly bookish type, never stood a chance. It was over in seconds. All the same, Sir Dorian did a lap of honour around the village green as if he'd just defeated the Minotaur. Edwin thought that would be the end of it, but Isadora insisted on thanking Sir Dorian for defending her honour – as she put it – by inviting him to dinner with her family. Sir Dorian was squeezed between Isadora and her mother, a sapphire-eyed beauty who must have been a child bride. Edwin, meanwhile, was seated at the far end of the table, next to Isadora's seven-year-old brother whose only topic of conversation was horses, and a profoundly deaf great-aunt. On the subject of deafness, Edwin was too far away to overhear Sir Dorian's conversation (and far too bored to listen to his neighbours) so he didn't know what pretext it was that took Sir Dorian and Isadora away from the table midway through the meal, though he could guess why both of them were pink-cheeked when they returned some time later.

And so it continued. Edwin had never seen so many damsels in distress in his life, though in his opinion a lot of them weren't particularly distressed. Like Isadora, most had had some kind of lovers' tiff and wanted a knight to fight for their supposed honour. It seemed to Edwin that fighting for the honour of these damsels was a clear case of closing the stable door after the horse had bolted – bolted into the field of a welcoming stallion. While he usually didn't object to a damsel of that ilk – far from it – these ones only had eyes for Sir Dorian. And Sir Dorian was incapable of saying no. *'Always do ladies, damsels, and gentle women succour,'* he'd say cheerfully, and, *'Be for all ladies and fight their quarrels.'* Since this was part of the Knights' Code, apparently, Sir Dorian claimed that he was obliged to take on every single one of these so-called quests. 'I'm sorry,' he'd say to Edwin with an exaggerated sigh, 'but there's nothing I can do.' He didn't look very sorry as he picked up his jousting lance to knock yet another toothless philanderer off his nag. He looked even less sorry when he came back from being thanked by the damsel, who insisted on offering him something for his trouble, not money of course, perhaps a bite to eat, why don't you follow me into the larder and help me get something off this high shelf, oops, the door has closed . . .

So progress was slow. Still, at least it gave Edwin time to think of all the tortures and indignities he would inflict on Martha when he finally caught up with her. If she wasn't in distress when she ran away she'd certainly be in distress after he found her. The longer it took, the more 'succour' Sir Dorian gave the damsels they met, the more baroque Edwin's imagination got. His errant – in every sense of the word – wife would pay for every second of boredom and embarrassment that Sir Dorian was subjecting him to. After all, if it wasn't for her, he wouldn't even be on this miserable quest. It was only fair. And Edwin prided himself on being fair.

Thirty-Two

As the days passed, the heat of the summer grew. The air was thick with it, a terrible, invisible blanket they were forced to push through. Elaine appeared to be suffering most, emerging from her tent late and unrested, sweating greenly on top of her horse, picking listlessly at her food when they stopped for meals, and offering little by way of conversation. Humphrey worried that she might be ill, but she brushed off his concern.

'It's this weather,' she said. 'I can't stand it. I can't wait for it to break.' She glowered at the blue sky, which stubbornly refused to produce even one small cloud.

'We could reduce our hours in the saddle,' suggested Humphrey. 'Only ride first thing in the morning and then late evening before it gets dark. Stay in the shade in the heat of the day.'

'No!' said Elaine. 'We've got to press on. Don't worry about me. I'll be fine.'

Humphrey agreed, even though the temperature was driving him mad too. And Conrad and the boy. The only one of the group unaffected was Jemima, who seemed in her element, though when they stopped to drink she'd suck up half a river with her trunk and squirt the rest over her head. Conrad, caught in the spray, didn't object at all.

Spending time in the infernal heat of the forges interrogating blacksmiths was a particular ordeal. Humphrey found himself plotting routes that, while broadly following Leila's instructions, avoided villages and towns as much as possible. Devoid of knights in black armour, Elaine turned to Leila more and more, hoping that the sword would be able to tell her where her fiancé was.

'Where is Sir Alistair?' she'd ask Leila, but when Martha spun the sword, she just went round and round and round until Martha had to put a boot down to stop her.

After one of these disappointments, Elaine burst into tears. When Humphrey tried to comfort her, she shouted at him, 'You don't know what you're doing. My father was right, I should have got a real knight!'

Humphrey turned and walked away, over to the fire pit where Conrad was peeling carrots, while Jemima loitered nearby, hoping for scraps.

'I used to be better at this,' he said to his squire.

Before Conrad could respond, Martha wandered over. 'Better at what?'

'Well, the old days were the glory days,' said Humphrey, perking up at the sight of a receptive audience. 'You've heard of the Questing Beast, I'll bet? Turned out to be just a big stray cat. You should have seen King Pellinore's face . . .'

The pair drifted away from Conrad, who wielded his peeling knife with new irritation.

Later, after the sun had dipped beneath the horizon and the sky was turning from indigo to black, Elaine took Humphrey aside to apologise for her harsh words.

'I don't want another knight,' she said, resting her hand on his shoulder for emphasis.

'It's fine, I'd already forgotten about it,' Humphrey said, shrugging her off, but the ghost of her touch lingered for hours.

The heat barely dropped that night. Martha, wedged between Humphrey and Conrad, stopped even trying to sleep. She missed the way Deborah used to fan her during heatwaves at the castle. Bored and uncomfortable, she slipped out of the tent, onto the expanse of heath where they'd set up camp.

The air was a little fresher outside, though there wasn't so much as the hint of a breeze. She sat on a log next to the embers of the campfire and looked up at the stars scattered in fistfuls across the sky. She could take Silver and run away, she realised. But where would she go? Leila was strapped to Humphrey's hip even at night. Leaving would mean leaving the sword, leaving Humphrey – though why should this matter? Staying with these people was her best chance of finding Jasper. Whether she liked them or not was irrelevant.

'You're still here.'

Martha looked up. Humphrey had followed her out of the tent. He was wearing only the long underwear he slept in. Black hair curled all the way down his broad chest and crept beneath the waistband of his underwear to whatever lay below. Martha found herself thinking of the book she'd looked at the night before her wedding, and felt a renewed surge of disgust, but this time tinged with a strange, slightly frightening curiosity.

'I was just trying to cool down a bit,' she said.

'If you run away, Conrad will devote the rest of his life to finding you, and when he does he will disembowel you and hang you with your own guts.'

'I couldn't sleep before,' said Martha. 'But I'm sure I'll have no problem dropping off now.'

Humphrey sat down next to her. He wiped the sweat from his forehead. 'It's hotter than a whore's cunt.'

'I, um . . .' said Martha, her already feminine voice coming out in a distinctly unmanly wobble. 'I wouldn't know.'

'Never been with a whore?'

'No.'

'Ever been with anyone?'

'No.'

'How old are you?'

For a mad moment, Martha thought to herself, *I mustn't say too young or he won't be interested in me.* Then she reminded herself: *He won't be interested in me because I am a BOY.*

'Fifteen,' she said.

'Same age as Conrad, and he's had plenty,' said Humphrey.

'Really?' said Martha, aghast.

'Sure,' said Humphrey. 'I could take you, if you like.'

'Take me?'

'To a whorehouse. There's one just outside Camelot called Mother Superior's House of Shame. It specialises in nuns.'

'Nuns?'

'Well, the madam says her girls are fallen nuns. None of them could exactly be described as a novice. She reckons she can charge extra to corrupt a virgin who's dedicated herself to the divine.'

Martha felt she had to say something, and the only thing she could think of was the truth. 'I don't know what a whorehouse is.'

'You're not joking, are you?' said Humphrey.

'I'm afraid not.'

'No, you don't joke very much – Conrad's right about that.' Humphrey paused. Then he said, 'A whorehouse is a place where people have sex for money.'

'Who pays?' said Martha.

'Who . . . ? The men pay. Though if you can find somewhere where the women pay, I would like very much to hear about it.'

Martha felt a dry-mouthed panic, half from discussing these things with Humphrey, half at the thought that she might actually end up in a whorehouse with him. It would hardly take long for the whores to find out that she was carrying the wrong equipment.

'I don't know what a cunt is either,' she found herself confessing.

Humphrey laughed in disbelief. 'Weren't there any other boys at the castle, when you were growing up?' he said.

'I was always in the Princess's chambers,' said Martha. 'The only people I spent any time with were the Princess and her maids.'

'You don't have a father? A brother?'

'They died,' said Martha. Sensing an explanation was necessary, she added, 'Smallpox.'

'I should have guessed. The scars on your face.'

'Yes,' Martha made herself agree. 'Smallpox. I got it too, as a baby, but I survived.'

'Well, that's lucky, isn't it? You're immune now.'

'Yes.' In fact Martha had never had smallpox. She would probably catch it now, and die, and how would she explain that to Humphrey? He would realise that the scars on her face were from acne and it would be so humiliating.

'And your mother?' he said.

'Smallpox too,' said Martha, for want of a better answer. She was sick of talking about smallpox now. 'I was raised in the castle, from before I can remember. Queen Martha was amused by children, so I was something of a jester to her, before I became her page.'

'A jester?' said Humphrey, amused. 'You?'

Why did nobody here think she was funny? Everyone at the castle always laughed at her jokes.

'Only when I was very small,' she said. 'They dressed me as a little dog, and I used to toddle around and fall over.'

Humphrey took a moment to picture this, chuckling. Then he said, 'So I take it nobody bothered to teach you about sex.'

'I know enough,' said Martha hurriedly. 'There is no need to enlighten me further.'

'And what about the other things a man needs to know? You can ride, at least.'

'The Princess liked my companionship on horseback.'

'You're bloody awful at pitching a tent, though. And you can't light a fire.'

'That's true,' acknowledged Martha.

'You have no swordsmanship – we learned that early on. What about archery?'

'Nope.'

'That I can teach you. If you like.'

'Archery? Why on earth do you want to teach me archery?'

Thirty-Three

That was exactly the question Conrad asked Humphrey the next morning.

'Archery? Are you out of your mind?'

Martha, quietly reading a book of poetry in the shade of a sycamore tree, pretended not to listen.

'I think it would be useful,' Humphrey replied.

'Useful how?'

'If the Queen's fallen into hostile hands, it would help to have another fighter on our side.'

'Hostile hands? You know who has hostile hands? Marcus!'

Martha did not react, though her hands weren't remotely hostile – she rubbed shea butter into them morning and night.

'Marcus isn't a threat,' said Humphrey.

'He tried to kill you!' insisted Conrad. 'And now you're going to arm him?'

'I'm not going to give him his sword back.'

'Oh well, that's fine then. We all know that murderers are very weapon-specific.'

'He's not a murderer.'

'I don't know what else you'd call him. Is this because he's got a crush on you? Are you that vain?'

Martha felt her face redden, and bent more deeply over her book. She'd been staring at the same poem for several minutes now without taking in a single word of it.

Humphrey looked at Martha, then took Conrad's gigantic arm and dragged him out of earshot.

'I've got a theory about Marcus,' he whispered.

Conrad refused to look interested, but shrugged one shoulder as minimal encouragement.

'I don't think he's who he says he is,' continued Humphrey.

'No shit.'

Humphrey ignored Conrad's tone. 'Have you noticed how much he looks like Jasper?'

Conrad nodded reluctantly. 'I suppose.'

'I believe him when he says he comes from Puddock Castle, and he's obviously obsessed with the royal family there. Last night he was telling me he used to be the Princess's jester, which didn't ring true at all . . .'

'When were you talking to him last night?'

'After you were asleep. It doesn't matter, listen. I think he might be the dead King's bastard.'

Conrad snorted. 'Oh come on.'

'Seriously. He's hopeless at everything. That's the mark of a king's son. Have you seen his hands? They're like a girl's! He's obviously never done a day's work in his life.'

Conrad couldn't deny that there was some truth in this. 'So, what, you're favouring him because you think he might be royalty? Since when does that matter to you?'

'I'm not "favouring him". I just think if we treat him well there could be something in it for us, when we find the Queen.'

'Or we could end up dead long before then.'

'Conrad. I'm not stupid. I was at the business end when he attacked me, while you sat up on your elephant and did nothing. But there's no way that kid can actually fight like that without his magic sword, and I've got it.' Humphrey pointed to Leila at his hip. 'Right now Marcus is our prisoner. And he's an asset, especially if he's the Queen's half-brother. I'm just saying that we should exploit that asset. Make him our friend, keep him sweet, and if he can come in handy at the same time, so much the better.'

Conrad looked back at Martha, who was peering at them over the top of her book.

'You're still arming him.'

'I'll keep hold of the bow and arrows. I'm just giving him some lessons.'

Conrad shook his head. 'I still think you're insane.'

Humphrey was losing patience now. 'It doesn't matter what you think. I am the knight, you are the squire, and you do as I say.'

'Do as you say.' Conrad's voice started to rise. 'You mean make friends with him? Is that what you want? Can't you see that I'm the one being loyal here, and he . . .' Conrad pointed at Martha. 'He . . . isn't!'

'It is not for you to question my judgement!'

'Your judgement?' replied Conrad. 'Because you're such a well-known judge of character? What about your wife – were you such a good judge of her?'

'Do not bring her into this,' warned Humphrey. He took a threatening step towards his squire, and Conrad flinched back, as if they didn't know that Conrad could snap any of Humphrey's bones with his bare hands. But before matters could escalate, Elaine poked her head out of her tent. Her hair was frizzy from the heat and she looked bilious.

'What's going on?' she said. 'Why are you two arguing?'

'Humphrey's decided to give Marcus archery lessons,' Conrad spat.

'Marcus,' said Elaine. 'Do you want archery lessons?'

Martha turned to her, surprised, as if she was only now aware that a conversation was taking place. 'Archery?' she said. 'I suppose it would be useful.' She resumed her reading.

'See?' said Humphrey, as if this proved something.

'Oh, the assassin agrees with you,' said Conrad. 'What a surprise.'

Elaine emerged fully from the tent, modestly wrapped in a dark blue robe.

'When?' she said.

'When what?' said Humphrey.

'When were you planning on giving Marcus these lessons?'

'I don't know,' said Humphrey. 'As we go along?'

'I think it's a great idea,' said Elaine.

Humphrey grinned. Conrad looked betrayed.

'Because we've got all the time in the world,' said Elaine. 'There's no rush. No rush at all! I can't think of one single other thing that we could be doing!'

Conrad and Humphrey swapped facial expressions while Martha calmly turned a page in her book, to another poem she would fail to read.

'I could go back to Camelot by myself, you know,' said Elaine. 'Tell them how you stole my quest from the Round Table and then let it be hijacked by a runaway.'

This, Martha could not ignore. 'What do you mean, stole from the Round Table?'

Elaine just turned and swept back into her tent.

'What did she mean?' Martha asked Humphrey and Conrad.

'Your bastard asked you a question,' said Conrad.

'Are you jealous?' Humphrey said to Conrad. 'Is that what this is? You're jealous?'

'Don't be ridiculous,' said Conrad. 'Why on earth would I be jealous of him?'

Realising that there was no hope of getting an answer out of either of them, Martha got up and followed Elaine to her tent. She stood outside it and cleared her throat. 'Do you mind if I come in?'

'Do whatever you like, you always do,' said Elaine.

Martha opened the flap of the tent. Inside the light was dim and the humid air smelt of tramped grass. Elaine's saddlebags were open next to her bedroll, with a few dresses pulled out and thrown to one side. She was digging her way through one of the bags, still dressed in her robe.

'That's not fair,' said Martha. 'I don't do whatever I like.'

'You never do a stroke of work, you just sit on your arse the whole time making daisy chains while the rest of us fuss around you . . .'

'I'm a prisoner!'

'I know. Though I imagine you err on the lazy side at the best of times.'

Elaine ran a hand through her hair. She looked as though she were about to burst into tears.

'Would you like me to return when you're dressed?' said Martha.

Elaine shook her head. 'None of these dresses fit,' she said. 'I'm too fat for them.'

'How can you be too fat? You never eat anything.'

Elaine trawled around the bottom of the bag and pulled out a drab grey gown with laces down the front. 'Forget I mentioned it. I'm sure this one will be fine. I can loosen it at least.' She straightened. 'What can I do for you, Marcus? You know it's an insult to my honour that we're alone in my tent together.'

'You don't have to worry about me.'

'I know. I was joking.'

'Oh,' said Martha, disappointed that she wasn't enough of a man to constitute a credible threat to a maiden's good name. She pulled herself together. 'What did you mean about Sir Humphrey stealing your quest?'

Elaine sighed. 'I shouldn't have said anything. But you may as well know. Humphrey's not from the Round Table.'

'He's not a knight?' said Martha.

'No, he is a knight. But he's from . . . he's from the Table of Less Valued Knights.' Elaine felt doubly ashamed, for betraying Humphrey's secret and for finding the secret shameful in the first place.

Martha thought back to the knight she had met in the tavern, who was so stinking and drunken and rude. 'He can't be,' she said, in horror.

'He is,' said Elaine. She felt a wave of sympathy, for the naive child in front of her and for the damaged man outside. 'Listen, don't take it to heart. Anyone can see how much you admire him.'

Martha looked away, embarrassed.

'There's no reason for that to change,' Elaine continued. 'He's a good man. It doesn't matter what kind of knight he is.'

'If he's such a good man, why are you always shouting at him?' asked Martha.

'Am I?' said Elaine, shocked. Then she composed herself. 'You're right – I have been taking out my own worries on Sir Humphrey. It's not fair on him.'

'I'm sorry this is so difficult for you,' said Martha. 'I know how important it is for you to find your fiancé, though Lord knows I have no idea why anyone would want to be married. Or . . .' Suddenly she stopped, thinking of something – or someone. 'Perhaps I do. A little. Anyway, it matters to you. I can see that. And I am very grateful to you for saving me before, when I was fighting Humphrey – when Leila was fighting Humphrey, I should say. I am not sure that I have thanked you for that. When all this is over, I shall see that you get the proper reward.'

Elaine smothered a laugh. 'Thank you,' she said.

'But it's very important that we find . . .' Martha hesitated. 'The Queen. I understand that your happiness depends on finding Sir Alistair, but the happiness of an entire nation rests on us restoring the proper monarch to the throne. You haven't met Edwin. You have no idea. He is a beast. A stupid beast, which is worse. I'd sooner have Jemima rule Puddock than he.'

'Those are fine words,' said Elaine. 'But I don't think much of a queen who would run away from her country and leave a man like that in charge, just as I don't think much of a page who would do the same for a handful of stolen gold.' Martha looked down at the ground, stricken. 'And besides,' Elaine continued, 'Humphrey is *my* knight. If you want a knight to track down your Queen, you should go and get your own.'

'I didn't go and get Humphrey,' said Martha, her pride returning. 'Leila did. I had no choice in the matter.'

'And yet you seem to have everything going your way,' said Elaine. 'That's quite a useful skill you have there, manipulating others to get what you want.'

'Something you would never do, of course,' Martha retorted.

The two of them stood staring at each other, with the hot dissatisfaction of two people who fundamentally like each other but have nevertheless found themselves in a hurtful argument.

'I should go to my archery lesson,' said Martha.

'Don't want to keep Humphrey waiting,' said Elaine spitefully.

'Maybe if I learn to shoot, I can be of use, instead of, you know – making daisy chains.'

'Maybe.'

Martha knew she should go, but hated leaving when things still felt so awkward.

'Before,' she said, 'when I spun Leila and she said that she could help you. She doesn't lie.' Martha had no evidence for this, but she was certain it was true. 'I promise you, as soon as we've found . . . the person I'm looking for . . . I will help you, Leila will help you. We'll find your fiancé.'

'By then it will be too late,' said Elaine, now with more sadness than anger.

Thirty-Four

Martha picked up archery quickly, much to her own surprise as well as her teacher's. The steadiness and focus required to shoot accurately came easily to her, perhaps a result of the patience she'd cultivated as a princess, always required to sit quietly, never to rush. On top of this, she had a natural eye and an instinctive understanding of how to find and adjust her aim. Humphrey was impressed, and Martha was delighted to have pleased him and to have finally found something she was good at. After only a few lessons he determined she was ready to have a go shooting at live targets.

'You mean animals?' said Martha. 'Killing animals?'

'That's the idea,' said Humphrey.

Martha felt suddenly sick.

He took her deep into the woods, leaving Conrad and Elaine behind in the clearing where they had camped the previous night. He stood close behind her, both of them shielded by the trunk of an old chestnut tree, scanning for prey. She could feel his breath on her neck. Was it this that made her hands tremble and sweat, sliding on the bow so that even if she did have it in her to kill a living beast, the arrow would disobey her? Or was it that yet again she was going to fail in her task of assumed masculinity? Or was it both: his proximity, and the certainty of disappointing him?

'I can't,' she said miserably.

'Yes you can,' said Humphrey. 'You were doing fine on the targets.'

'This is different.'

'No it isn't. It's exactly the same.'

A stag appeared through the trees, handsome and strong.

'Now,' said Humphrey.

Martha, shaking, drew the bow. The stag turned his head, seeming to look her in the eye. 'I'm sorry,' she said, not knowing whether she was speaking to the stag or to Humphrey. Either way, it was too late. In half a moment, the stag was gone.

'You can't hesitate, even for a second,' said Humphrey.

'I could see his heart beating through his skin.'

'They all have hearts, you know.'

'I know. But it's not usually me who has to stop them.'

'If you can't kill a deer, what are you going to do if the Queen's been taken prisoner and we have to fight our way through her captors?'

Martha imagined herself shooting arrows at Jasper's captors. Then she imagined failing to shoot arrows at them, and Jasper being killed. 'I'll try again,' she said.

They waited. After an eternity, a rabbit crept out of a patch of bracken. It was soft and brown, its fur like silk. It didn't notice them, but hopped its way into a cool patch of the glade.

Humphrey nodded towards the rabbit. Martha raised her bow. The rabbit wrinkled its little bunny nose. Martha aimed her arrow at the rabbit. The rabbit nibbled on a blade of grass. Martha drew her bow. The rabbit did a shimmy with its ears.

'I can't,' wailed Martha.

'Oh, for crying out loud,' said Humphrey, raising his own bow, but the rabbit had heard them, and bounced away out of sight.

'It was too cute,' said Martha.

'Cute?' said Humphrey. 'Do you want us all to starve? Or are we not cute enough to live?'

'We can go to the market and buy meat.'

'You do know that meat has always been alive first?'

'Of course I know.'

'Well then, next time, you shoot.'

Nothing stirred for quite a while. Martha wondered whether this might be a good moment to ask Humphrey about the Table of Less Valued Knights. She'd been trying to find the right words for days, ever since Elaine had mentioned it. She still couldn't believe that Humphrey belonged there. There must have been a terrible mistake, or maybe Elaine had misunderstood. She was formulating a question when suddenly they heard something crashing towards them through the trees, something big. Humphrey leapt to attention and pointed an arrow towards the sound.

'Aim,' he said, 'but wait for it to get closer before you shoot.'

'What is it?' said Martha, raising her bow again, heart beating hard.

'I don't know,' said Humphrey. 'But it's big.'

There was a flash of white through the bushes.

'Cow?' said Martha.

Humphrey shook his head. 'Horse, I think.'

'Well, don't kill it if it's one of ours,' said Martha.

As the creature passed between two trees, they both got a good look at it.

'Unicorn,' breathed Humphrey, lowering his bow.

Unicorn! Martha didn't wait another moment. She started to run. She couldn't afford to let a unicorn anywhere near her. Unicorns sought out virgin maidens and laid their heads in their laps. Virgin *maidens*. Not virgin boys. Bloody animal! Why couldn't it have gone for Elaine?

'Marcus!' shouted Humphrey.

'I'm not running away!' she yelled. 'Don't send Conrad! I will come back!'

She heard hoof-beats behind her, growing closer. The unicorn was drawn to her, as surely as a fleck of iron is drawn to a lodestone.

'Piss off!' she shouted at the creature.

The unicorn accelerated, galloping after her through the trees.

Trees. Unicorns couldn't climb trees.

She spied a trunk with low branches, and started hauling herself up. The bow and quiver of arrows were getting in her way, but she was glad to be in men's clothes, much easier than in a dress and heels.

At the foot of the tree, the unicorn stopped. It stared up at her, a soppy look on its face.

'Go away,' said Martha, grabbing a branch, hitching her leg up, pulling herself ever higher.

The unicorn leaned against the trunk of the tree and looked up at her lovingly.

Martha was nearing the top now. There was nowhere left to go except some thin branches that would not take even her slight weight. She sat on the highest of the firm branches and looked down. The unicorn was still gazing adoringly at her.

'Get lost! I'm married.'

The unicorn was undeterred. It made a noise that sounded alarmingly like purring. For the first time ever, Martha wished she'd had marital relations with Edwin.

'Go find Elaine! *Elaine!* She's that way!'

Martha gestured with her bow. The unicorn continued to stare up at her with limpid eyes.

Maybe she could just climb down quickly and let him do it.

She heard Humphrey calling her. 'Marcus! Where are you?'

What if it followed her back to camp? Unicorns were said to be loyal for life. How would she explain herself then?

'Come back or I'm sending Conrad to kill you,' shouted Humphrey.

That's me, thought Martha. *Caught between a unicorn and a hard place.*

There was only one thing for it.

Martha smiled down at the unicorn. Unicorns don't smile, but it looked up at her with a contented and trusting air. Martha shot it between the eyes, just beneath its alabaster horn.

Thirty-Five

'Conrad!' Humphrey marched back into camp, where the giant and Elaine were busy packing their tents up.

'What now?' Conrad was sitting backwards on Jemima, stuffing scrumpled-up canvas into her saddlebags.

'Marcus has run away.'

Conrad laughed. 'I told you so.'

'You need to find him. He was heading south.'

'Right you are.'

Conrad swivelled round on Jemima's back and kicked her forwards.

'Conrad? Don't hurt him.'

'Why not?'

'He's the only one who can spin the sword.'

Conrad shook his head but didn't say anything as he steered Jemima towards the trees.

'Oh, and Conrad?'

'What?'

'Be careful. He's got the bow and arrow.'

'For fuck's sake,' muttered Conrad as he rode away.

'Marcus didn't take Leila with him, did he?' said Elaine. She was sitting on the ground leaning against a tree, looking uncomfortable in the ugly grey dress she hadn't changed out of for days.

'No. She's right here.' Humphrey patted the sword at his belt.

'Thank God.'

Elaine reapplied herself to the blanket she had been folding. Humphrey stood watching her for several seconds.

'You're pregnant, aren't you?' he blurted out. 'That's why you're in such a hurry to find your fiancé.'

Elaine's head shot up. She stared at him for several moments, breathing hard. Then she slumped. 'How long have you known?'

'I just figured it out. We saw a unicorn in the woods. I was thinking about how if it followed us back to camp, it would lay its head in your lap. The virgin maid,' he said bitterly. 'And then . . . I don't know, the pieces somehow fell into place.'

Elaine put a hand on her belly. 'I suppose it will be obvious to everyone soon enough.'

'Is it Sir Alistair's?' said Humphrey.

Elaine hesitated, then she shook her head.

'Whose?' said Humphrey.

'It's none of your business.'

'We're on a quest to find your kidnapped fiancé. I think the identity of your baby's father . . .' Humphrey began self-righteously.

'It's Frank's,' snapped Elaine.

'Frank?' Humphrey tried to remember. It came to him. 'The guard? The one who left your parents' castle?'

'That's right. He couldn't get out of there fast enough once I told him. And before you start, we've already ruled him out of the kidnapping – too tall, remember?'

'Do your parents know?'

'Yes. I had the foolish idea that they might help me. And they did, I suppose, by arranging the tournament for my hand. But after Sir Alistair went missing they wanted nothing more to do with it. They'd suffered humiliation enough. They told me to find him or forget about being their daughter.'

'So the plan was that you'd wed Sir Alistair in haste, consummate the marriage and then pretend the baby was his?'

Elaine nodded. She was pink-cheeked and looked beautiful and innocent and not nearly as ashamed as Humphrey thought she deserved to be.

'You . . . you bitch!' he said.

'What?' Elaine was as stunned as if he'd slapped her.

'You would lie to your husband.'

'For the good of my child.'

'For the good of yourself.'

'What would you know? Are you telling me that you've never touched a woman other than your wife?'

Humphrey said nothing.

'Exactly. You can spread your favours without any fear of repercussions. If a child is conceived, you can run away like Frank, and even if it is known that you've fathered a baby outside marriage, it just demonstrates your virility! There's no shame in it as there is for a woman. Even before this I knew that I must be someone's daughter or someone's wife, or else, I suppose, I might go to the convent or the brothel, but I am not allowed to be simply myself, ever! And now, even though I was one of a pair who chose freely to lie together, and I have been abandoned, I am the only one who must carry dishonour, I am the one who will be shunned by society and turned away by my parents if I raise this child on my own.'

'So you would trick a man into believing that he is the father of somebody else's child?'

'Why not! He will love it all the same.'

Humphrey thought over everything that had passed between them. 'That night when you tried to seduce me,' he said, 'you were lining me up as an alternative, should Sir Alistair not materialise.'

Only now did Elaine's face show contrition. 'I changed my mind,' she said.

'You decided that a Less Valued Knight would not be a worthy enough father for your bastard?'

'No! I thought you were too good a man to trap like that.'

'So you agree that it is a trap.'

Elaine was crying now. 'Would it really have been so bad? You've done it before.'

Humphrey could feel himself softening at Elaine's tears, and so he forced his voice to be harder. 'Don't bring Conrad into this.'

'He's your wife's son, isn't he? That's why he's so short. He's half human.'

'It doesn't matter whose son he is. He's not mine.'

'But you love him.'

'He's my squire. Love has nothing to do with it.'

As he spoke, Jemima emerged from the trees, a stony-faced Conrad on her back. Sitting in front of him was Martha, and in front of Martha was the body of the dead unicorn, slung over Jemima's neck. Conrad leaned over and pushed the unicorn onto the ground where it landed with a thud.

'Seven years' bad luck,' he said.

'What did you hear?' Elaine demanded, wiping her eyes.

'That there's no love lost between him and me. As if I didn't know.'

'What else?'

'Nothing. So whatever precious secrets you have are safe.'

Meanwhile Martha was babbling to Humphrey. 'I'm sorry, I wasn't trying to run away, I'm scared of unicorns, did you see that I killed him, Sir Humphrey? I mean I know you're not supposed to, but it shows that I can do it, like you said.'

'Finish packing,' Humphrey told her. 'You've wasted enough of our time as it is.'

'Humphrey,' said Elaine, standing up and taking a step towards him.

'I have nothing more to say to you,' said Humphrey, walking away.

Thirty-Six

While the rest of them packed, Conrad, surlier than ever, cut the unicorn flesh into strips and rubbed it with salt so that they could take it with them on the road. The meat tasted pungent and gamey and, to Martha, of guilt, and of triumph. She couldn't believe she was eating an animal that she herself had killed. Perhaps it hadn't been for the most honourable of reasons – felling the finest creature of the forest just to keep her secret – but she had done it all the same. Now that she knew what she was capable of, the next time would be easier.

'Mount up,' Humphrey told the group. 'We've got a lot of ground to cover.'

'Don't you want me to check the direction first?' said Martha.

Humphrey squinted at her as if he couldn't remember what she was doing there. 'We don't need directions,' he said. 'I've got a map.'

'But we don't know where the Queen is.'

'We're not looking for the Queen. Lady Elaine has lost her fiancé and is in a terrible hurry to find him. Isn't that right, Lady Elaine? The sooner we find Lady Elaine's fiancé, the sooner Lady Elaine can have her big romantic wedding and the rest of us can go home.'

Humphrey tied Silver's bridle to his saddle, something he hadn't bothered to do in days.

'But . . .' said Martha. 'But I don't want to go home.'

'It doesn't matter what you want. We're on Lady Elaine's

quest and we must do Lady Elaine's bidding. Isn't that right, Lady Elaine?'

'That's right,' said Elaine, chin raised, fingertips flicking tears from her cheeks as though they were nothing more than raindrops. Though Martha was pleased to see that even Elaine's pretty nose ran when she wept. She was not as perfect as all that.

She had no idea why Elaine was crying, seeing as she had got her own way. For that matter, she had no idea why Conrad was in such a sullen mood. It couldn't possibly be that stuff they'd overheard Humphrey saying about love – he was an employee. Martha was the one being punished for having run away, she was the one who deserved to be upset. Humphrey was acting as if she wasn't even there, riding alongside him, though obviously that mattered much less than the fact that he'd given up on looking for the Queen. They were heading doggedly towards Sir Alistair Gilbert's home town, which was in a completely different direction to the one they'd been going in before. Humphrey was using his map to find forges along their route, and the only times that Leila was deployed were to determine the innocence or guilt of the men (and occasional women) who'd commissioned black armour. There was no way that Martha could co-opt those spins to help her find her brother.

She knew what she had to do. She had to get Leila back and leave this group behind. She had no loyalty to them. Any sentiment that she experienced was just weakness on her part. Grabbing Leila during one of their spin sessions was the most obvious way of going about it – they were the only times she had her hands on the sword – but then she'd have to fight her way out. Martha felt a cold finger trailing down her spine. Even with Leila on her side she had lost that fight with Humphrey, and a less compassionate man – Conrad, say – would have killed her. And she couldn't rely on Leila cooperating with her anyway. She was a sword with a mind of her own. Why she had attacked

Humphrey in the first place was as mysterious to Martha now as it was the day she'd done it.

She decided to take Leila at night, while Humphrey was sleeping. By the time they noticed she was gone she'd have several hours on them. It wasn't much of a plan, but sometimes the simplest was the best.

The night she chose was sultry, with storms that circled but never came. Martha thirsted for rain. She lay sweating in the oven-like tent, waiting for Conrad's breathing to slow, for the reliable saw of Humphrey's snore. Once she was sure they were both asleep, she gathered what things of hers she could find in the dark and then slipped out to saddle Silver. She considered loosing the others' horses, chasing away Jemima, to give herself more of a head start, but these people had treated her adequately, for a captive; there was no need to leave them stranded.

She went back into the tent and knelt down by Humphrey's bed. All the habitual tension was gone from his face, leaving behind a surprising innocence. She began to slide her hand around under the covers searching for Leila, trying not to touch him. Their faces were close together now. His elephantine snores (no offence to Jemima, who was a relatively quiet sleeper) did spoil the moment somewhat, but even so she wondered whether he would wake up if she kissed him. If it was a very light kiss. Just the slightest brush of lips. And another part of her wondered, if he woke up, exactly what he would do . . .

Humphrey had never had a problem with sleeping. Even in the weeks after he'd returned from Castle Maudit he had dropped off as soon as he closed his eyes. This was more of a curse than a gift back then. When awake, he had some control over his thoughts, the ability to open a book, say, and distract himself, even if only for a few minutes at a time. When asleep, it was just his wife laughing, the sword sweeping towards him, her scream and then her silence, over and over again.

So he was surprised that night to open his eyes to absolute

darkness and silence. Something was wrong. He waited – the slightest movement – there was someone in his bed – a woman! He could tell by the weight, the scent of her. Elaine? His heart jumped. He reached out and grabbed her by the wrist – there was a cry, high and light – he pulled her towards him – felt the stubble of her cheek against his. Stubble?

'*Marcus?*'

Silence. Then, 'Yes.'

He gripped the boy's wrist harder, angry.

'What are you doing?'

He could feel the boy's breath on his face – hot – fast – frightened.

'Taking Leila,' said Marcus.

Humphrey realised with shock that he was aroused.

He threw Marcus's wrist from him.

'Go back to bed. Go back to bed now.'

'I'm sorry,' the boy choked.

'Get away from me before I hurt you.'

'I'm sorry,' Marcus said again.

Humphrey watched the shadowy form of the boy as he scuttled away from him to the mess of blankets, where he huddled, shaking. Humphrey thought he heard him crying.

How could he have mistaken Marcus for Elaine?

He was still aroused.

His hand found its way to his cock, where it moved, quietly.

But Marcus was a boy.

This was wrong, this was all wrong.

Thirty-Seven

The next morning, Marcus looked bruised, skinny limbs twitching with fear, the skin of his face pale and blotchy with last night's tears.

If he had got the sword, thought Humphrey, *would he have run away, or would he have killed me first?*

He made Marcus ride next to him, same as ever. He had to. He couldn't trust the boy. Every time he looked over at him, Marcus looked down. Had the boy felt the charge between them in that moment? Humphrey felt certain that he had. If Marcus was one of those men who preferred other men, that would make sense of so much. In fact it was obvious, now he thought about it. But it wouldn't explain his own feelings. He had never wanted a boy. Plenty of knights did. There was always talk about what went on between certain knights and their squires. It was against the law, but as long as it wasn't blatant, it was tolerated.

And if it had been Elaine in his bed? Elaine's draw on him was like the hum of a mosquito, impossible to ignore. But when he thought of her he thought of Cecily, glowing and excited in the early days of her pregnancy, wanting him more then than she ever had. The shock of her disappearance, the terror that he had lost not only her but their child. The months of miserable searching with his brother knights. The heartbreaking realisation of her betrayal. Her blood on his sword. And then Conrad.

So those were the twin poles of his attraction: a woman

carrying a bastard, and a boy who was probably a bastard himself. Both liars. And he'd thought these things were meant to get easier as you got older.

Meanwhile, beside him, Marcus just looked sick.

'I haven't decided what to do with you yet,' said Humphrey.

The thoughts that accompanied this sentence were best not spoken out loud.

'It was foolish,' said Marcus. 'I'm sorry. Only, you've decided to return to Lady Elaine's quest, and I still need to find the Queen.'

If Humphrey's hunch about Marcus was correct, he could understand, even admire, the boy's urgency to find his half-sister. But king's bastard or not, Marcus's problems were none of Humphrey's concern. And until they found Sir Alistair and offloaded Elaine, the sword stayed with him. (His mind went back to last night. The boy in the darkness, the hand beneath the sheet. He felt a stirring which he made himself ignore.)

'I can't find her without the sword,' Marcus said. 'Give Leila back to me and I will leave you, I promise.'

'The last time that sword was in your possession you tried to kill me.'

'Leila tried to kill you.'

'In your hand.'

'I've spun her dozens of times since then. She's never done it again. Maybe she made a mistake the first time. Maybe she's changed her mind.'

Where would be the harm in letting Marcus go? Humphrey asked himself. He was sure that the boy would take the sword and disappear, never to be seen again. There was no risk in it, none at all.

'No,' he said.

He didn't want to let Marcus go.

They rode on.

Thirty-Eight

It was, as usual, blisteringly hot in the forge. Elaine wished she were outside with Conrad and Marcus, even in the thick torrid weather, anything to get away from the heat of the fire. She missed drizzle. Sweet, cool drizzle. The stuff that crawled through your clothes and skin and flesh until it coated your bones in icy slime that would never dry. What could be lovelier?

This smith, a man by the name of Roddy, was a Christmas pudding of a man with a holly berry of a face. Elaine was becoming an expert in smiths. They were rarely small. They tended towards loud voices and excessive perspiration, which wafted as they moved, their stench blooming in clouds through the elemental aromas of fire and metal and horse shit that surrounded them.

I will spend the rest of my life amongst these men, thought Elaine. *We will visit each and every one of them on these islands. Have you shod a black stallion? Oh yes, too many to count. No, I have no records, for I can neither read nor write. Have you forged a suit of black armour? Black armour, me? By my lady, I have never heard tell of such a thing.* They were hardly going to answer, 'Yes, I do forge armour for criminals,' were they?

Roddy was friendlier than most, though. When Humphrey had explained their business to him, he had sent his boy for tankards of ale, had ushered them over to a table from which he swept a mountain of bridle parts onto the floor, and bid them to 'rest their weary souls'. As if her soul could ever find succour sitting on a stool of which one leg was shorter than the other three, while drinking sour hops bound to give her wind. Lord, but the baby inside her was a veritable machine for producing wind.

'Look at these good tankards – I made them myself,' said Roddy as his apprentice handed out the beer. Elaine examined hers. The handle had been soldered on wonky. 'I'm doing a special deal on them, buy three get the fourth one free.'

'Is that so?' said Humphrey.

'It is, it is. Drink up now, good gentleman, good lady. What an honour it is to have a Knight of Camelot here, in my most humble workshop.'

'Knight of Camelot' was the formulation that Humphrey was using to avoid saying 'Less Valued Knight'.

'These stools were made by an associate of mine,' added the smith. 'I'm sure I can get you a preferential rate.'

'That's very kind of you,' said Humphrey. 'But, as I said, we are looking for a gentleman who wears distinctive all-black armour.'

'I do armour of all varieties,' said Roddy. 'Hauberk, haubergeon, partial plate, full plate (man and horse), engraved, embossed, for self or gift, or as a gift for yourself, ha ha, all very reasonable, especially if you're buying in bulk, I doubt you'll find a better offer within a hundred miles.'

'We're not actually buying.'

'Everybody's buying. If you think you're not, it's just that the price isn't right. Now, I don't like to haggle, but I am always open to a spot of gentlemanly negotiation.'

'I assure you that I have all the armour I need. Now, about that man in the black armour I mentioned earlier,' said Humphrey, trying to steer the smith back to the point.

'I can see you in a suit of black armour, my lord. It would go very well with your complexion. My boy can measure you up while you wait, if you like.'

'I am not shopping.' Humphrey's voice got surprisingly

squeaky when he was annoyed. 'Have you ever made a suit of black armour? That's all I want to know.'

'I am well versed in all types of armour, as I said.'

'Have you or haven't you?'

'The colour of the armour doesn't affect the skill that it takes to make it. Black, silver, blue, green, it's all built the same way. Crafted by these very hands.' The smith held up his two huge cracked and blackened palms. 'If you'd like, I can get my lad to show you a few prototypes, see which you prefer. They come in every price bracket from the basic suit to the "regal" range featuring gold and mother-of-pearl inlay, carved to your specifications.'

'Yes or no. Just say yes or no.' The tankard actually started to bend in Humphrey's furious grip. 'Have you ever forged a suit of completely black armour?'

Roddy's face fell. 'No,' he said.

'Right,' said Humphrey, 'we're off.'

He and Elaine got up from their stools, Elaine barely bobbing a curtsey in her desperation to get back outside.

'I've worked for King Leo!' the smith cried at their retreating backs. 'I oversaw the retooling of the castle dungeons! That's a lot of metalwork! Shackles, chains, bars for the windows. I did him an iron mask!'

At the words *iron mask*, Leila started clattering furiously back and forth in her scabbard. Elaine's eyes shot to the sword, then to Humphrey. Could King Leo be holding Queen Martha in an iron mask? It would make sense. He benefited from her being out of the way, leaving his brother to hold the throne. Or could it even be Sir Alistair? He was wealthy and popular – maybe Leo saw him as a threat. Perhaps they were finally on the brink of finding him! Elaine wasn't sure how she felt about this. It certainly wasn't happiness. Humphrey meanwhile was staring at the sword by his side, no doubt thinking along similar lines.

'I can do you a mask,' said Roddy eagerly. 'A matching set, if you like. Buy one, get one half price.'

Elaine didn't need to spin a sword to know where they were heading next.

Thirty-Nine

Just when Edwin was giving up all hope, he found her. He had almost forgotten that they were looking. Sir Dorian had developed the sleek, satisfied look of a well-fed seal, fat with gratitude from all the damsels they had encountered. Edwin, meanwhile, felt that his balls were set to explode. He blamed Martha for this. If she hadn't run away he'd be safe at the castle, banging every serving maid who took his fancy, and her, of course, when duty insisted upon it. Instead he was playing second fiddle to a priapic cavalier. Plus he had lost so many games of piquet to Sir Dorian's squire while they were waiting around that he was going to have to raid the castle coffers when he got home to cover his debts. They were Martha's castle coffers, true, but even so.

The lake where the Lady finally appeared was in a valley that straddled the Camelot–Puddock border. It wasn't much of a lake, though it probably looked more impressive when not surrounded by a ring of cracked mud where the water level had fallen. It was the same story everywhere. Rivers were turning into streams, streams were drying up entirely. They could no longer rely on finding drinking water at wells, so Silas and Keith loaded up the cart with barrels of water wherever they could. The added weight was slowing them down, and that afternoon Sir Dorian had hung back to remonstrate with his tardy squire and page, leaving Edwin to ride ahead to the lake, unable to wait another moment to strip off his clothes and plunge into the cool water. How Dorian was feeling inside his tin box in this heat Edwin could barely imagine, though he wouldn't go so far as to say that he felt sorry for him. Nobody was forcing the berk to ride in full armour.

Edwin dismounted from Storm and peeled off his shirt, and was loosening his boots when he heard a woman's voice calling him from across the water.

'Prince Edwin of Tuft?' she said.

'King of Puddock,' Edwin said automatically as he looked up.

'The King of Puddock is dead,' said the woman, a brunette in a blue gown, pretty enough, in fact definitely worth a poke, except that she was standing on the water in an unnatural way that made Edwin queasy.

'So is the Queen by now, probably,' he said, ignoring the discomfited way she was making him feel.

'No,' said the woman. 'Martha is still alive.'

'What?' said Edwin, suddenly alert. 'How do you know? Have you seen her? Who are you? Are you the Lady of the Lake?'

'Martha is still alive. I know because I am the Lady of the Lake. I have seen her. I am the Lady of the Lake. Yes.'

'What?' said Edwin again.

'Martha is still alive. I know because –'

'It's all right, I got it.' Edwin started to pull his shirt back on.

'There's no need to dress on my account,' said the Lady of the Lake, fixing him with a gaze that he could only describe as flirtatious. Actually, now that he thought about it, he could also describe it as come-hither, though he had no intention of trying to walk on water, and also sexy, or possibly slightly short-sighted. 'I've been watching you,' the Lady continued. 'Waiting to get you alone for weeks. But there's always that knight there, spoiling things.'

Edwin pulled his shirt off again and squared his shoulders, showing off his chest to its best advantage.

'I know,' he said. 'I can't shake him. He's so annoying.'

'I hate knights,' said the Lady. 'They treat you like their own personal library. All they want is information.'

'They think they're better than everybody else,' agreed Edwin. 'And they hog all the maidens.'

'But not the Ladies,' said the Lady of the Lake with an unlady-like leer. 'The Ladies like a prince.'

For once, Edwin resisted the urge to point out again that he was actually a king. 'The thing is,' he said instead, 'I need your help finding my wife. But I don't love her or anything. It doesn't need to come between us.'

'I think I can give you some pointers,' the Lady of the Lake said. 'God, it must be awful being married to her. She's a right little madam. Not nearly good enough for you.'

'Thank you,' said Edwin, in heartfelt tones. 'Nobody else gets it.'

'The things I could tell you about her,' said the Lady of the Lake. 'You should see the way she looks these days! Unfortunately I signed a confidentiality clause. Secrecy is the cornerstone of the Sorcery industry.'

'I don't suppose you would consider letting slip a morsel or two,' said Edwin. He winked.

The Lady of the Lake giggled. 'I wish I could,' she said. 'We don't get a lot of men in the Lake. It's just Ladies, Ladies, Ladies. It's a real treat to meet a handsome fellow like you. Although you could say, in some significant ways, that meeting Martha was a lot like meeting a handsome fellow like you.'

She winked back, and watched to see if what she said had sunk in. Edwin couldn't make head or tail of it, but he wasn't about to ask for an explanation. He concluded that she meant that meeting a woman was an awful lot like meeting her husband, which he supposed he agreed with. He nodded intelligently.

'To be honest with you, I've had enough of the Lake,' the Lady confided. 'I'd love an excuse to leave. It isn't even my proper job. I'm just filling in for Nimue, since she ran off with Merlin. The Ladies do that, you know. Run off with men. I've often thought about –'

'Is there anything else you can tell me?' Edwin interrupted. He hated it when females didn't know when to stop talking.

The Lady paused, annoyed. Apparently she didn't like being interrupted. Typical female. Edwin was disappointed that the magic ones were no better than the normal ones.

'They're heading towards your brother's castle,' she said, a little brusquely.

'They?' said Edwin. 'Who's they?'

'Can't tell you.'

'Has she been captured? Did she have help running away? Does she have a lover?'

'Can't say.'

'Has Leo kidnapped her? That's so typical of him! He won't let me have one thing for myself.'

'I can neither confirm nor deny.'

'What bloody use are you then?'

The Lady of the Lake put her hands on her hips. 'You're just as bad as she is! Five minutes ago you didn't know where to look, and I've just told you exactly where to find her, for all the thanks I get. You probably won't be able to find her there anyway. You seem like the type who couldn't find his own dick if he was holding it with both hands.'

The Lady of the Lake began her descent into the water, muttering, 'That's it, I've had enough, I'm putting in for a transfer.' But then she stopped. 'One last thing,' she said. 'Just out of interest. What's Martha's favourite colour?'

'I couldn't give a fuck,' said Edwin.

Forty

Taking Roddy with them, they rode as far as the edge of the woods that grew within reach of Tuft Castle, close enough to see the turrets in the distance. Roddy's expertise regarding the dungeons would be invaluable, which is not to say that a value hadn't been placed on it by Roddy, and paid in advance. They squatted in a circle round a patch of earth that was clear of grass, and Roddy used a stick to scratch out the dungeons' layout in the dirt.

'Between you and me and these four walls,' said Roddy, ignoring the fact that there wasn't a wall anywhere near them, 'I scrimped a bit on the materials, so the bars at the entrance here –' he pointed with his stick '– and on the windows, here, and on these cells, and, well, all over the place really, are a tad flimsy. Don't get me wrong, usually I'm straighter than a cock in a brothel, pardon me, but that King Leo never pays his invoices on time, and to be frank, he's a shit, mind my French.'

'So I keep hearing,' said Martha.

'He visited my parents' castle just after he was crowned, on his tour of intimidation of the region,' said Elaine. 'He has the charm of a toad, the kindness of a snake, and the wit of a dog who hasn't figured out it has to dip its head to go underneath a low-hanging branch.'

'Like I said, a shit. Far be it for me to suggest tactics when there's a knight in the room,' said Roddy, again overlooking the fact that they weren't in a room, 'but if it were me I'd arm myself to the teeth and just kick down the door and go in. Or snap off the bars. Same difference.'

'What do you mean, "If it were me"?' asked Humphrey. 'You're here, aren't you?'

'I'm not coming with you,' said Roddy.

'What do you mean, you're not coming?'

'You haven't paid me nearly enough for that. I could get myself killed. Or lose an arm. These are craftsman's hands.' He held up his two immense paws.

'Con man's hands, more like it,' Conrad muttered.

'Fine,' said Humphrey. 'Roddy and his hands aren't coming. They can wait with Elaine and keep her safe, or at least entertained. Or failing even that simple task, they can try to sell her things.'

'All right with me,' said Roddy.

'You're not leaving me behind,' said Elaine.

'Yes I am,' said Humphrey.

'No. You can't make me stay. I know you all think that Queen Martha is in that mask, but it might be Sir Alistair. And if my fiancé needs rescuing, I'm going to be the one to do it.'

'But it's dangerous.' Humphrey glanced meaningfully at Elaine's belly, but she affected not to notice.

'I'm coming,' she said. 'And you can't stop me.'

The two of them locked eyes, both with expressions of implacable determination.

Humphrey caved in first. 'Very well, if you insist. But it is entirely against my wishes and my best advice.'

'I have no problem with that,' said Elaine.

'Right then,' Humphrey resumed. 'Elaine will do her best to get killed for no reason. Conrad, you'll break the bars where Roddy's indicated the weaknesses. I'll cover you with the bow and arrow. Marcus, you –'

'Me?' interrupted Martha. 'I don't even know which hand I'm supposed to hold a sword in.'

'You'll be fine,' said Humphrey, 'I'm going to give Leila back to you, and she'll do all the work.'

'What?' said Conrad. 'You're going to give him the magic sword he used to try to kill you?'

'The sword wants to find the Queen, and she only cooperates with Marcus.'

'He, she or it, it's still sharp and it still wants your neck.'

'We don't know that.'

'And giving it back to Marcus is the best way to find out?'

Humphrey looked at Martha. He saw a very young, very pale face with worried eyes. But behind that worry shone a fierce tenacity.

'We need Marcus,' Humphrey said. 'And I trust him.'

'Because you think he's got blue blood?'

Elaine frowned as she looked from Martha to Humphrey and back. Roddy considered the previously unimportant boy in a whole new lucrative light. Martha's mouth fell open, her heart pounding. 'What? What do you mean, blue blood? Don't be absurd. Humphrey, what did he mean?'

'It's got nothing to do with that,' Humphrey said to Conrad. 'Since that first day, he's done nothing to make us doubt him.' *Nothing except run away in the woods. Nothing except try to steal Leila back from me.* Humphrey knew that Conrad was right to be cautious, but his instincts told him to have faith in Marcus. That his instincts might be clouded with lust or greed was a possibility that he refused to consider. 'Stop acting like a brat, Conrad. You're the one who's slowing us all down.'

Conrad got to his feet and crossed his enormous arms. 'Fine. Do what you like. I've had enough. When we get back to Camelot I'm asking for a new knight. Marcus can be your squire, seeing as you're so fond of him.'

'You're being childish,' said Humphrey.

'For the rest of this quest, I follow orders, but that's it. You can keep your personal observations to yourself. I'm done pretending that we're some kind of happy family. Consider this my notice.'

There was a long silence. Even Jemima looked embarrassed.

Then Roddy said, 'Can I just make sure – I'm still not coming, right?'

Forty-One

Edwin and Dorian skirted around the Lake, which was perhaps just a lake now that the Lady was gone, and this took them briefly into Puddock before they finally crossed the border into Tuft. The dwarf at the border post recognised Edwin immediately as the Prince of the Realm, jumping from his stool and kneeling down in the dirt, his head so low that his bushy eyebrows grazed the ground. Edwin looked over to see if Sir Dorian had noticed, but he was busy picking a stone out of his horse's hoof, and Keith and Silas were down the road, hurling contraband apples out of the cart before they were fined for smuggling. By the time anyone was paying attention the dwarf was back on his feet.

It was gratifying to finally get some recognition, but unfortunate too, because the last thing Edwin needed was Leo getting wind that he was on his way. If he had Martha in his custody, it would be just like him to kill her before Edwin had a chance to do it himself. The dwarf had to be silenced. Edwin considered cutting out his tongue, but that was gross. He couldn't figure out how to do it without holding onto the tip, and who wanted to hold onto a dwarf's tongue? And killing him would just attract more attention once the body was discovered. In the end, Edwin merely relieved the dwarf of his employment and told him to report to Puddock Castle for incarceration. The dwarf slunk away down the road in tears. Edwin had no sympathy. He probably wouldn't even show up to prison.

Dwarves were notoriously duplicitous. He hoped that the others would be impressed at his show of power, but Dorian said something patronising about how they were supposed to protect the weak, not lock them up, while Keith and Silas were annoyed at the waste of apples, now that there was no longer a customs officer to inspect the cart.

'We can't have more encounters like that,' Edwin told Sir Dorian as they rode away from the customs post. 'Now that we're in Tuft, I need a disguise. Everybody here knows what I look like, and they revere me. There's no way I can get to the castle without being recognised.'

Dorian, who was still annoyed that Edwin had had the entire encounter with the Lady of the Lake without summoning him, had started pretending that he hadn't heard anything Edwin said, waiting three seconds, then saying, 'What was that?'

'What was that?' said Dorian after three seconds.

Edwin fought back the urge to kick Dorian in his (inferior) teeth. If Dorian insisted on pretending he hadn't heard Edwin, Edwin could only respond by pretending that he didn't care.

'Now that we're in Tuft, I need a disguise so that Leo doesn't find out I'm coming,' he repeated.

'Hmm,' said Sir Dorian. 'We could dress you in rags and say you're a mendicant?'

This was not at all the type of disguise Edwin had in mind. 'I could drape myself in rare silks and darken my skin with clay, and pretend to be an Arabian potentate?' he suggested in return.

Sir Dorian made a great show of looking around the wide, empty valley. 'Where are we going to get rare silks from?' he said. 'They are, by definition, rare. How about . . . you lie in the cart under a blanket until we get to the castle, and pretend to be a heap of turnips?'

There was a certain appeal in being able to sleep the whole journey, not to mention getting away from Sir Dorian, but Edwin was damned if he was going to lie under a blanket in direct sunlight in this weather. Also, he was not a man who could easily be mistaken for a turnip.

'I know!' he said, as if he'd just thought of it and it wasn't what he'd had in mind all along. 'Why don't I borrow your other suit of armour and pretend to be a Knight of the Round Table? It's the perfect cover. What could be more unremarkable than two knights travelling together? I could keep the visor of my helmet down so that nobody would recognise me, and if I'm called to undertake a few quests, comfort a few damsels, then so be it.'

'You can't pretend to be a Knight of the Round Table,' said Sir Dorian in genuine horror. 'That's fraud. And quite possibly treason.'

'Treason? That's going a bit far, isn't it?' said Edwin. 'Anyway, I'm the King. I'm pretty sure I can't commit treason.'

Sir Dorian – as he had done many times before – swallowed back the urge to point out to Edwin that he was not, and never would be, a king.

'You are not the King in Camelot,' he said instead, 'and the Round Table is a holy order, a compact with God. You cannot put yourself above God.'

Even Edwin had to concede that no, he probably couldn't do that.

'If you wish,' Sir Dorian said, a hint of amusement entering his voice as he came up with a particularly mean idea, 'you could claim to be on the Table of Less Valued Knights. I don't think God is particularly bothered about them.'

Edwin did not like the idea of being a less valued anything. 'No, no, you were right,' he said. 'I'm sure we can come up with something else. The last thing I want is to commit fraud. Or for that matter treason.'

'Don't worry about that,' said Sir Dorian. 'They let pretty much anybody be a Less Valued Knight. And it would be a good disguise. Who could possibly believe that the great Prince Edwin of Tuft is a Knight of Lesser Value?'

Edwin – as he had done many times before – swallowed back the urge to point out to Sir Dorian that he wasn't a prince, he was a king. And anyhow, it occurred to him that he probably wouldn't have to say what kind of knight he was anyway. People would assume he was a Knight of the Round Table, and appearances were the most important thing.

'All right then,' he said. 'A Less Valued Knight it is.'

They pulled up and waited for Silas and Keith to catch up with them in the cart. The child inside Edwin was excited about the idea of dressing as a knight, any kind of knight, while the adult inside him was looking forward to taking advantage of his new-found status with the maidens.

'Though of course,' said Sir Dorian, as if reading his mind, 'you can't actually raise your visor at any point. If anyone recognised you, that would completely defeat the object of being in disguise.'

Edwin toyed with the idea of keeping his helmet on while he removed everything else, but even he could see that this was absurd. The bits you did with your face were some of the best bits.

With Silas's help he put the armour on. It was more comfortable than he'd expected. It was a combination of mail and plate, which meant that it was more flexible and less heavy than he'd imagined, and he could easily bend his arms and legs and get on and off Storm without help. What bothered him more was the padded gambeson he had to wear underneath. It was saturated with Sir Dorian's sweat and the stench was almost unendurable. With the armour on top, he was unspeakably hot in the thick summer swelter. Edwin had seen people burned at the stake who looked cooler than he was. Sir Dorian had never complained, though, and so Edwin refused to as a matter of pride. The knight's forbearance filled Edwin with reluctant admiration, and this only made him resent Sir Dorian even more.

To Edwin's delight, though, where one knight had attracted

attention, two sent the population into raptures. Ladies ran out of their houses, waving and cheering as they rode by. Children chased after them until their little legs gave out in fatigue. Men bowed and saluted them as they passed. Edwin had never felt so adored. But although he now rode up front with Sir Dorian as his equal, although he now shared the love of the crowds, when push came to shove and shove came to poke, it was still Sir Dorian who fought the duels ('We can't risk a prince getting hurt,' he said with maddening accuracy and to Edwin's slight relief) and still Sir Dorian who reaped the rewards in the bedroom (or on top of the haystack or up against the back of the barn). Edwin was incensed. *But this is my childhood dream*, he told himself, as he tried not to faint from the heat, *and one way or another I am going to bloody well enjoy it.* The platonic love of the populace would have to do.

And it was good to be home. Tuft, land of his childhood! And early adulthood! Its rolling hills, its boggy dales! Edwin felt his heart swell with pride. Although as they drew close to Tuft Castle, he had to admit that it was a bit crappy-looking in comparison with Camelot. When he was growing up, he'd thought it was the grandest castle he had ever seen, but this may have been partly because it was the only castle he had ever seen. It did have some storybook charm, but it was quite small. Very small, in fact. He should have known it wasn't normal for two princes to have to share a bedroom. The king's quarters were bigger, as one might expect, but as soon as he was crowned, Leo had stuck a KEEP OUT sign on the door. Still, at least from then on Edwin could sleep on whichever bunk he preferred.

Looking at the castle now, he couldn't believe how lazy Leo was, leaving it in the same state he'd inherited it in. If Edwin ran the place, he'd keep the main body of the castle as it stood for public functions – heritage impressed the lower orders – but add two new wings: one as living quarters for himself, and one for his child. Martha would be dead by then – they'd put the story about that she'd died in childbirth – so he'd have to hire a wet nurse. Bonanza! Wet nurses always had massive jugs. He wondered if he could design some kind of one-way door so that he could go in to visit the boy, but the boy could not come out. (It never occurred to Edwin that his baby might be a girl.) That would work nicely for the nurse as well, of course.

Leo's laissez-faire attitude to the castle extended to the nation around it. Rolling hills were one thing, but the boggy vales didn't have to be quite so boggy: if only he would instigate some kind of proper drainage programme! You couldn't imagine a king like Arthur letting things slide to this extent. If Edwin were in charge, he'd hire somebody to deal with that and any other civil engineering projects that needed doing, aqueducts or whatever. Then he'd get his own knights, and send them off on quests just as daring as Arthur's, not for the Holy Grail of course, that was taken, but the Bible was full of stuff. The Holy Plate They Ate The Bread Off – they could look for that.

People would respect him. People would adore him. And if they didn't, he'd have them put to death. That was what being king was all about.

He could do all of this in Puddock, of course – he was sure you could bung an aqueduct into Puddock, no problem – but it wouldn't be quite the same. No matter how much he might protest, he knew that he was never really going to be King of Puddock. For as long as Martha was still alive, he'd be Prince Consort, and then after he killed her, he'd be Regent for his son. People didn't write epic poem cycles about regents, no matter how numerous their knights and effective their irrigation solutions. More than anything – more even than wanting to be a Knight of the Round Table – Edwin realised that he wanted to be king.

He was thinking all of this as he rode towards the castle gates.

The castle belonging to Leo, his brother, the King. The unmarried King, with no legitimate issue. The unmarried King, with no legitimate issue, who was his only brother.

A plan was forming, but, this being Edwin, it was forming very slowly.

Forty-Two

The plan they finally came up with was quite straightforward. Martha couldn't decide whether that was its strength or its weakness. They would disguise themselves as servants and enter the castle through the kitchens. Once inside, they would calmly follow Roddy's directions to the dungeons. Conrad, with his superior strength, would incapacitate the guards and break the man in the iron mask out of his cell, and then they would bring the prisoner back to Roddy, who would free him.

They rode their horses and Jemima as far as they could without risking being seen from the castle, then dismounted and left the animals with Roddy. Martha wouldn't put it past Roddy to sell the animals, if offered a good price or even a mediocre one, but that could not be helped. Everyone put on their cloaks to hide their weapons and make it easier for them to pass as servants. They took a spare with them for the man in the iron mask. Humphrey had to leave his armour behind because it was too obvious, even under a cloak. Martha tried not to imagine him being slit from gut to throat. It was easier than it might have been, because she was so busy imagining herself being slit from gut to throat.

Just before they set off, Humphrey removed Leila from his side and strapped her to Martha's hip.

'I'm trusting you,' he said.

Conrad swore under his breath and kicked at a clump of dirt.

Martha put her hand on Leila's hilt, tears of gratitude springing to her eyes, but she didn't pull the sword out of the scabbard. She was still too afraid of what Leila might do to Humphrey.

'Humphrey,' she said, 'what did Conrad mean, about you thinking I have blue blood?'

Humphrey smiled a half-smile. 'Just that I realise this quest might be a bit closer to home than you've let on. But don't worry, Marcus. If that is Queen Martha in there, we'll get her out safe.'

If he doesn't think I'm Martha, who on earth does he think I am? Martha shook her head. Whoever he thought she was, it didn't matter. He hadn't tried to drag her back to Puddock and hand her in for some reward. He trusted her, and she would have to trust him.

The road to the castle was busy, and nobody gave them a second glance. That is to say, they didn't attract more attention than Conrad usually got, which was quite a lot. But nobody regarded them with suspicion. By the time they reached the gates, there were dozens of people pushing their way through, abuzz with excitement. All around them, the talk was of two Knights from Camelot who were said to be making their way to Tuft Castle.

'Do they mean us?' asked Conrad.

'I doubt it,' said Humphrey. 'No mention of Jemima. Bollocks, though. Do you think someone else has got wind that Queen Martha's there?'

'Do you think it might be Sir Gordon?' said Martha, remembering the so-called knight she'd met in the tavern.

'Possibly,' said Humphrey. 'That wouldn't be so bad. Even if he found the Queen, he'd be far too inept to get her out. It had better not be Sir Dorian, though. I'm not letting him have her, not after all the work we've put in.'

Martha was silently satisfied by Humphrey's use of 'we'.

The castle gatekeeper appeared to have lost interest in

controlling the crowds, and was slumped listlessly on a stool, watching people pass, a spear lolling in his hand. But when he saw Conrad, he snapped to attention.

'You,' he said. 'Stop there. No giants.'

'Fine by me,' said Conrad.

'But he's my –' Humphrey stopped himself from saying 'squire' just in time. 'Friend,' he finished, lamely.

'I don't care if he's your mother, he's not coming in,' said the gatekeeper.

'All right. Wait for us here,' Humphrey said to Conrad. 'Don't move. Any sign of trouble . . .'

'Do what, exactly?' said Conrad. 'Send a pigeon?' He sat on the grass beside the castle wall and leaned back against it, closing his eyes. 'Wake me up when you get back.'

Without Conrad's reassuring bulk, Martha felt even more nervous as they squeezed with the crowds through the castle gates and started along the track towards the inner keep.

'What are we going to do now?' she said to Humphrey.

'We don't need him,' said Humphrey. 'Roddy said the metal-work is like twigs.'

'But what about the guards?' said Elaine.

'Don't worry about them. In my experience guards are more easily incapacitated by gold than by fists, and I took the liberty of helping myself to a selection from Marcus's supply.'

Martha was too relieved to be annoyed at the theft. Well, not very annoyed, anyway.

Tuft Castle was dainty and pretty, with a small turret at each end and crenellated battlements across the top. The battlements would be less picturesque when manned with soldiers shooting arrows from them and pouring down barrels of pitch and burning oil, but on a sunny peacetime day, framed by a blue sky with little fluffy clouds, the place had a fairytale appeal.

'It's tiny,' said Martha, not unpleased.

'In Camelot we'd call this a shed,' agreed Humphrey.

'I don't know, I wouldn't object to living here,' said Elaine. 'You two are spoilt.'

They were halfway along the path when they heard a child near the gate shout, 'They're here! They're here!'

All at once, everyone started jostling for position. The people who'd been walking along the road started to shove their way to the grassy slopes which rose on either side, and the people who'd already taken up position there complained loudly about their view being blocked. Martha, Humphrey and Elaine found themselves bundled together close to the front, to the vocal annoyance of someone who'd set up a sausage stall just behind them. The entrance to the castle kitchens was frustratingly out of reach, the crowd too thickly packed to push through. Meanwhile, on the far side of the gate, they could see two knights on horseback, dressed in full armour – silver, not black – and flying a richly embroidered pennant.

'Boar, rampant regardant on gold,' said Humphrey, as the crowds began to cheer. 'Terrific. That's Sir Dorian. But who's the other one?'

Forty-Three

The adulation was jolly gratifying, thought Edwin, but it was only what he deserved. He thought back to the handful of doddering ancients who had provided his desultory welcome in Puddock. It had been insulting. In Tuft, they were treating him like royalty. True, he was royalty, but they didn't know that. He waved and bent down to shake people's hands, drinking in the adoration as a dry flowerbed soaks up water. Here in the castle, if not between the damsels' sheets, he was getting as much attention as Sir Dorian was.

As much. But not *more*.

The time had come to reveal himself, Edwin decided. Yes, he had wanted to surprise Leo, but it would still be a surprise, wouldn't it? The only difference was that Edwin wouldn't get a chance to see Leo's face when his brother found out he was there. Never mind, he would ask him to act it out. Then Leo would be, like, 'Bro, what are you talking about, I'm not going to do that, don't be a dick.' It would be like old times. In his thirst for attention, Edwin had forgotten that the purpose of keeping his arrival secret from Leo was to give him a chance to find Martha before his brother could dispose of her. He no longer cared about Martha. He cared only about the crowd.

He reached for his helmet and ripped it off his head, revealing his enormous smile to his subjects. He hoped that he didn't have helmet hair.

'People of Tuft!' he cried. 'It is I, your Prince!'

The response wasn't quite what he anticipated.

Forty-Four

'We've got to get out of here,' said Martha, as the crowd groaned with disappointment. Behind them the sausage seller swore and started packing up his wares.

'We can't leave now,' said Elaine, 'We're so close.'

'We don't have to leave the castle but we've got to get off this road,' said Martha. 'That's Edwin, Queen Martha's husband. What if he recognises me?'

'Recognises you?' said Elaine. 'Marcus, who are you?'

Humphrey shook his head at her. 'Not now,' he said. 'Anyway, we'll be in just as much trouble if Sir Dorian sees me. I'm not even supposed to leave Camelot, let alone be gazumping his quest. So pull your hoods up over your faces and let's try to get into the castle at the back.'

They all pulled their hoods up. Around them, everyone was trying to leave, but the castle gate was narrow and the crowd was bottlenecked. In the middle of the confusion, Dorian was attempting to pull his horse aside and out of the way, but Edwin was still trying to act as if he was surrounded by adoring admirers, grabbing the hand of anyone who came near him and shaking it vigorously.

To her horror, the momentum of the crowd pushed Martha directly into Edwin's path. Her stomach lurched. She kept her eyes fixed on the ground, hoping that he wouldn't notice her. But he looked straight down at her and smiled his awful smile.

'There's no need to be shy, lad,' he said.

He stuck out his hand. Martha held hers up, trembling. Edwin took it. He had a terrible handshake, limp and clammy: it was like shaking hands with a snot-soaked handkerchief.

'God save the King,' said Martha.

'What king? Fuc-king!' said Edwin.

In shock, Martha looked up, right into Edwin's eyes. Edwin's grip tightened on her hand as he stared at her for several long seconds, trying to place her. Then he shrugged, laughed and let her go.

'It's an oldie but goodie,' he said. He kicked his horse onwards into the crowd.

Martha realised she had been holding her breath, and let it out, in a long tremulous exhale. He hadn't recognised her.

'Thank God for that,' said Humphrey behind her. 'Now, if you've finished making friends, let's go.'

Forty-Five

Smile and wave, thought Edwin. *Smile and wave, smile and wave, smile and wave.*

Sir Dorian was sniggering, which was interfering with Edwin's ability to pretend that there was nothing wrong. He couldn't wait to find Martha so that he could send this smug-bag back to Camelot with all the other smug-bag knights. Or maybe he could persuade Leo to arrest him? They could stick him in an iron mask and shove him in the basement. It would be fun to have a pet knight to torment.

In the meantime, Edwin carried on shaking as many hands as people would allow. There was one boy, a terrified-looking lad of about fifteen, he could swear he'd seen before, but he couldn't figure out where. Just a servant boy from the castle, like as not, but there was something about him that bothered Edwin.

His mind picked at the memory for a minute or two, until a burly man jogged his arm, causing him to drop his helmet. It landed with a clang. A young girl picked it up and threw it in the air. Then someone else caught it and threw it up again.

'Can I have my helmet back?' Edwin called.

But nobody gave it to him. The helmet was tossed back and forth like a brilliant steel balloon, cheers going up whenever it was thrown, and again whenever it was caught.

Sir Dorian turned to Edwin. 'That is quite an expensive helmet,' he said.

'They're just having fun,' said Edwin, 'I'm sure they'll give it back in a moment.'

But the helmet game went on. Hadn't these people ever seen a helmet before? Maybe they hadn't. Or maybe they were too poor to afford balls and so a helmet was all that they knew how to throw. Edwin didn't want people like that touching his helmet.

'Give me back my helmet!' he commanded.

Someone tossed the helmet towards him, but so high he couldn't reach it, and it went sailing over his head to the crowd on the other side. Then the person who caught it threw it back over his head to the original side.

They're playing piggy in the middle with me, Edwin realised. *That's my least favourite game. When I played it with Leo and Daddy, I was always the piggy. They never let me catch the ball, not once. I was the piggy for fifteen years.*

'Give me my helmet right now or I'm having you all put to death!' he shouted.

The helmet dropped down and landed on the ground.

'I am not the piggy!' he yelled. 'Do you all hear me? I am not the piggy!'

The crowd went very quiet, apart from a small child who started to cry. A middle-aged woman picked the helmet up off the ground and handed it up to Edwin.

'It was just a bit of fun,' she said.

'Don't you tell me what's fun,' said Edwin. 'I decide what's fun.'

He passed the helmet to Sir Dorian. It was covered in dirty handprints and dust, and had a large dent in one side. 'There you go,' he said. 'I told you they'd get fed up with it eventually.'

Sir Dorian looked down at the helmet and then back up at Edwin. 'And you're revered here, are you?'

Edwin fought the desire to knock Sir Dorian into the dirt. He had seen the knight joust. If he tried to dislodge Sir Dorian from his horse, it was assuredly Edwin himself who would end up on the ground. He refused to undergo that particular humiliation, especially in front of this crowd who were now shuffling silently towards the gate, uttering the occasional muffled jeer.

'You know,' he said to Sir Dorian instead, 'it seems to me that it would be better if I went to see my brother on my own. He might take it the wrong way if I turn up with a knight from an enemy realm.' Officially Arthur was no enemy of Leo's, but then again, officially nobody was. Leo didn't pay much attention to what was official.

'Whatever His Highness wishes,' said Sir Dorian. Apparently he was as frustrated with Edwin as Edwin was with him. Edwin couldn't think why. 'I'll go and wait with Silas and Keith outside until His Highness is ready to resume his quest.' The knight turned tail and followed the dregs of the crowd towards the castle gate.

Forty-Six

Edwin had hoped that once word reached his brother that he was there, Leo would come down to meet him at the entrance in person, but instead he had sent Noah, the deputy head steward, a freakishly tall and gaunt individual with a long nose, deep-set eyes and a film of sandy hair.

'Where's Olivier?' asked Edwin, dismounting and handing the reins of his horse over to some kid or other. Olivier was the head steward.

Noah shrugged. He was a man of few words.

'Why did Leo send you?' said Edwin.

Noah shrugged again. Edwin didn't like having to look up at this lanky lunk. Maybe it would be better if he got back on Storm, but the horse had already been led away, and anyway that might give the wrong impression, make him look like he was leaving again, or was the kind of indecisive person who didn't know if he wanted to be on a horse or not.

'Where's Leo?' he asked Noah.

Noah jerked his chin. Which was a different response, at least.

'So, Noah, it's been a while,' said Edwin, as he followed the deputy steward into the main hall of the castle. 'There must have been lots of changes around the old place, eh?'

Noah didn't reply. Edwin tried to remember if he'd ever heard Noah speak. Perhaps he had a disease, or was mentally defective. But in fact there didn't seem to be that many changes around the old place at all. It still smelt the same, of beeswax with a hint of blood, and Leo hadn't bothered to repaint or knock down any walls or do any of the things that Edwin would have done in his place. The one difference that Edwin noted was that there were a lot more paintings of Leo hanging on the walls. He was glad to see that the painting of himself as a boy with Leo and Daddy was still there, although he did notice that his bit of the painting was somewhat obscured by a potted plant. The portraits of himself on his own were all gone.

Noah led Edwin up the stairs, which creaked in the same places they always had. When he was a boy, he had learned how to sneak out of the castle by climbing down the stairs without making them creak, and Leo had learned how to creep up behind him, make the stairs creak and then run away, leaving Edwin to get into trouble. *Those were the days*, thought Edwin, but it was a hollow thought. He was starting to remember why he hadn't been that upset about being sent away to marry Martha No-Tits.

When they reached the tall double doors of the throne room, Noah held up a finger, then slipped inside. Edwin supposed that meant wait. He waited. There were candles burning in the two alcoves that flanked the doors. Edwin pulled some wax off one of them and tried to mould it into a shape, but it was really hot and burned him, and then it hardened too fast. First the helmet and now this. He was starting to get into a really bad mood.

Noah came out of the throne room. He lifted another finger. His fingers were really long. Then he just stood there. So Edwin supposed that meant wait again.

'What's the weather like up there?'

Noah didn't say anything.

'You're very tall, aren't you?'

Noah still didn't say anything, but he looked down at Edwin as if Edwin were a streak of pondweed he'd got tangled in his boots.

Now Edwin didn't say anything. He'd used up all his best material.

After an age, a familiar voice from inside the room called, 'Come!'

Noah – without a word, of course – opened the double doors, then stepped aside. Edwin entered alone.

Forty-Seven

Getting into the castle kitchens was easier than they'd expected. Lots of the servants were heading back that way, slightly subdued after the aborted excitement of Edwin's arrival. According to Roddy, the prison tower was in the north-west corner of the castle, with one entrance on the inner courtyard, and a service entrance from the kitchens for the delivery of food, inasmuch as the prisoners were ever fed. Inside the kitchens, which Martha considered barely large enough to put together a modest picnic, they found some heaps of vegetables that had been gathered for the next meal, so Elaine, doing her best to look filled with legitimate purpose, piled up a trencher, and the group headed together to the service entrance.

The prison tower was the largest part of the castle, but even so, only a certain class of prisoner was held there for long. Wealthy prisoners bribed their way out; famous ones were rescued; the most and the least important ones were swiftly killed, for opposite reasons. Those who were kept locked up for years on end either had information that was more useful when their heads were still attached to their bodies, or were from families over whom the King wished to exercise leverage. A little bit of torture could go a long way. Though having said that, with Leo, it was rarely just a little bit of torture.

The man – or woman – in the iron mask was being held in the basement dungeon. This was the darkest, dankest hole; the prisoners kept there were the lowest of the low, literally and figuratively. Roddy had said that he didn't know who he'd made the mask for and that he had never seen him.

'It was for a special prisoner, though?' Martha had insisted.

Roddy had shrugged. 'As far as I know he might just have been an ugly blighter.'

The would-be rescue party headed to the prison tower door, a sturdy-looking wooden affair, but with bands of iron which, according to Roddy, might as well have been paper chains.

Humphrey knocked. A panel at head level slid aside and a cloud of halitosis emerged.

'Lunchtime,' said Elaine.

'Piss off,' said the cloud. 'We haven't had vegetables in here since Leo's great-grandfather's reign. Transparent rescue attempt.'

The panel slid shut. Elaine put her vegetables down. Humphrey knocked again. The panel slid open again, and the cloud re-emerged.

'We're friends of the King,' said Humphrey.

'Bullshit,' said the cloud.

Humphrey held up a gold coin with Martha's father, King Peter's, face printed on it.

'This King,' he said.

'How good friends are you?' said the cloud.

'We're extremely close,' said Humphrey. He shook the bag of coins so that it audibly clinked.

The door opened. The halitosis cloud turned out to be emanating from a man of middle age, middle height and middle weight, whose main distinguishing feature was that both of his teeth were black.

Humphrey handed over the bag of coins, leaning back as he did so to try to avoid the full force of the guard's breath. The guard dug into the bag and took out a coin, but he couldn't bite it because his teeth were too far apart. He scratched at it instead with a filthy fingernail. Martha couldn't see what that achieved, but he seemed satisfied. He stepped aside, and they entered the tower.

'Going up?' said the guard.

'Down,' said Humphrey.

The guard's forehead creased with consternation. 'Down? Are you sure?'

'We're sure.'

'I should give you some of this back if you're only going down.'

Martha assumed he was joking, but he raked through the sack, carefully picked out some coins and handed them back to Humphrey.

'Fair's fair,' said the guard. 'I'll give you back even more if you let me hang on to that one.' He pointed at Elaine.

'She's not for sale,' said Humphrey.

'Not unless you want your nuts to end up in that sack,' added Elaine.

The guard seemed sanguine at this prospect, but Humphrey shook his head.

A long, stone staircase wound down in a spiral from the base of the tower. As they began to descend, Martha remembered how she and Jasper had been taken to visit the man in the iron mask in her own castle's dungeon once, when she was very small. Martha had thought he was a monster with a huge metal head, and had cried and been carried away. She had never gone back, although the man had periodically reappeared in her nightmares. She wondered what had become of him. She supposed that he was still there. Guilt buzzed around her like a fly. She swatted it away.

The stench of the guard's rotten breath was soon replaced by the cloying funk of the cheap tallow candles that illuminated the dank underground passageways, and the encroaching miasma of piss, shit, vomit, sweat and low-quality foodstuffs that outweighed oxygen in the air of any self-respecting basement dungeon. They continued along a downward-sloping bare-brick passageway, with small holes in the roof through which guards, if needs be, could shoot arrows or other missiles at absconding prisoners. Eventually, the passage opened out into a low, square room, lined with three iron-bar-fronted cells. They stopped, and looked first to one side, then to the next, then to the next.

'Well,' said Humphrey, 'I hadn't anticipated this.'

All three of the prisoners were wearing iron masks.

Forty-Eight

Good old Leo. Even when he was supposed to be ruling, he was shagging. Not that he was shagging right now, because that would be awkward. But he was sprawling on his throne – a huge jewelled one he'd had made, not that spindly old thing that had been around for donkey's years and went straight on the woodpile when he became king – with no shirt on, and he had a comely damsel on his knee, naked except for a silk sheet wrapped around what was quite clearly a top-notch bod. Her hair was messy and she looked a bit dazed.

'Hello Leo,' said Edwin.

Leo stared at him. He didn't even smile.

'What?' said Edwin.

Leo inclined his head just slightly.

Oh yes! Bow. Leo was the King, so Edwin had to bow, even though they were brothers. Edwin bowed, making a mental note to ensure that Leo bowed to him if he ever came to Puddock.

'So,' said Leo, 'to what do I owe the . . .' He yawned and made a vague gesture with his hand. Edwin waited for him to finish his sentence. After a while it became obvious that he wasn't going to.

'Well,' said Edwin, 'I'm sort of on honeymoon, so I thought I'd drop in.' He had decided to put a positive gloss on things until he figured out how much Leo knew. And, in any case, it was semi-true. He and Martha were both travelling after their wedding. Just not together.

'On honeymoon?' said Leo. 'Really? I heard about your wife getting snatched. You couldn't hold on to her for more than a day. That's pretty shoddy, even for you.'

'I'm going to have her killed when I find her,' said Edwin, 'once I've managed to get a sprog out of her, anyway. So it doesn't really matter.'

'Ever the romantic,' said Leo. He pinched the damsel's nipple through her sheet. She squealed and then laughed, but it didn't look as if she found it very funny.

'I should introduce you to my fiancée,' Leo said.

'You're getting married?' said Edwin.

'I wouldn't need a fiancée if I wasn't,' said Leo.

'Congratulations, brother.' *Ha ha, I got married before you!* 'It's a pleasure to meet you,' he said to the maiden in the sheet.

'Oh, this isn't her,' said Leo, 'don't be absurd. No, I'm marrying a fat milch cow from a good family who'll breed me lots of brats. Her name's Annabel or Arabella or something. She's already knocked up. The physician said she's having twins. She didn't want to submit to me before we got married, but I've always believed you should try before you buy. She was all right. Cried a bit, but I can beat that out of her.'

'Well, gosh,' said Edwin. 'So you're going to be a father now. Lots of sleepless nights for you! Of course you're used to that, from all the carousing and bonking and stuff. But I mean, sleepless nights with a baby! Two babies. Wow! Imagine if Daddy had lived to be a grandfather!'

'He did live to be a grandfather. I sired my first child at fourteen.'

'Oh. Yes. But you know, a real grandfather, to real kids.'

Edwin was starting to feel, as he so often did with Leo, like someone trying to climb a steep slope of loose pebbles. The harder he strove, the more he fell backwards. 'Well, congratulations anyway,' he said. 'I'll send you a pair of silver spoons. That's traditional, isn't it? Although how do you get the spoons into their mouths before they're born?'

'My God, Edwin, you are thick.' Leo looked up at the ceiling in a pantomime of exasperation.

'Ha ha,' said Edwin. 'You're so funny, bro. Ha ha.'

It was like old times. Two brothers together.

Leo's hand slid up underneath the sheet of the maiden on his lap, and she started to move and moan. Edwin took the opportunity to look around for somewhere he could sit down. He'd been riding for days and he was bloody knackered. He wouldn't mind a drink too, and a bit of grub. Leo's throne was on a high dais, and on the floor beside him on a thick Persian rug was a golden jug with matching goblets, cool beads of condensation slipping tantalisingly down its side, and a silver dish filled with exotic fruits and those little continental biscuits that come wrapped in pieces of thin paper that fly up into the air when you set fire to them. The paper, not the biscuits. The rest of the throne room had a floor of bare stone, and was decorated with the stuffed carcasses of animals that Leo had killed. Just the big ones, the bears and wolves and stags. Not the bunnies, which would probably go into the nursery after Leo's sons were born. There weren't any chairs, and Edwin was buggered if he was going to kneel to his brother, king or no king, so he was forced to carry on standing. Christ, he was starving.

Once the moving and moaning of the girl in the sheet had been completed to Leo's satisfaction, although not perhaps her own, Leo wiped his hands on his britches, slapped her on the arse, and told her to go and wash. She giggled again and started to leave.

'Stop. I'm keeping the sheet,' said Leo.

So the maiden unwrapped herself and walked naked across the throne room and out of the double doors to where Noah, presumably, was still waiting. She didn't smile or say goodbye to Edwin or anything. She was a very unfriendly girl, but he'd been right – her body was tip-top.

Leo tossed the sheet at Edwin. 'Have a whiff of that,' he said. 'Remind yourself what pussy smells like.'

Edwin caught the sheet but he couldn't tell if Leo was joking so he only half sniffed at it before dropping it in a heap beside him.

'I suppose you want help finding this missing bitch of yours,' said Leo. He poured himself a goblet of wine and drank deeply from it.

'Well, actually,' said Edwin, 'I went to Camelot, and Arthur, that's the King, King Arthur, but I just call him Arthur because we're friends now, anyway Arthur gave me one of his best knights from the actual Round Table to look for her, because that's the kind of high esteem I am held in by King Arthur.'

'Is that right?' smirked Leo. 'Well, actually, I heard about your little trip to Camelot, and the tit you made of yourself there. They're laughing about it from here to Cornwall. Arthur gave you one of his best knights, did he? What's the name of this most excellent knight?'

Edwin hesitated for a moment before saying, 'Sir Dorian.'

'Sir Dorian? As in, Sir Dorian and the . . . ?'

'What do you mean?' said Edwin.

'Well, the best knights all have something famous that they're associated with, don't they? Sir Gawain and the Green Knight. King Pellinore and the Questing Beast. Sir Dorian and the what, exactly?'

'Maybe it's Sir Dorian and me,' said Edwin.

'Sir Dorian and the Foolish Prince? I suppose it's possible,' said Leo. 'Well, if he's doing such a good job of looking for your lost chit, what on earth are you doing here?'

'The Lady of the Lake told us – told me – that this is where Martha was heading.'

For a split second Leo looked genuinely surprised. If you didn't know him as well as Edwin did you would have missed it – Leo hated to betray any real emotion, and had steely control of his face – but Edwin caught it. *He didn't know she was here*, he thought. *So she's not his prisoner.*

'How interesting,' Leo said coolly. 'That would explain why I caught another knight sniffing around here the other day. I had him arrested for questing outside his jurisdiction. And wouldn't you know it, he wasn't even a Knight of the Round Table. He was from the Table of Less Valued Knights. Do you know what that is?'

'Yes,' said Edwin.

'It's the table where they put the cowards,' Leo went on anyway, 'the invalids, the talentless, the lazy, the decrepit, the battle-maddened, the corrupt, the incompetent, the stupid, the useless idiots they can't trust not to wet themselves at the first sign of trouble. Those are the people who are looking for your runaway cunny. That's the esteem in which you are held by your dear, dear friend King Arthur. That's your table, Edwin. That's where you belong.'

Edwin, incensed, drew his sword and advanced on his brother.

'Oh, are you planning to kill me, now?' said Leo, without a flinch. 'Is that the idea? So that you can finally be King of Tuft like you've always wanted to be? Might I remind you that I've got a couple of legitimate heirs in Abigail's belly, so if you kill me, whichever one pops out first will be the King, and you'll just be a rotting head on a pole?'

'They're not legitimate. You haven't married her yet.'

'I'm not stupid, unlike you. I signed a document naming them as my heirs. I can do that. Unlike some people, I'm the King.'

Edwin wavered for a moment. Then he recovered his resolve.

'Fine,' he said. 'I'll kill you and then I'll kill her.'

'You won't kill her. You don't know who she is. Even I don't know what her name is. Anthea? Alicia?' Leo furrowed his brow in a show of trying to remember. 'It definitely begins with A.'

'Then I'll kill every woman whose name begins with A in the whole kingdom!' cried Edwin.

'No you won't. You're not a good enough speller. Go home, Edwin. Go home, rule your backwater kingdom, polish your teeth, and hope that your Queen gets bored with running and comes back, dragging her tail behind her.'

'She doesn't have a tail,' said Edwin.

'You're a loser, Edwin,' said Leo. 'You always have been. Prince Consort of Puddock is the best that you can hope for. Accept what you are and go home.'

Forty-Nine

All three men had their hands in shackles behind their backs, and were attached by chains from their wrists to the walls of their cells. None of the masks had eye-holes. Two of them were ornately fashioned, even beautiful, the curlicues of the faces frozen in eternal terror. The third was artless and misshapen, an upturned bucket with a slit for a mouth.

'I think we can guess which one was made by our friend Roddy,' muttered Humphrey.

Apart from the iron masks, the three men were dressed identically, in itchy-looking floor-length sackcloth tunics, with *Property of the King – Never to Leave Dungeon* stitched on the front. They had heaps of rotting potato peel in front of them, which was evidently all they were given to eat. Water had been left for them in dishes to be lapped up like dogs. A hole in the corner of each cell served as exactly what you'd expect a hole in the corner of a cell to serve as. It wasn't an escape route, that was for sure.

'Well, we evidently haven't found the Queen,' said Humphrey. 'They're all men.'

Martha thought of a few things she could say to that, but kept quiet. Humphrey stepped forward to speak to the prisoners, but Elaine grabbed his arm and motioned them all into a huddle.

'What is it?' whispered Humphrey.

'How do we know which one's Sir Alistair, or even if any of them are?' said Elaine.

'We'll take all their masks off.'

'I'm not sure if I'll recognise him,' said Elaine. 'I only met him once.'

'Now that's true love,' said Humphrey. 'I suppose we'll ask. Unless anybody's got a better idea?'

Leila rattled in her scabbard. Martha raised her eyebrows at Humphrey.

'Better not,' said Humphrey. 'That thing's got an agenda and we don't know what it is. We don't want her acting up the way she did when she first met me. Save her for emergencies.'

He stepped away from the group and cleared his throat. 'Which one of you is Sir Alistair Gilbert?'

Total silence.

'Let me rephrase that,' said Humphrey. 'We're here to rescue Sir Alistair Gilbert.'

All at once, two out of the three men started shouting, 'Me! Me! Sir Alistair Gilbert? That's me!'

The other man – the one in the bucket-like mask – said nothing.

'Perhaps that wasn't the best approach,' said Humphrey. He turned to Elaine. 'Ask them something.'

'What do you mean?'

'Something only Sir Alistair would know the answer to.'

'Oh Lord, this again,' muttered Martha.

'I don't know anything about him,' said Elaine.

'Names of his parents?'

'Lord and Lady Gilbert! We weren't on first-name terms.'

'Siblings?'

'No idea.'

'And you're marrying this man?'

'Yes,' said Elaine, 'I'm marrying him. I'm not studying him for an exam.'

One of the vocal prisoners started yelling again. 'I'll marry you, darling! I'll marry you right here, just bring your quim closer to these bars!'

'I hope it isn't that one,' said Elaine.

'Maybe you should ask them how much money they've got,' said Humphrey.

'That isn't fair,' said Elaine, stung.

Humphrey turned back to the prisoners. 'Gentlemen,' he said. 'What is the name of your fiancée?'

There was a pause. Then: 'Mary Margaret Elizabeth Margot Nadine Angela Esmeralda Buttercup Susannah Jane Elvira Catherine Lucy . . .'

Elaine shook her head. 'Maybe it's him.' She pointed at the third man, who so far had remained silent.

Humphrey stepped up to the third man's cell.

'Are you Sir Alistair Gilbert?' he said.

'I'm afraid not,' he said. 'Sorry.'

'Are you sure?' said Humphrey.

'I think I know my own name,' said the man in the iron bucket.

'What is your name?'

'Not telling.'

'Why not?'

'I'm here in an iron mask. Not revealing your identity kind of goes with the territory. I can't see you. You could be anybody.'

'It doesn't matter who he is,' said Martha. 'We'll take him with us and Roddy will take his mask off and then we'll find out.'

'I don't want to go with you,' said the man in the iron bucket. 'And I don't want to marry that woman.'

'Maybe you're pretending not to be Sir Alistair so that you don't have to marry her,' said Martha.

The man in the iron bucket laughed. 'No. But then I would say that.'

'He doesn't want to come with us,' said Humphrey, 'and the other two aren't Sir Alistair, and they certainly aren't Martha. Let's leave them and get out.'

'Wait!' said Martha. 'The sword wouldn't have brought us here for no reason.' She turned to the man in the iron bucket and said, 'Are you Jasper?'

The man in the iron bucket jumped, making his chains clang against one another.

'No,' he said, after a short silence.

'I'm Jasper! I'm Jasper!' the two other prisoners cried immediately.

'You mean Jasper, the Queen's brother?' said Humphrey.

Martha ignored him. 'You don't seem sure,' she said to the man in the iron bucket.

'I'm not Jasper,' he replied.

'If you're Jasper, you've got to come with me.'

'I don't have to go with anyone.'

'Please.' A note of desperation entered Martha's voice. 'I've been looking for you for a long time.'

'What do you mean, you're looking for him?' said Humphrey. 'Jasper's dead.'

'No, he's not,' Martha said. 'That's what the Lady of the Lake really told me. That Jasper's still alive. That's who I've been looking for.'

'Marcus, you're so full of lies I don't know what to believe any more. What about the Queen?' said Humphrey.

'She's still alive too. But she doesn't want to be found.'

'So this whole thing's been a colossal waste of time,' said Elaine.

'Not if this man is Jasper.'

'And who are you?' said the man in the iron bucket to Martha.

'I'm your . . . I'm his . . .'

Martha looked at Humphrey. Then she looked back at the man in the iron bucket.

'I can't tell you who I am,' she said. 'And frankly even if I did, you wouldn't believe me. But I mean you no harm. And if you come with me, you'll make Leila very happy.'

'Leila?'

'Yes, my magic sword. She was very keen on us coming to this dungeon.'

'Your sword's name is Leila?'

'I know, I know. Swords are male, everyone keeps telling me.'

There was a long pause.

'Well, I've got to admit this is intriguing,' said the man in the iron bucket. 'But I don't want to leave here under false pretences. And I'm not Jasper.'

'I don't believe you,' said Martha.

'That's as may be, but it's fairly easily proved.'

'How?'

'Come here and look at my feet.'

'What?'

'My feet. Come up to the bars of the cage, lift up my tunic, and have a look at my feet. Come on.'

Martha approached the cell. She hesitated.

'Don't kick me in the face,' she said.

'Wouldn't dream of it,' said the prisoner. 'Cross my heart and hope to die. Though it's quite hard to cross my heart with my hands chained behind my back, and I've hoped to die for some time now. But you know what I mean.'

Martha knelt down. The man in the iron bucket walked as far forward as his chains would allow. Martha lifted his tunic. In the murky light of the dungeon, neither Humphrey nor Elaine could see the man's feet. Martha dropped the tunic and sat back on her heels.

'It's not Jasper,' she said.

'Sorry,' said the man who was not Jasper. 'I did warn you.'

Martha put her head in her hands and began to weep.

'We should go,' said Humphrey.

'He's right,' said Elaine. 'But we'll take them all with us, of course. We can't possibly leave anyone here, regardless of what they've done.'

'If you take us out of here, I'll be Jasper, Sir Alistair, his fiancée and anyone else you like,' said one of the other two prisoners.

'But how are you going to get us out?' said the other of the two prisoners.

'Oh, that's easy,' said Humphrey. 'If you give your chains a really good tug, they should just break.'

One by one the prisoners did so. 'Why didn't we think of that?' said one of them, snapping off his manacles.

'I feel like a bit of an idiot now,' said the other, rubbing his wrists.

'It just goes to show one should never take anything for granted,' said the prisoner with the un-Jasper-like feet. 'You get thrown in a cell and chained up, you just assume that the metal-work is sound. No point trying to escape, I thought. Better to accept my fate with good grace. Well, more fool me.'

Something occurred to him. 'These masks,' he said. 'Will they come off just as easily?'

'There's only one way to find out,' said Humphrey.

All three of the prisoners attempted to undo their masks. The two with the ornate masks failed to break them open. But as the metal inevitably snapped on the iron bucket, Humphrey saw the third prisoner's face emerge, and realised what Marcus had seen when he'd looked at his feet. The prisoner had the dark skin of a Moor.

The Moorish prisoner blinked in the dim, but to him blinding light, and shook out his long, matted black hair and beard.

'Karim!' cried Humphrey. 'It's you!'

Fifty

Conrad was angry. Several times he thought about leaving the castle behind, picking up Jemima from Roddy and riding her away, but some stupid sense of loyalty stopped him.

He'd never had many illusions about Humphrey. There were seventeen tenets of the Code of Chivalry and Humphrey had broken all but one of them. *To fear God and maintain his Church*: Humphrey only went to church to steal the wine. *To serve the liege lord in valour and faith*: Humphrey had been known to hide behind a pillar to avoid Arthur. *To protect the weak and defenceless*: Marcus was hardly weak and defenceless, and Humphrey was protecting him with all his might. *To give succour to widows and orphans*: Humphrey had only given Conrad succour in order to indenture him as his squire. *To refrain from the wanton giving of offence*: Humphrey believed that offence was the gift that kept on giving. *To live by honour and for glory*: abstract terms, said Humphrey, which meant that they did not exist. *To despise pecuniary reward*: Humphrey had made no secret of his interest in the reward for finding Queen Martha. *To fight for the welfare of all*: Humphrey hadn't fought for the welfare of anyone in fifteen years. *To obey those placed in authority*: Humphrey delighted in tormenting anyone in authority over him. *To guard the honour of fellow knights*: Humphrey loathed most of his fellow knights. *To keep faith*: the only thing Humphrey believed in was that everyone would let him down in the end. *At all times to speak the truth*: except where it would be more convenient for Humphrey to lie.

To persevere to the end in any enterprise begun: Humphrey's motto was 'If at first you don't succeed, give up'. *To respect the honour of women*: best not dwell on that one. *Never to refuse a challenge from an equal*: Humphrey had been known to try to resolve challenges by tossing a coin. *Never to turn the back upon a foe*: the very first thing Humphrey had taught Conrad was how to run away.

To eschew unfairness, meanness and deceit, though. Despite everything, Conrad had always thought that Humphrey was fair, lacking in true malice, and honest at heart. So why had he taken in Marcus, a self-confessed liar and thief, a boy who had tried to kill him? Why was he lavishing so much attention on someone who was supposed to be his captive? Why did he always take Marcus's side against Conrad?

Conrad was loyal to Humphrey. He had sworn fealty to him. He would lay down his life for him, even though this was not part of the squire's oath, because nobody would sign up for it if it was. Though he'd strenuously tried to avoid thinking in these terms, Humphrey was the closest thing he had to a father. It was too ironic. He'd heard what Humphrey had said back in the woods, that Conrad was just his squire, and love had nothing to do with it. But he'd also heard what Humphrey had said just before that: that Conrad was Cecily's child. It was silly of him ever to have thought that Humphrey might love him. But he'd never realised, as was now so obvious, that his master hated him. Conrad was a constant reminder of his wife's betrayal. It must make Humphrey sick to look at him. Well, now he had a new boy to play Daddy to – a king's son, no less. He didn't need a pet giant any more. Conrad was better off without him. If he could get a position with one of the Errant Companions, he might even end up being a squire at the Round Table one day. Not a knight, obviously. Giants didn't become knights, they were killed by them.

Submerged in these thoughts, Conrad was barely aware of his surroundings. People were still streaming out through the castle gates, and if someone hadn't cheered for Sir Dorian, the knight would have been upon him before Conrad had the chance to hide. Hide he did, and quickly, because the last thing Conrad needed was to be spotted by snotty, superior Sir Dorian and hauled back to Camelot for a bollocking. Conrad scurried along the side wall of the castle and ducked around the corner. It wasn't very far away; it wasn't a very big castle. Conrad peered around the wall as Sir Dorian emerged from the gate, pulled his helmet from his handsome head, shook out his hair, and began kissing babies, accepting colours from maidens, and generally basking in adulation like a cat in a sunbeam. *It's not you, you dickhead*, Conrad wanted to say. *It's the position. Get yourself busted down to Less Valued Knight and they'll forget all about you toot sweet.* He was lucky that Sir Dorian hadn't spotted him on the way into the castle, but then again he wasn't wearing a tight bodice. Sir Dorian was more blinkered than his horse. Meanwhile Sir Dorian's squire and page stood by, looking bored. Conrad knew how they felt.

When the crowd finally dispersed, Sir Dorian stayed on, pacing his horse up and down and glaring with growing irritation at the castle gate. Evidently he was waiting for someone. Eventually, just as Conrad was giving up hope that anyone was going to arrive, a man on horseback came out of the gate, dressed in full armour, aside from his helmet, and looking furious.

'Edwin,' said Sir Dorian. 'Finally.'

Edwin! So this was Queen Martha's famous husband.

'It's *Your Majesty*,' Edwin said to Sir Dorian.

'I'm sorry,' said Sir Dorian, '*Your Royal Highness*. Did you find her?'

Edwin looked behind him at the gatekeeper.

'Perhaps we should discuss this somewhere more private.'

To Conrad's horror, Edwin began to steer Sir Dorian towards the corner where he was hiding. Conrad scuttled back to a huge horse chestnut tree and hid behind the trunk. A normal-sized giant would never have been able to conceal himself behind a tree of any size. There were some advantages to being a runt. Edwin and Sir Dorian soon rounded the corner, with Silas and Keith trailing behind.

'Martha's dead,' Edwin told Sir Dorian.

To his surprise, Conrad was dismayed. This should have been a major triumph over Marcus, but he felt sorry for the poor young Queen.

'How do you know?' said Sir Dorian.

'Leo killed her. He told me himself. It was murder.' Edwin rolled the word around his mouth like a delicious sweet.

'But . . .' Sir Dorian shook his head. 'That doesn't make any sense. Why would your realms go to all the trouble of making such a key alliance through marriage, only for the King of Tuft to kill the Queen of Puddock before you've even had the chance to be crowned?'

'I don't know why Leo does things,' snapped Edwin. 'I'm not his keeper.' He took a breath and added, in a tone he probably felt was more regal, 'It was jealousy. Leo can't stand that I'm a more important king than he was, of a country with a bigger castle.'

'But you're not the King of Puddock,' said Sir Dorian. 'You're the bloody Prince Consort.' Conrad thought that Edwin's eyes were going to pop out of his head, but Sir Dorian didn't seem to care. 'We've got to get back to Camelot right away,' he said. 'King Arthur will know what to do.'

'No,' said Edwin. 'Why is it always about what King Arthur wants? This has nothing to do with him. This is between Leo and I.'

'Leo and me,' said Sir Dorian.

Conrad wasn't sure that correcting Edwin was a wise move. From the look on the face of Sir Dorian's squire, he agreed with him.

'I'm going back to Puddock, to prepare for war,' said Edwin.

'War?' said Sir Dorian, appalled.

Conrad's heart started beating so hard, he was surprised that the two men didn't start clapping along. He'd heard war described as glorious, but it terrified him: a brutal and bloody tide of death, almost always waged for no good reason. Yes, a young woman had been killed, and that was a dreadful thing. But why it would improve matters for tens of thousands of men to die too was not at all clear to him.

'Stop and think,' said Sir Dorian, causing Edwin to pull a face. 'Have you actually seen the Queen's body? Perhaps Leo was trying to antagonise you by pretending that he'd killed her. One should not go to battle unless there is absolutely no alternative. Before you do anything, you need to verify that Leo's claim is true.'

'Of course it's true,' said Edwin. 'Everyone knows that my brother is the killing kind. Don't get your knickers up your bum. You can tiptoe back to Camelot and leave the war to the real men. War is what men were made for! War and fucking. War and fucking and – no, just those two.'

'I think, perhaps, King Arthur, with his experience –'

'You're a patronising git, Sir Dorian,' Edwin interrupted. 'You always think you know best. Don't you?'

Sir Dorian paused. 'In certain matters, possibly. It depends on whom I'm speaking to.'

Oops, thought Conrad.

'You think I'm an idiot, don't you?' said Edwin.

Sir Dorian paused again. Conrad had a very bad feeling about that pause. It was the pause of someone who could keep silent no longer, and who was about to say something that would be far better left unsaid.

'You want to know what I think? I think you are all vanity,' said Sir Dorian. 'There is nothing else to you. That's why you want to go to war, to sacrifice countless lives – though not your own, I'll bet. In fact I'll bet you all the money in Puddock, Tuft and Camelot that you don't give two shits about your wife, that you're just annoyed with King Leo for breaking your plaything, so now you want to send innumerable men to their deaths simply to teach him a lesson. Grow up! There are things in this world that matter more than you, astonishing as this news may be. And yes, I do think you're an idiot. Frankly, it's not a matter of opinion. Get a dictionary and a mirror. And while we're on the subject of mirrors, your teeth are ridiculous!'

A scrape as Edwin removed his sword from its sheath, a swish, an unpleasantly wet chopping sound and two thuds. Sir Dorian's head fell from his shoulders, and his body fell from his horse after it.

'Well,' said Edwin. 'That was easy.'

Conrad felt paralysed. But when Edwin plunged his sword into the neck of Sir Dorian's squire, he started to run. Not away from Edwin, but towards him, throwing himself between Edwin's sword and the page. It was too late. Edwin beheaded the child, and then, Conrad's head being too far away for him to reach, he rammed his sword deep into Conrad's belly.

Fifty-One

They clambered up the dungeon steps, half carrying, half dragging the prisoners with them. It was slow going. All three prisoners were weak and emaciated. Two of them were blinded by the masks they were still wearing, while Karim was wrapped in the spare cloak they had brought with them, the hood drawn up to hide his tangle of hair. Everyone was bursting with unanswered questions, but the time for those would be after they'd escaped.

'You're taking them all?' said the halitosis guard in the anteroom at the top of the stairs.

'We were hardly going to leave two of them behind,' said Martha.

'Punch me in the face, then. The King won't believe me otherwise,' said the guard. He sighed. 'I'm always getting punched in the face, every time there's a rescue.'

Humphrey punched him, then flicked him an extra gold coin. 'Treat yourself to some false teeth.'

They left by the main door, forcing themselves to walk slowly across the courtyard and out through the front gate of the inner keep. Humphrey and Elaine walked in front, with the two men in the iron masks following behind as if they were prisoners, arms behind their backs and Roddy's flimsy chains wrapped around their wrists. Martha drew up the rear with Karim.

'You two know each other?' she said to him, indicating Humphrey.

'Quiet,' said Humphrey. There were a few castle servants milling around, and it was impossible to know which of them were loyal to Leo, or were frightened enough of the consequences to feign loyalty.

When they reached the drawbridge, the gatekeeper was a little more alert than he had been on their way in. Clearly people breaking into the castle was less of a problem than people breaking out. Either that, or men going for a walk wearing iron masks tended to arouse suspicion in even the sleepiest guard.

'What's going on here, then?' he said, looking up from his game of marble solitaire.

'We're taking these two out to be executed,' said Humphrey.

'What's wrong with the execution ground?' said the gatekeeper.

Humphrey hesitated.

'We're taking them to be drowned,' said Elaine.

The gatekeeper's eyes widened. 'Witchcraft?' he said.

'That's right,' said Elaine.

The gatekeeper's eyes narrowed again. 'But they're men.'

Before any of them knew what was happening, Karim had picked up a stone and thrown it with devastating accuracy, hitting the gatekeeper square between those disbelieving eyes. He tumbled from his perch into an unmoving heap on the ground. They all stared at Karim, apart from Humphrey, who began to laugh.

'Still got it,' he said.

'He'll be out for a while,' said Karim, 'but I think we'd better get away before anyone finds him.'

'Right you are,' said Humphrey. 'Now, where's my hairy lump of a squire? I see he paid no attention to me telling him to stay put.'

The road was empty – fortunately, as nobody had seen Karim knock out the gatekeeper.

'He probably went off chasing skirt,' said Humphrey. 'Wait here, I'll go and look for him.'

Humphrey headed off round the side of the castle wall, while the others hovered near the gatehouse, hoping the gatekeeper would not wake up.

'So how do you two know each other?' Martha said to Karim.

'From Camelot,' said Karim.

'You're a Knight of the Round Table?'

'I was a squire,' said Karim. 'Would you mind if I took a look at your sword?'

'Please do,' said Martha, 'but watch out. She's a bit temperamental.'

'I know,' said Karim, strangely.

Martha drew Leila from her scabbard and handed her over to Karim. She didn't feel the usual wrench of loss as she let her go. Karim took Leila by her emerald-studded hilt and turned her gently so that her obsidian blade caught the rays of the sun. His eyes filled with tears.

'She's beautiful,' he said.

He handed the sword back to Martha, who looked with curiosity at his handsome, saddened face and didn't know what to say. She sheathed the sword without a word.

'You know,' said Karim, 'back in the dungeon, from your voice, I thought you were a woman.'

Martha laughed awkwardly, but before she could come up with a reply they heard Humphrey screaming from behind the castle wall.

'Elaine!' he cried. 'Elaine!'

Without waiting a moment, Elaine began to run. Karim and Martha grabbed the arm of a masked man each and tried to run after her, but the staggering men, blinded by their masks, slowed them down and Elaine soon disappeared around the corner ahead. They heard her shriek, while Humphrey continued to yelp wordlessly, a strange low sound like a wounded wolf. In tacit agreement, Karim and Martha left the men where they were and hurried to find their friends.

When Martha came upon the scene, she was so appalled she staggered backwards, fighting her rising gorge. There were three dead bodies on the ground, all without their heads, one a child of no more than ten. A blood-spattered horse trembled nearby, taking a few paces here, a few paces there, shaking its head from side to side, shuddering. And in the middle of it all, Conrad lay motionless, in a huge pool of red-black blood, his guts ripped open. Elaine was kneeling beside him, weeping.

'Sir Dorian,' said Humphrey, pointing at the dead knight. 'Silas,' he said, indicating the squire. 'And little Keith.' His voice caught as he looked at the dead child. Then he dropped to his knees beside his fallen squire. 'Conrad, you idiot, what did you have to go and get yourself killed for?'

'He was a good kid,' said Karim in a tight voice. 'He grew up tall.'

'Actually he was always a short-arse for a giant, and he hated it,' said Humphrey. He drew Conrad's enormous head up onto his knees and ran a hand through his hair. 'You never stopped giving me trouble, did you? Silly boy.' And then the catch in his throat exploded into huge heaving sobs, and Elaine crawled over, her skirt trailing in Conrad's blood, and held him close as he cried. 'I'm sorry, I'm sorry,' he said. 'He was like a son to me, he was the only son I had.'

'I think he's breathing,' said Martha. Her voice sounded odd, floating thinly in the air above the carnage. 'I saw his chest move. I think he might be alive.'

Humphrey shook his head. 'It's not possible.'

'Even if he is, he won't survive long with those injuries,' said Karim.

'I can help,' said Martha. She felt as though she were in a terrible dream.

'You can't,' said Karim.

'I can,' said Martha. 'I have, I have, a, this . . .' She pulled the tiny bottle of universal panacea that Nancy, the young apprentice crone, had given her, out of her pocket where she always carried it. 'It's supposed to cure everything.'

'It won't cure this,' said Karim.

'I'm going to try,' said Martha.

She went over to Humphrey, who was still holding Conrad's body, and unstopped the bottle. Conrad was lying with his eyes shut and his mouth slightly open. Barely daring to hope, she poured the tiny dose of precious liquid between his lips until it was all gone. Then she stood back to see what would happen.

It took less than a minute. As the companions watched, astonished, the hideous wound on Conrad's belly closed and the skin healed. His clothes were still shredded and covered in blood – apparently the universal panacea didn't stretch as far as tunics. His chest swelled with an enormous, shuddering breath, and his eyes popped open. Martha gasped, astonished that the potion had actually worked. Elaine leaned over and kissed Conrad's perfect brow. The panacea had cleared up his spots too.

'It was the King,' Conrad said. 'He got Keith. I tried to stop him, but he got Keith.'

'Shush,' said Humphrey, laughing joyfully through his tears.

'Why are you crying? Are you a woman now?' said Conrad, trying to smile.

'You're alive,' said Humphrey. A huge bubble of snot and spit burst out of his nose and mouth, and he wiped it away with the back of his hand.

'But he got Keith,' said Conrad again, and now tears were running down his own face. 'Poor kid. And Silas, God. And Sir Dorian. I know we never liked him, but he didn't deserve that.'

'He got *you*,' said Elaine. She still had her arms around Humphrey. 'We thought he'd killed you, Conrad.'

'Me? I'm fine, don't worry about me,' said Conrad.

'I know,' said Elaine. 'It was Marcus. He saved your life.'

Conrad looked over at Martha in confusion.

'We thought you were done for, but he gave you some kind

of magic potion,' said Humphrey. 'Where the hell did you get that, Marcus?'

'I was given it,' said Martha.

'I wouldn't mind getting my hands on a bit more,' said Humphrey.

'The woman who made it has disappeared. That's all there was.' *And the woman who was me has disappeared*, she thought. *Now I will always be caught between male and female.*

'Thank you,' said Conrad simply.

Martha looked down, unable to respond.

Humphrey and Elaine helped Conrad to his feet, but Karim stayed with Martha, sensing her distress, his comforting arm around her shoulders.

Fifty-Two

Lacking the means to bury them, they placed the bodies side by side, heads reunited with torsos, eyes closed, hands crossed on chests. Humphrey said that he would send word to Camelot to let them know what had happened, so that they could be laid to rest with full honours.

'I suppose that means there's room on the Round Table for a new knight,' observed Conrad.

'Let's not think about that now,' said Humphrey.

They borrowed Sir Dorian's horse for Karim to ride, intending to return it to Sir Dorian's family as soon as they could. They left Silas and Keith's little cart behind, not realising it had belonged to them. The two prisoners in iron masks were understandably confused, but Humphrey filled them in as they made their slow way back to where Roddy was waiting for them.

'So that's you, Humphrey du Val, is it?' said one of the prisoners, as Humphrey finished his tale. 'I thought I recognised your voice.'

'Typical,' said Conrad. 'We rescue three prisoners from a dungeon in Tuft, and you know two of them.'

'Yes, it's me,' said Humphrey to the prisoner, giving his squire a friendly, if somewhat ginger, cuff. 'We know each other, do we?'

'We do indeed,' said the man in the mask. 'It's me, Gordy, from Camelot.'

'Sir Gordon Pencuddy!' said Humphrey, raising his eyebrows at Martha. 'This is a surprise.'

'Oh my God,' mouthed Martha silently back.

'How on earth did you end up in King Leo's dungeon?' Humphrey asked Gordy.

'Got picked up by one of Leo's goons for questing in Tuft without permission,' said Gordy. 'I don't know how long I've been down there, but it was plenty long enough. The sooner you can get us some food, the better.'

'What about your squire, is he all right?' Martha asked.

'I don't know, my lady,' said Gordy.

Conrad chuckled at Marcus being mistaken for a woman.

'He's probably still in that prison somewhere,' Gordy went on. 'Don't worry about it though, squires are two a penny.'

Conrad stopped chuckling and took an angry step towards Gordy, but Elaine put out a hand to restrain him.

'Not now,' she mouthed.

'How about you?' she said to the other man in the iron mask, who could barely walk. 'You're not an old friend of Humphrey's too, are you?'

'I doubt it,' said the man. 'My name's William, but I prefer to be called Gwendoline. And apparently that's enough of a reason in Tuft to end up in one of these.' He indicated the mask.

'Gwendoline, my dearest friend, for so many years all I had was your voice in the darkness,' said Karim. 'I'm so glad to see you finally free.' He reached out and squeezed Gwendoline's hand.

'And me you,' said Gwendoline. 'Thank you all,' he said turning his head to where he approximated the group to be. 'I will never be able to express how grateful I am to you for getting me out of there.' They could hear tears in his voice.

'There is no gratitude enough,' agreed Karim. 'We are forever in your debt.'

Martha was about to ask Karim why he had refused to be rescued at first, but Gordy spoke over her.

'You're in deep shit with Arthur for running off without permission, Humph,' he said to his fellow Less Valued Knight.

'Word got back to Camelot that you've been fighting unauthor- ised duels all over Tuft. The Round Table are up in arms.'

'You can talk,' said Humphrey. 'I heard you were out looking for the missing Queen.'

'Where did you hear that?' said Gordy. He shook his iron head. 'Never mind, that Queen's way more trouble than she's worth. The minute this mask is off I'm heading back to Camelot and I'm never going on a quest again.'

'There's no point looking for her anyway,' said Conrad. 'She's dead.'

'What?' said Martha. 'No, she isn't.'

'She is,' said Conrad. 'I heard Edwin say so.'

'When did you see Edwin?' said Martha.

Conrad looked at her as though she was crazy. 'Um, just before he killed Sir Dorian, Silas and Keith, and tried to kill me?'

'That was Edwin?' said Humphrey. 'You said *the King*. I assumed you meant Leo.'

'No, King Edwin,' said Conrad. 'Of Puddock.'

'He's not the fucking King of Puddock,' said Martha furiously. 'He's the Prince Consort.'

'Well, whoever he is, he said that Leo had murdered Martha and now he was going to take Puddock to war with Tuft to get his revenge.'

Everyone stared at Conrad.

'War?' said Humphrey.

'We cannot let this happen,' said Karim.

'And it isn't even true,' said Martha. 'Martha's still alive. I know she is. And anyway, the only reason that Edwin would go to war with Leo is because he hates Leo and he wants Tuft for himself.'

'Well, short of Martha walking back into Puddock and reclaim- ing the throne, I can't see what's going to stop him,' said Conrad.

Martha turned to Humphrey. 'We have to find Jasper,' she said. 'Jasper is the rightful King of Puddock. If we find him, we can depose Edwin and stop this war.'

'But Jasper's dead,' said Conrad.

'He's not,' said Martha.

'Jasper's not dead, Martha's not dead,' said Conrad. 'You've certainly got enough insider knowledge about the state of health of the Puddock royal family.'

'Marcus is right,' said Karim. 'Jasper's not dead. Not as far as I know. And assuming he hasn't moved house in the last six years, I know where to find him.'

Fifty-Three

The trouble with war, Edwin reflected as he rode for Puddock, is that you can't just decide to wage it and then off you go. In that respect it differed greatly from killing a few (say, four) people at a time. No, there was all this boring organising you had to do first. For example, it was one thing to decide to conscript all of the men in the realm of fighting age into your army (which meant everyone over the age of twelve, except for the rich ones whose families you didn't want to piss off), but it was quite another to actually do it. You had to send people to go and get them. If you just stuck a couple of notices up on trees, nobody would turn up. So Edwin would have to send Puddock's existing army off to round everybody up, which meant that they wouldn't be available for getting the war started in the meantime. Also, even when you had everyone in place, you still had to arm them, and feed them, and train them to march and stuff. Although Edwin wasn't planning to do that with all of them, it would take too long. Only the ones at the front had to learn how to march and the others could just follow them. And only the ones at the back needed to be armed, because the ones at the front always got killed straight away – there was no point wasting weapons on them. Except, now Edwin thought of it, if the ones at the front were all going to get killed straight away, then the ones at the back were going to need to learn to march after all, because there would be nobody left to follow.

It would be worth it, though, if he could wipe the smirk off Leo's face. And then wipe the face off his head, and the head off his body. Edwin thought back to the moment just before he'd sliced off Sir Dorian's head, and felt annoyed all over again. That remark about his teeth had been uncalled for. Then he laughed. Sir Dorian had looked so surprised when Edwin had sliced through his neck. The squire and the little page had looked frightened, which was satisfying in a different way. As for the giant – Edwin had killed a giant! He felt taller just thinking about it. True, it hadn't been a very big giant, but you had to start somewhere.

All in all it had been a very successful trip. True, Leo had been a prick, but that would make defeating him in battle even more pleasing. True, he hadn't found Martha, but either she'd turn up in her own time, in which case he would kill her then, or she'd never come back, in which case it didn't matter that he was claiming she was dead. True, the people of Tuft had not been as welcoming as he might have wished, but once he'd subjugated them in the coming war, there'd be no more piggy-in-the-middle, no more wenches giving all their favours to unworthy knights, no more boys who –

He drew his horse up sharply. That boy. That boy he thought he'd recognised. He knew where he'd seen him before now. He – she – it? – was Martha! Oh Lord. He felt cold all over. He'd had Martha within a sword's length – he'd had her by the hand! – and he'd just let her go. It was a good disguise, he gave her that – she definitely looked like a boy. God knows how she'd managed to grow a beard, even a patchy one. Maybe she was naturally bearded and usually shaved – you saw ladies like that in circuses. Anyway, he couldn't worry about that now. The question was, what was he going to do about it?

He couldn't leave her be. Sure, that was the decision he'd made only a few seconds ago, but a great leader always knows when to change his mind, plus now he knew where she was. And now he knew that she knew that he hadn't recognised her! How she must be laughing at him! It could not be tolerated. And what had she been doing at Leo's castle, disguised as a boy?

Maybe she was planning to go to war with Leo herself. Maybe she was planning to assassinate him. That was unacceptable. Only one person was going to bring Leo down, and that was he, himself, Edwin, King of Puddock, future King of Tuft!

The decision was made. He would send word to Puddock to begin preparations for war. And while they did all the boring stuff, he was going back to find Martha.

Fifty-Four

They left Gordy and Gwendoline with Roddy, who agreed to take the two prisoners back to his forge and release them from their masks, as part of a two-for-one special deal. Then Karim led the way with Humphrey, as Elaine, Martha and Conrad – whose notice to quit had been quietly forgotten by all parties – rode behind. Or at least that was the way it was supposed to go. Martha found herself drifting forwards to ride beside Karim, while Humphrey hung back closer to Elaine and his squire. Jemima seemed to sense that something terrible had happened to Conrad since he'd been gone, and kept reaching up to touch him with the tip of her trunk. Conrad in return scratched her ears the way that she liked best.

Karim's presence made Martha feel safe. He had a calm, composed way about him that she wanted to be near. She liked him. It was a simple feeling. At the same time she had so many questions that she barely knew where to start.

'You were a squire at the Round Table?' she said.

'Yes,' said Karim.

'You don't seem like a squire.'

Karim was a tall, imposing man, even with his matted hair and emaciated limbs.

'I was younger then,' he said.

'So . . . whose squire were you?'

'Can't you guess?'

'Humphrey's?' This wasn't really her guess. Her real guess was too frightening to say out loud, in case it wasn't true.

'No,' Karim laughed. 'I wouldn't squire for that lazy goat turd for love or money.'

'As if I would offer either for you,' retorted Humphrey.

'I was Prince Jasper's squire,' Karim told Martha, which was exactly what she'd hoped.

'But Jasper's squire died,' she said, the words sounding foolish even as she said them.

'Surely by now you've realised that hearing that someone has died, and someone actually dying, are not the same thing,' said Karim. 'Jasper didn't die, and neither did I.' It seemed as good a time as any to tell his story, and so he began.

'My parents were brought to Camelot from the Maghreb as – well – King Arthur does not have slaves, of course; he does not believe in them. Shall we say instead as indentured labour? They were more or less willing, I suppose. My father was a field worker, my mother a necessary woman.'

'Is that the same as a whore?' asked Martha, proud of her new vocabulary.

'No,' said Karim. 'It means that she emptied the chamber pots.'

Martha was mortified. 'I'm sorry,' she said, apologising both for her error and for the job Karim's mother had had to do. It had never occurred to her before to give a moment's thought to the person who emptied the chamber pots.

'So am I,' said Karim. 'It was not a dignified position, although she remained a dignified woman. As for me, I don't remember a time when I didn't work. Up the chimneys at first – they used to joke that the soot didn't show on my skin. Then, when I got too big for that, I was put to work in the kitchens, helping to prepare food. I became very skilled with a knife. So much so that when the kitchen boys had their breaks, I graduated from chopping and slicing to throwing. Another boy would stand with an apple on his head and I would toss a knife and hit the heart of the fruit. Every time. Well, except for that child I blinded.'

'I never heard about that,' said Humphrey.

'That is because I am joking. Anyway, one day Prince Jasper came out into the kitchen gardens, looking for somebody, I suppose. And he caught me at my knife-throwing game. I was terrified. I thought I'd be turned out of the castle, my parents and sister with me – my sister was a scullery maid. But Jasper was impressed.'

'It does sound very impressive,' said Martha.

'I can demonstrate on you, if you like. Though I may be a little rusty after years with my head in a bucket.'

'Maybe demonstrate on Conrad.'

'Maybe not!' said Conrad.

'Well, anyhow, Jasper said that I was wasted in the kitchens. Actually I was not wasted at all in the kitchens, the kitchens are exactly where a boy with exceptional knife skills should be. But I was bored in the kitchens, and bored and wasted are close enough kin. So when he asked me if I would like to be his squire, I said yes. I even thought that I might become a knight myself one day, like Sir Palamedes, although the other squires used to say that Arthur already had one black knight, so why would he want another one? But I was hopeful. And Jasper was kind to me. So much so that my sister fell in love with him, but that is another story. He did not have eyes for her, anyway. To continue with my tale, I was very happy as Prince Jasper's squire until one summer when we returned to his home in Puddock to visit his family. He was heir to the throne there, as you know.'

'Of course,' said Martha.

'He and his father argued very badly.'

Martha was shocked. 'What about?'

'I am not at liberty to disclose that. And in any case, I was not there when it happened. The King had requested that I keep to the servants' quarters. But perhaps Jasper will choose to tell you himself what they argued about, if and when we find him. Anyhow, afterwards, Jasper came to fetch me and told me that we were leaving the castle immediately and that we would never return. Once we got away, he told me that he was going to pretend to die on a quest so that he didn't have to become king.'

Martha stifled a gasp. Like her, her brother had run away from the throne. She could hardly blame him for that. But he'd let her believe that he was dead? He'd let her grieve?

'Nobody wants to rule that place,' observed Conrad. 'It must be one hell of a dump.'

'Puddock is the most beautiful place in the world, actually,' said Martha.

'Really?' said Conrad. 'You've been everywhere in the world?'

Ever since Martha had saved his life, Conrad's attitude to her had changed, if not to open affection, at least to fraternal teasing.

'I've been to Tuft, and Puddock is similar but nicer,' Martha said to him. 'Karim, please carry on with the story. Jasper was about to pretend that he'd died.' There was a crack in her voice as she said this.

'Yes,' said Karim. 'I am still ashamed of what we did next. We took the body of a hanged corpse from a gibbet, boiled up the bones, and sent them to his father saying that it was him.'

'You mean the bones that are displayed in the chapel in Puddock as being Jasper's belong to a common criminal?'

'Yes.'

'Do you know what he was hanged for?'

'It could have been anything. Theft, brawling, throwing a stone at a soldier . . . Things we have all done, perhaps. Would that make a man unworthy to be laid to rest in a chapel rather than rot on a gibbet?'

There was a note of reproach in his voice. Martha looked down, chastened.

'Finally,' Karim continued, 'with my help, Jasper found somewhere to live, a secluded place where nobody knew who he was. We bid each other farewell, knowing that in order to keep him safe we could never see one another or communicate again. It was an extremely sad time. I returned to Camelot where I told King Arthur that Jasper had died, and tried not to feel ashamed of all the mourning that ensued. I was assigned to another knight, on the table of Errant Companions.'

'Nobody on the Round Table wanted a brown squire?' said Conrad.

'I prefer to think that is not the reason. I like to think well of the Knights of the Round Table. They are, for the most part, the best of men. Perhaps none of them needed a new squire, perhaps I was considered unlucky now that my master had died. Perhaps I simply wasn't a very good squire.'

'It sounds like you were an excellent, loyal squire,' said Martha.

Karim grinned at her. 'Whatever the reason, I adjusted to my new life and my new master, Sir Dennis du Pont, who was, in a word, a dolt.'

'The Errant Companions all are,' said Humphrey.

'One day, we were out on a minor quest – as I recall, retrieving an unbreakable shield from a dwarf who'd stolen it from a damsel – when a gang of King Leo's soldiers ambushed us and took me captive. I do not know what became of Sir Dennis.'

Humphrey filled him in: 'Took a challenge from a purple knight, slept with his wife, stole his girdle of invincibility which turned out to be a piece of string, got his head cut off.'

'A worthy end,' said Karim. 'As for me, it turned out that I had been less discreet about Prince Jasper not being dead than I should have been. I'd trusted the wrong person . . . My own weakness was to blame for this. After I was captured, King Leo sent word to Arthur that I had died, so that nobody would come looking for me. Then he kept me in his dungeon in an iron mask, swearing never to release me until I had revealed Jasper's whereabouts. Leo's brother was set to marry the princess who is now this missing Queen of Puddock, and through this union, Tuft planned to annex Puddock. If Jasper were to turn up alive, then the plan would be for nothing.'

'All the more important that we find Jasper!' This was from the unlikely source of Elaine, who hadn't said a word about looking for Sir Alistair since they'd left Tuft Castle.

'Karim, does that mean you've been in that iron mask for six years without ever revealing where Jasper is?' said Martha.

'I don't know exactly how long I was in there for, but I believe so. That's why I didn't want to be rescued at first. I thought it was another trick, a way of getting me to lead Leo to Jasper. But I trust Humphrey. I trust you all. And you have the sword, of course.'

'What's so special about that bloody sword?' said Conrad.

Karim smiled. 'It's magic.'

'We know that,' said Conrad.

'You don't know everything,' said Karim. But he refused to be drawn any further.

Fifty-Five

That night there wasn't enough room for Karim to fit into the men's tent with Humphrey, Conrad and Martha, so he borrowed Humphrey's bedroll and took it out under the stars. Martha lay awake wondering what it was like for him, out beneath the huge sky, after so many years locked away in his mask, underground. After several restless hours, she crept outside to join him. She found him sitting up cross-legged on his mat.

'After years in perpetual darkness, it is too light for me to sleep,' said Karim. 'The moon is like a flaming torch.'

'I couldn't sleep either,' said Martha, sitting down next to him. 'It seems like I never can.'

'No,' said Karim. 'Something is bothering you.'

'Yes,' said Martha.

'What is it?' said Karim.

She felt that she could trust him. Not absolutely, perhaps. But enough.

'My father died,' she said. She started to cry. 'And I've been running so fast I haven't even let myself think about him.'

Karim put an arm around her and held her quietly as she wept, sobbing out the anguish not only of those weeks since her father had died, but of the months and years she'd suffered before that, as she'd slowly, agonisingly lost him. Eventually her tears slowed. They sat together in comfortable silence. Karim didn't move his arm away. Martha wondered how it could possibly be that she felt she'd known him for so long, when in fact it was less than a day.

'There's something else,' she said.

'Yes?' said Karim calmly.

'You know that other prisoner? William?' she said.

'Gwendoline,' said Karim.

Martha took a deep breath. Not once had she been close to being truthful with anyone since she had left the castle on her wedding night.

'I'm like her,' she said. 'I look like a boy, but really I'm a girl.'

She could feel fresh tears welling in her eyes.

'Is that all?' said Karim. He laughed softly. 'Don't worry. You will find that there are people who don't mind.'

He drew her to him, and kissed her, very gently, on the mouth.

Fifty-Six

There was no point looking for Martha by himself, that would take far too long. It was possible that she was still at Leo's castle but equally likely that she was not. Edwin didn't like to think of himself as lazy; the word he would have chosen was *efficient*. He found a small body of water. Not a lake. A lake would be too big for his purposes. A stream too small. In the end he settled on a little pool made from a dug-out quarry that had been filled by an underground spring.

He stripped off Sir Dorian's third-best armour and plunged into the water. The coolness was pleasant in the heat, but he barely noticed. He made sure he swam on his front and on his back. You never knew exactly what it was that people liked to look at. Then he got out and lay down in the sun by the side of the pool, nude. Bait. If you wanted to catch a fish, it was all about bait.

Edwin knew he'd got to the Lady of the Lake the first time around, even though she'd left in a fury. Maybe especially because of it; he'd managed to get under her skin. When a maiden appeared not to like Edwin it was a sign that she liked him really. And when she appeared to like him, that was also a sign that she liked him. *Not enough men in the Lake*, that's what she'd said. Well, he was nothing if not a man.

He waited. Time passed. In another man doubts would have set in. In Edwin, doubts presented themselves, decided that this was not a hospitable environment, and left again. If she didn't come, why, then, she was playing hard to get; or she was washing her hair; or she was stupid. It couldn't be because she had no interest in him, or because it wasn't a good plan. It was Edwin's plan. What more was there to say?

'You're going to get sunburnt.'

He had drifted off. He sat up with a start, feeling indeed a little burned, and queasy from the heat. Nevertheless, he flexed the muscles in his chest and gave her his best smile, the one that showed all of his teeth.

'I haven't stopped thinking about you,' he said.

'Really?' said the Lady of the Lake. She was standing on the surface in the middle of the pool, twirling a length of her midnight hair around her finger. Her face was too eager. It was sad.

'I was ungrateful before,' said Edwin. 'You have such a difficult job. It's hard for a king like me to understand.'

'You're actually not a . . .' The Lady of the Lake stopped. She bit her thumb coquettishly. 'Aren't you going to get dressed?'

'Aren't you going to get undressed?' said Edwin.

Come closer.

She took a step closer, across the surface of the water. Then she stopped.

Damn it, thought Edwin. The pool was deep all the way across. He should have picked somewhere shallow that he could wade into. He would have to be patient. Patience didn't come naturally to him.

'We've been warned to stay away from men like you,' said the Lady of the Lake. 'Because of how Nimue ran off with Merlin.'

'I'm not Merlin,' said Edwin.

'No,' said the Lady of the Lake. She licked her lips. 'You most certainly are not.'

'Come closer so that I can show you my magic,' said Edwin.

'You don't actually have any magic,' said the Lady of the Lake.

'No,' said Edwin.

'You shouldn't joke about that kind of thing,' said the Lady of the Lake. 'We take it very seriously in the supernatural community.'

'I'm sorry,' said Edwin.

'You can't go around claiming to have powers that you don't have.'

'I understand.'

'I didn't just fall into this, you know. I had to take exams.'

Edwin raised an eyebrow. He was very proud of being able to do that. 'That's impressive,' he said. 'What kind of magic can you do?'

The Lady of the Lake took several steps closer now, flattered by Edwin's interest. 'Well, finding things mostly,' she said.

'And people?' said Edwin.

'Yes. That's how I started off, being the Child at the Crossroads. Then I got my module in Future Divining, which is how I became the Woman by the Well, which is my proper job. Did I mention I'm just covering here?'

'You don't like the Lake, do you?' said Edwin.

'No,' said the Lady of the Lake. 'It does terrible things to my skin. I'm getting all wrinkled.'

'So what do you see in the future for us?' asked Edwin.

The Lady of the Lake concentrated. Then she broke into a smile. 'Really?' she said. 'You're going to take me away from here?'

'That's right,' said Edwin, nodding encouragingly.

Now the Lady of the Lake was beaming. 'Nimue thinks she's so special! Like she's the only one who could get a man! Wait till she sees I got myself a k –' The Lady of the Lake broke off, too honest to say *king*. Then something occurred to her. 'Oh Lord, they're going to be furious with me down in the Lake. Maybe I can sneak out. What am I saying? They probably already know I'm leaving. Bloody sorcerers!'

Hurry up, woman, thought Edwin.

'I hope they don't make me pay back my tuition fees,' the Lady of the Lake continued. 'I wonder who'll take my place? Not the Girl by the Gate, surely. Her incantations are really derivative.' She caught the bored expression on Edwin's face. 'Oh, sorry. Wait here, and I'll go and pack my things. Hopefully I won't run into anyone while I'm down there.'

The Lady started to descend into the water.

'Wait!' shouted Edwin.

The Lady stopped and looked at him quizzically.

'Come and give me a kiss before you go?'

The Lady smiled. 'Of course, my dearest love!'

She fairly skipped across the water towards Edwin. Edwin rose to his feet, and the Lady, no longer of the Lake, threw her arms around him with delight. They kissed for several long and very enjoyable moments. Then he reached down behind himself, picked up his sword and clubbed her over the head with the hilt. There was no point taking chances. As she crumpled to the ground at his feet, he did wonder whether he'd be better off with someone a little more adept at divining the future, but it couldn't be helped.

Fifty-Seven

'We're here,' said Karim.

It was a village. There was nothing remarkable about it. They had ridden up to a pleasant enough green where some children were playing some kind of bat and ball game under a sky that had started to fatten, at long last, with thunderclouds. There was a tavern and a church, and some houses that were neither pretty enough nor ugly enough to be of any note. The trees were trees, the grass was grass, the mud was mud. Daisies and dandelions competed to be the less obtrusive.

'Why here?' said Martha. 'It's so ordinary.'

'Exactly,' said Karim.

Martha blushed. She blushed whenever Karim said anything at all. She felt that everyone could tell what they had been doing, which was nothing more than kissing. Suddenly all those images from the book had come flooding back to her, and to her astonishment, instead of being disgusted, she longed to try them with Karim. (Karim! Why had she ever even looked at Humphrey?) Except, of course, that she couldn't. She was sure he had taken her words, 'Really I'm a girl', as a metaphor, and now she was afraid to disappoint him when he found out the truth. Could anything be more ironic? When they were together, she kept having to move his hands in strategic directions. Thinking of it, she blushed once more. And now he would notice her blushing and he'd never want to kiss her again.

'I can't believe that Jasper would choose to live in Grint,' she said, to cover her embarrassment. 'The people here are cranks. They don't have a king, all decisions are made by committees of commoners, they barely have any laws, just the obvious ones like murder, and they never put anybody to death.'

'That was the appeal,' said Karim. 'What exactly do you consider to be the disadvantages?'

'I . . .' said Martha. 'Um . . . It's just so strange. They don't have a *king*.'

'I'd sooner a committee of commoners than one King Leo,' said Elaine. 'Or Edwin, for that matter.'

Karim led the way past the green and into a nest of narrow streets that curled behind the churchyard where Martha hoped her brother wasn't buried. Her heart was racing and her hands were so slippery with sweat that she could barely hang onto her horse's reins. What if Jasper wasn't there? What if he was? What was she going to say to him? What if he was married now? What if he had children? What if he was dead? What if he didn't want to come home? How was she going to explain to him that she was a boy? What would the others do when they found out the truth? What would Karim do? But joy and excitement edged out the fear. *I'm going to see my brother again!* Jasper wasn't dead. The Lady of the Lake had said so. What else mattered, really?

Karim brought his horse to a halt.

'There,' he said.

The cottage Karim had stopped in front of was modest but in good repair, with a well-tended vegetable garden in front of it, and roses climbing up beside the front door and into the thatch above. They all dismounted. Karim handed the reins of his horse to Humphrey, unlatched the front gate and walked up the path. Martha thought she could see his hands tremble. She tried to think of what she was going to say when she saw her brother. *Hello, Jasper, it's me, Martha. And . . . and . . . and . . .* At her side, Leila bounced in her scabbard in time with the beating of her heart.

Karim knocked.

For a few seconds nothing happened.

'There's nobody home,' said Martha, awash with the certainty of disappointment. But then from inside the cottage Karim heard footsteps.

'He's coming,' he said.

Martha could hardly breathe. The door opened. A slim, blond man with sparkling blue eyes peered out from behind it. Martha had never seen him before in her life.

'Sir Alistair!' said Elaine.

The man slammed the door in Karim's face.

Martha felt dizzy. She'd gone over every possible scenario, but she had never thought of this.

Humphrey turned to Elaine. 'Are you sure?' he said. 'You said you wouldn't recognise him, back in the dungeon.'

'I'm sure,' said Elaine.

She hurried up to the door and knocked again.

'Sir Alistair, it's Lady Elaine. I just want to talk to you.'

'Are you there, Jasper?' called Karim.

'Is it definitely the right place?' said Martha.

'It was,' said Karim. 'But it's been six years.' He shouted through the door again. 'Jasper! Are you there? It's Karim!'

'It doesn't look like a prison,' observed Humphrey.

'What do you mean?' said Karim.

Humphrey looked at Elaine. 'I mean, he just walked to the door and opened it.'

Elaine didn't say anything to this.

Humphrey turned to Conrad. 'Knock the door down.'

'That doesn't seem to be striking the right note,' said Conrad.

'Conrad!'

'Fine. Stand back, everyone.'

Conrad pulled back his fist to punch through the door, but before he could, it opened again, this time revealing a taller, round-cheeked man with auburn hair.

'Steady on,' said the man.

'Sorry,' said Conrad, lowering his arm.

'Jasper!' said Martha.

'Who are you?' said Jasper. Then he smiled, a broad, infectious grin. 'Karim!' He took his former squire in his arms and hugged him closely. 'What are you doing here? I never thought I'd see you again! I wasn't supposed to see you again. But I can't say I'm sorry. Are you well?'

'I am,' said Karim.

'Except that he's been in an iron mask for the last six years,' said Humphrey.

'Christ, Karim. Why didn't you say? You look bloody good on it. And . . . Sir Humphrey?' said Jasper. 'My God, is that you?'

'It is.'

'So that must be little Conrad all grown up. With an elephant, no less!'

'I haven't necessarily stopped growing yet,' said Conrad a little gruffly.

'And who else have you brought with you? Lord, this is like Christmas!' Jasper scanned the group. Martha took a breath, ready to step forward, but before she could speak, Jasper said, 'Leila?'

Martha, surprised, looked down at her hip. But the sword, and its scabbard, were gone.

'Yes, it's me,' said a voice from behind them.

They all turned to see a young woman standing behind them, with dark hair and skin and bright green eyes, wearing a simple brown leather shift.

'Hello Jasper,' she said. 'Hello Karim. Humphrey, Conrad, Martha.'

'She's the . . . sword? You're the sword? You're Leila?' Martha stammered.

Karim ran to Leila and embraced her. 'I knew it was you,' he said. 'I just knew.' The girl began to sob against his shoulder, and Karim held her close and cried too. If Martha hadn't been so agape at her sword taking human form, she would not have liked the way they were holding each other one bit.

'I told you she was female,' she muttered to Conrad.

'It doesn't count, because she wasn't really a sword,' Conrad retorted.

As the group stared, amazed, at this new arrival, Jasper took Martha by the arm, turned her towards him and looked closely at her face.

'She said *Martha*,' he said.

'Yes,' said Martha.

'You look an awful lot like my sister,' said Jasper. 'Although in some ways, not so much. I know a lot can change in six years, but . . .' He reached out and gently touched her stubbled cheek. 'Can it be you?'

Martha nodded. 'Yes,' she managed to say. 'I thought you were dead. You let me think you were dead.' Then all she could do was cry.

Jasper hugged her close. 'I'm sorry,' he said, 'I'm sorry.' Martha's travel companions, who had been marvelling at the sword that had transformed into a woman, now turned to marvel at the boy who was really a queen.

Jasper loosed her from his hug. 'I think you'd all better come inside,' he said.

Fifty-Eight

At the back of the cottage was a small, cosy parlour with a large fireplace. The furniture was old and faded but comfortable, with plenty of cushions on the settles and chairs, rugs on the flagstone floor, and thick tapestries on the walls. Sir Alistair and Jasper had had to push everything to one end of the room to allow space for Conrad to squeeze inside. He'd crawled in through the low door, and now sat on the floor. Martha had been given the larger of the two armchairs, which was gratifying after weeks of being the most junior man present – second fiddle to a squire! Elaine sat in the other armchair, while Karim and Leila shared the settle, sitting close together in a way that Martha disliked. The rest of the men stood. The tears had stopped flowing, and the wine had started. They were all getting through it pretty fast.

Martha told her story first. When she had finished, Humphrey said, 'I'd figured you for the King's bastard. I should have guessed you were Queen Martha in disguise. Marcus, Martha, it's bloody obvious now I know. Anyway it explains a hell of a lot.'

'Such as?' said Martha.

Such as why my body responded to you as though you were a woman, Humphrey thought but didn't say. 'Well, for example, most men don't begin every day by filing their nails and – what was it you did with the little stick?'

'I was retracting my cuticles,' said Martha.

'Exactly. I don't even know what that means.'

'And you're stuck like this for good,' said Conrad, 'because you gave me the antidote.'

Martha hadn't actually mentioned this part. 'Yes,' she said. 'But it's just my appearance. It doesn't matter.'

'I think it probably does matter,' said Conrad. 'To you. Doesn't it?'

'I'm fine,' said Martha, with an attempt at a smile.

'I owe you my life,' said Conrad. 'You will always be able to count on me no matter what. Also I think I can probably mention now that you have the worst moustache I've ever seen, and please let me teach you to shave properly.'

'Done,' said Martha. Then she turned to her brother. 'Karim told us part of your story,' she said. She tried not to look at Karim, who seemed very cosy with his arm around the maiden who had until recently been her sword. 'How you argued with Father, and decided to pretend that you had died, and how the two of you found a place for you to hide. But I don't understand why Sir Alistair is here.'

'Karim told you that Father and I fell out,' said Jasper. He was standing at the centre of the group, with his back to the empty fireplace. 'But did he tell you why?'

'I didn't think it was my place to say,' said Karim.

'I'm not ashamed of it,' said Jasper. 'The fact of the matter is that I am a lover of men.'

It took Martha a moment to realise what he meant. Then her jaw dropped open with surprise.

'And you're not the only one, I assume,' said Elaine, with a glance at Sir Alistair. She had caught on faster.

'When I told Father my preference,' Jasper continued, 'he called me debauched, disgusting and evil. He said that if I did not marry a woman, not only would he disown me utterly, but he would ensure that I was burned at the stake for my crimes against nature. He said that he would light the pyre himself.'

There was a silence.

'Father was sick before he died,' said Martha. 'In the mind. I'm sure he didn't mean what he said.'

'That's as may be, but those are the laws of our country,' said Jasper. 'They're not the laws of Grint, and that's why I'm here. I refuse to live a lie and I certainly don't want to die an agonising death. Here, people leave you alone, what you do in your own home is your business. And so I lived peacefully, occasionally taking a lover, though never anyone I had deep feelings for. Then one day Al came to the village.'

'I was on a reconnaissance mission for King Leo,' said Sir Alistair. 'He'd been talking about an invasion. He often did. I went back and told him that Grint was a barren hellhole inhabited by bloodthirsty bandits and he'd be wasting his time. Hopefully he won't check. Anyway I met this one quite by chance in the marketplace when I was shopping for pears.'

'It was love at first sight,' said Jasper.

'The pears were excellent. Perfectly ripe. Oh, you mean with you? Yes, darling, it was. But the point is that I hadn't yet come to terms with who I was. Obviously there had been dalliances – the odd roll in the hay with a frisky shepherd. But I always thought that I would marry a maiden and leave all that behind.'

'You and me both,' said Elaine.

'Yes, and I'm truly sorry about that,' said Alistair.

He looked over at her but she refused to meet his eye. There was an uncomfortable moment before Jasper resumed the story. 'I begged him to stay,' he said.

'I really wanted to,' said Alistair with renewed warmth. 'The man has the spirit of an eagle and the heart of a bear.'

'And the body of a lapsed knight with a weakness for cake,' said Jasper.

'But I was too afraid to let go of what convention demanded of me,' said Alistair. 'I went home.'

'So you were the Knight in Black,' said Elaine to Jasper. 'You kidnapped him.'

'You risked going back to Tuft for him, even though you knew what would happen if King Leo got hold of you,' said Martha.

'It was the only way,' said Jasper. 'I knew if I found a way to bring him back, a way that would spare him the shame of his family, he'd never leave me again.'

'He was right,' said Sir Alistair.

They looked lovingly into each other's eyes.

'That's very romantic,' said Elaine. 'But I'm the one who has to go home without a husband, and . . .' She tailed off, then shook her head. Her eyes filled with tears. 'I'm the one who'll have to face the shame.'

Humphrey opened his mouth as if to speak, then closed it again.

Jasper said, slightly awkwardly, 'But I don't understand – were you all looking for Alistair, or for me? And how did you know we were together?'

'We didn't,' said Martha.

'I did,' said Leila.

'You did?' said Martha.

'You find out a lot of things, living in the Lake.'

'How can you find anything out, being a sword?' said Martha. 'How did you come to be a sword? And how come you're a person again now? And . . . who are you, anyway?'

Leila looked at Karim, then at Jasper.

'I was in love with Jasper,' she said. 'Years ago, when I was still a scullery maid at the castle. I didn't know that it was hopeless, or why. Jasper, you were always so kind to me! But when you rejected me I was angry. I thought it was my lowly status or the colour of my skin. Part of me believed that if only you could see beyond those things you would love the real me, and part of me feared that you did indeed see beyond them and yet you did not love me all the same. Both of these thoughts only contrived to make me angrier. Even so, when I heard you had died I was inconsolable. I cried for days, I refused food, I sincerely wished that I would die too. Eventually, my brother took pity on me.'

'Your brother?' said Martha.

'Karim.'

Martha broke into a huge grin. 'Oh, Karim's your brother! Of course he is! That's why he's been hugging you. Because brothers hug sisters.'

'Indeed they do,' said Jasper, and he came over and hugged Martha from behind her chair. Martha leaned her head back against his forearm, and Karim smiled at them. Martha felt herself blush yet again.

'Karim told me that Jasper was not really dead but in hiding, and he explained why he had gone,' Leila continued. 'But instead of being relieved, I felt so humiliated! In my rage, I went to King Leo and I told him the truth. I thought he would track Jasper down and kill him.'

'She's quite bloodthirsty,' said Humphrey. 'When she was a sword she tried to kill me.' His tone was only half jocular.

Leila turned to Humphrey, a sheepish look on her face. 'Yes, I apologise for that. I promise I had no intention of killing you.'

'It didn't look that way from the sharp end,' said Humphrey.

'I knew that you were looking for Sir Alistair,' Leila explained, 'and that Sir Alistair was with Jasper. I just didn't know where they were. I thought that if I could get you and Martha to join forces, then you'd have a better chance of finding them. But there aren't that many ways a sword can bring two people together. Attacking you was the only way I could think of.'

'Thank you for your help,' said Humphrey. 'I think?'

'And Martha,' Leila added, 'I'm sorry I put you in danger. I know I was sworn to protect you, but I remembered Sir Humphrey from my days at Camelot. I knew he was a good man, and that what he went through with his wife had robbed him of any desire to kill. I remembered how he'd cared for Conrad even though he was his enemy's son, and I was almost entirely sure that he wouldn't hurt you, especially if he thought you were a child.'

'Almost entirely sure?' said Martha. 'That's slightly less sure than I'd like.' But she smiled at the erstwhile sword.

'Well this is lovely, but your story's only half done. We'd just got to the bit where you betrayed me to King Leo,' Jasper said drily.

'Jasper,' said Leila, 'I can't tell you how sorry I am that I told King Leo you were still alive. I'm only glad that I didn't know where you were hiding. But Karim knew, and so the King came and took him away. He told everyone that Karim had been killed, but I knew that he was being held prisoner. I was too ashamed to return to Camelot, so I went to the Lady of the Lake and asked her to help me get my brother back. She turned me into a sword, which wasn't exactly what I had in mind. I was hoping for a supernatural army or something like that, but you have to be careful how you phrase things with the Lake people. She told me that, as penance for my betrayal, I would stay a sword until I had reunited Jasper with his sister, and only then would I become a human again and be reunited with my own brother. But there is no penance great enough for what I did.'

'I forgave you long ago,' said Jasper. 'There is no joy in living in bitterness. And you have suffered enough.'

'Thank you,' said Leila, 'but I will never forget myself.'

Karim drew her against his side and kissed her temple.

'What's it like being a sword?' Conrad asked her.

'It's worse than you can possibly imagine,' said Leila. 'You're completely trapped, and almost completely powerless unless you're in someone's hand. And I can't describe the frustration of understanding everything that goes on and being paralysed in this form, unable to act, unable to communicate. As for being used in a fight, that's horrific, the way the other sword comes at you . . .' Leila flinched at the memory. 'Though I admit there is a thrill in fulfilling your purpose. But even when you're just in the scabbard, for some reason it's always unbearably cold, and you get terrible pins and needles. Oh, and lots of swords are female, by the way.' She winked at the squire.

'Well, all's well that ends well,' said Martha triumphantly. 'Karim is free, so are you, and the two of you have found one another again. Sir Humphrey has completed the Pentecost quest, and can return to Camelot and claim his place at the Round Table. And I've found Jasper, so he can come back to Puddock and be the rightful king, save the nation from Edwin, stop the war, and annul my marriage so that I can do whatever I like and marry whomever I like!' She couldn't help but glance at Karim here, and noticed that he was looking back at her, though whether that was because he was thinking about who she might marry next, or just because it is polite to look at whoever is talking at the time, it was impossible to say.

'I'm not going to be king,' said Jasper.

'What?' said Martha.

'I'm not going to be king. I intend to stay here, living my quiet life with my husband. I don't want to be King of Puddock. I don't want to be king of anywhere, but I especially don't want to be king of a country where the previous king, my own father, threatened to have me put to death in the most brutal way possible, just for being who I am!'

'I think hanging, drawing and quartering is more brutal,' said Humphrey.

'Not if the hanging kills you. Then it's just about disposal methods,' said Conrad.

'A really talented executioner would never let the hanging go on long enough to kill you, when there's drawing and quartering yet to come,' said Humphrey.

'Yes, but we've both seen men die prematurely from a clumsy hanging, whereas burning always goes on for ages, and looks incredibly painful,' said Conrad.

'As I was saying,' said Jasper, and waited for the other two to shut up. 'No.'

'You can't say no. You're the King,' said Martha. 'You don't have a choice, you just are.'

'That didn't stop you when you were the Queen.'

'Because you were never dead, I never was queen, so any actions taken by me under that aegis are null and void.'

'Fine. In that case, in front of all these witnesses, I abdicate. Congratulations, Martha. Long live the Queen.'

'You can't abdicate!'

'He just did,' said Alistair.

'In your own words, all's well that ends well,' said Jasper.

Martha leaned back in her seat and looked up at the ceiling. There was nothing stopping her from abdicating as well. She thought of her freedom and of her new friends, of Karim, and of the life that could still await her wherever she chose to go. Then she looked back at the room. She sighed.

'Long live me,' she said.

Fifty-Nine

There were no horses in the Lake so Edwin had to share Storm with the Lady. It wasn't comfortable. He tried tying her up and slinging her over Storm's neck but she kept sliding off, so then he untied her legs and got her to sit in front of him, but there wasn't enough room on the saddle. There was no way Edwin was riding bareback, so he shoved her forward as far as he could, but she kept bouncing back again and pushing him off the saddle onto Storm's bony back. They made terribly slow progress. He hoped they weren't going far. *Maybe I should just kill somebody and take their horse*, Edwin thought, when they passed other travellers, but it was probably a bad idea. If he gave the Lady of the Lake her own horse, she might escape. Anyhow, he was relieved when she told him to pull up on the outskirts of a village on the border with Grint.

'Is she here?' asked Edwin.

'I don't know where she is exactly,' said the Lady of the Lake, 'but she's close. And on the far side of this village there's a camp with somebody else who is looking for her, and he can help you find her.'

'Well, I suppose that's better than nothing,' said Edwin, gathering the reins and preparing to move on.

'Wait,' said the Lady of the Lake.

'What?' said Edwin.

'He's not going to want to help you. So you'll have to find a way to persuade him.'

'Oh, I can be very persuasive,' said Edwin, putting his hand on the hilt of his sword.

They rode into the village. It was like an ants' nest that had been kicked, with swarms of people hurrying in the same direction they were going, dragging handcarts piled with produce, while others scurried in the opposite direction hauling bundles of dirty clothes. On a corner, a madam was doing a headcount of her prostitutes.

'How many people are camped out there?' Edwin asked the Lady of the Lake.

'Only one that you need to worry about.'

'You mean only one who needs to worry about me,' said Edwin.

The Lady of the Lake didn't say anything to that.

The lane through the village curved at the far end and climbed a slight incline, so they were almost upon it when they saw the huge pavilion that had been erected on the side of the hill, surrounded by several smaller tents.

'Yellow and blue,' said Edwin. Leo's colours. 'Of course.'

There were soldiers everywhere. They were all bustling around as if they had something incredibly important to do, because if you didn't look busy around Leo, you got sacked or executed. Even the two guards at the entrance to the pavilion were standing to attention to the point of paralysis, silently exuding the message that standing still was itself a form of being busy, if you put your all into it.

Edwin rode up to them.

'Halt!' said both guards in perfect chorus. 'Who goes there?'

'I'm Edwin,' said Edwin. 'Prince of Tuft, King of Puddock.'

'Really?' said one of the guards, not entirely respectfully. 'Oh, I suppose you are. And who's that?'

The Lady of the Lake was sitting sullenly in front of him, barefoot, long black hair tangled from the ride, hands bound with rope, blue dress hitched up to her thighs so that she could straddle Storm.

'She's my whore,' said Edwin.

'Right,' said the guard, uninterested.

Edwin dismounted and dragged the Lady of the Lake after him. He handed Storm's reins to one of the guards and the Lady of the Lake's arm to the other one.

'Look after them both,' he said. 'And be careful. I am very fond of that horse.'

He started to go into the pavilion.

'You can't just go in there,' said the guard holding Storm.

'Yes I can,' said Edwin.

The guards exchanged sneering looks as he swept inside, but nobody tried to stop him.

The air in the pavilion was hot, close and fetid. In the dim blue light, soldiers seethed like maggots on carrion. Edwin grabbed the shoulder of a passing officer.

'Show me to Leo,' he said.

'What makes you think the King's going to want to see you?' said the officer.

'I'm his brother,' said Edwin.

'I know,' said the officer. He shrugged Edwin off and moved on.

Above the heads of the soldiers, Edwin saw a face he knew: Noah, the deputy head steward. Edwin forced his way through the military mass towards him.

'Noah!' he called out. 'Noah, it's me! Prince Edwin!'

Noah turned his head towards the approaching prince, his face as inscrutable as if it had been carved out of stone.

'I need you to take me to Leo. Immediately.'

Without moving a muscle, Noah somehow managed to convey his doubt that Edwin's undertaking could in any way be of importance. But from through the crowd, Edwin heard a bored voice say, 'Oh God, bring him here, then.'

Noah turned and, with a wave of his arm, parted the soldiers as easily as if he were drawing curtains. Beyond them, Leo was sitting at a large, ornate wooden desk that must have been a nightmare to transport from place to place. On the desk was a map, and on the map was a small silver eagle. Leo pointed to it.

'Me,' he said.

On the desk beside the map was a crumb.

'You,' said Leo.

Edwin did the smallest bow that he could manage, he hoped for the last time.

'So you're invading Grint, then?' he said.

It wasn't a bad idea. Grint was a nation of lunatics and floozies who needed a firm hand. Edwin planned to get around to invading it himself, when he'd taken care of a few more pressing grudges.

'What, this?' said Leo. 'No. Well, eventually, yes, when I can be bothered. But if you're asking what I'm doing here, I've had some prisoners stolen from me, one of them a very important prisoner. I've been tracking them. They passed this way, so I'm here to get them back.'

'And the important one is Martha?'

'Your runaway bint?' Leo smirked. 'How could she be, when, according to you, I killed her?'

Edwin looked around, but there was no hope of privacy.

'We both know that you didn't kill her,' he hissed. 'And the Lady of the Lake told me that you were here looking for Martha.'

'Then the Lady of the Lake is wrong,' said Leo.

'Are you sure? You said you were looking for some of your prisoners. You might not even know that you have her.'

'I think I would notice,' said Leo. 'For a start, they are all men.'

'Exactly. Martha is disguised as a man.' It was Edwin's turn to smirk.

Leo had looked startled in front of Edwin once before and he wasn't about to do it again. Even so, he took a breath before he answered. 'One of the prisoners did always insist that we refer to him as a woman. It seems unlikely that that ugly bastard is your wife, though, because he's been in the dungeon since –'

But Edwin had heard enough.

'King Leo of Tuft,' he announced in a loud voice, 'you have stolen my wife, the Queen of Puddock, and thus breached the sovereignty of the nation of Puddock. I challenge you to a duel.'

Leo had trained his soldiers to react to nothing without his cue. Edwin might as well have made his pronouncement in an empty room.

'A what?' said Leo.

'A fucking duel, you dick. Winner gets Martha and both nations.'

'You remember, of course, that I have a fiancée who is pregnant with not one but two of my heirs?'

'I'll take a spot as Regent,' said Edwin. *Just until she shows up to make her claim and I get a chance to kill her and her babies too.*

Leo leaned back in his chair. 'And why would I want to fight a duel with you?'

'It's either that or I'm challenging you to a war.'

'You don't challenge someone to a war,' said Leo. 'You declare a war.'

'It doesn't matter! I'll war you! So choose!'

'You'll lose either way,' said Leo.

'If that's what you really think, then get it over with.'

A soldier appeared beside Edwin at Leo's desk. Edwin recognised him as one of the guards from outside the tent. The soldier bowed with a huge flourish.

'Your Majesty,' he said, 'the prisoners have been found. The Lady of the Lake revealed their whereabouts in exchange for her liberty.'

'What?' said Edwin. 'You can't let her go. That's my Lady of the Lake!'

'Too late,' said the guard with a shrug.

'Well done, Brian,' said Leo.

'My name is George, my liege.'

'We must be on the move at once. Tell the men to pack up the tents.'

George hurried away. Leo looked back at Edwin as though he were an apple core he didn't know what to do with.

'A duel or a war?' Edwin reminded him. 'It's your choice. If you're so sure you'll win, what's the risk?'

'Fine, fine,' said Leo, 'a duel it is. It is the cheaper option, after all. I look forward to adding Puddock to my prizes, and to having a go on your bitch, of course, once I smoke her out. But let's make it snappy. I've got these prisoners to catch.'

Edwin was already wearing Sir Dorian's third-best armour and had taken his second-best helmet, Sir Dorian not requiring it any more, so he was ready to fight. Leo got Noah to dress him quickly. There was no dissenting voice amongst the soldiers as to the wisdom of the duel. Not one of the men there would dare contradict the King once he had made a decision.

Noah went ahead, to prepare a suitable site. It was clouding over outside, for the first time after the long stretch of summer heat, and in the distance Edwin could hear the first rumblings of thunder. Although he was focused on the forthcoming task of killing his brother, he couldn't help but wonder how often knights got struck by lightning. He hoped he would be able to take his armour off soon.

'I don't know why you're in such a hurry to die,' said Leo, as the pair of them walked together towards the designated field.

'On the contrary, I've been waiting to kill you ever since I was born,' said Edwin.

'Really? I've barely been aware of you at all. Ah, here we are.'

Edwin looked around at the field of his destiny. It was a large, rough rectangle, the grass knee-deep, interrupted here and there by molehills. Noah had picked a spot for them where the ground wasn't too uneven, lessening the chance of this encounter being decided by who tripped first. Thunder growled more loudly now, and Edwin felt the first few drops of rain clang against his armour. Apart from Noah, they were alone.

'Come on!' said Leo. 'Back to back. Three paces to Noah's count, then turn.'

Noah looked intensely annoyed that he was going to have to speak, but there was no way around it.

Edwin and Leo stood back to back, swords drawn, Edwin facing the tents. The soldiers were busy preparing to move the encampment, and none of them were looking in their direction. There was no question in their minds that Leo was going to win this duel. Anybody who might have doubted it had already been eliminated from the command chain. This view could be the last thing that Edwin ever saw, this ultimate expression of Leo's mastery, that he controlled even the thoughts of his troops.

Noah inhaled, ready to begin his count. Edwin wheeled around, sliced him in half through the belly and, even as the steward fell, plunged his wet sword through the one soft part of Leo's armour, the part that covered his buttocks, thrusting upwards through his arsehole and out the other side.

Leo collapsed to the ground. He looked up at his brother with pride for the first and last time.

'I was planning to turn on "one",' he gasped as he died.

Sixty

They almost didn't hear the banging on the door of the cottage, the thunder was so loud. They had pulled the shutters closed against the driving rain and were still gathered together in the parlour, discussing how best to deal with Edwin. When they realised there was someone at the door, they looked at one another with horror.

'Could anybody have followed you here?' Jasper asked.

'I don't think so,' said Karim. 'I was very careful.'

'Although even if they only got a general idea of where we were heading, there are four horses and an elephant in your front garden, which is a bit of a giveaway,' said Humphrey.

'Oh, for crying out loud,' said Alistair. 'Couldn't you have parked them somewhere else?'

'I'll move them,' said Conrad, starting to get up.

'No,' said Elaine. 'None of you can go out there. King Leo's looking for half of you lot, and Edwin's looking for the rest. Conrad, Edwin thinks that you're dead! If that's him out there, what's he going to do if you suddenly appear at the door carrying an elephant halter? He'll kill you all over again, and this time we don't have an antidote.'

The knocking at the door became more insistent.

'All of you stay put,' said Elaine. 'I'll deal with this.'

'What about me?' said Leila. 'I could come with you. Nobody knows I'm alive. You don't know how to use a sword. I can protect you.'

Elaine hesitated. Then she said, 'It's too risky. If King Leo's out there looking for Karim, he might recognise you. Look, everybody stay here. I'll answer the door. It's probably just a traveller caught out in the rain. And if it is someone we need to worry about, I'm the only one who won't be recognised. I'll come up with some story about the animals. Don't worry, I'll be perfectly safe.'

'But . . .' began Humphrey.

'Be quiet and don't move!' insisted Elaine. 'I'm going before they break down the door.'

It certainly sounded as if the knocking was heading that way.

'I don't like you going alone,' said Humphrey.

Elaine just left the room without another word, closing the door firmly. Then she put on her most innocent smile and opened the front door of the cottage.

On the threshold was a damsel with long black hair, a blue dress and no shoes. Elaine was surprised. She hadn't been expecting a damsel. She was also confused because, despite the torrential downpour, the damsel appeared to be perfectly dry.

'What can I do for you?' said Elaine.

'Let me guess,' said the damsel. 'You're not Martha and I'm pretty sure you're not Leila. Elaine?'

'You're mistaken, my lady,' said Elaine. 'Perhaps you are looking for another house in the village? As you can see, this is the home of the veterinarian.'

Jemima gave her a reproachful look, as if to say that no true veterinarian would leave an elephant out in a torrential downpour.

'Oh. Of course. You're being cagey. That's understandable. But I'm the Lady of the Lake. Well, I'm the acting Lady of the Lake.'

'I don't see a lake anywhere near here,' said Elaine, 'unless you mean one of those puddles.'

'The Lake is a metaphysical realm. It could be any body of

water. And to be honest, it's just a title. It could be any designation and location. So, actually, right now I'm the Damsel at the Door,' said the Damsel at the Door.

'That's very interesting,' said Elaine. 'I'm sorry I can't be of any help. I'd invite you in to shelter from the storm, but my husband isn't at home.'

'You're not married,' said the Damsel at the Door, 'otherwise that baby of yours wouldn't be such a problem, would it?'

Elaine stepped out into the rain and pulled the door shut behind her.

'What do you want?' she said.

'I just want to talk to Martha,' said the Damsel at the Door.

'There is no Martha here.'

'Of course not,' said the Damsel at the Door. 'Stupid me. You're all impossible, you know that? I'm only ever trying to help. Well, let me give you a message for Martha, just in case you happen to meet someone of that name. Tell her that Edwin is looking for her, that he's planning to kill her. Tell her I've staved him off but not for long. I've sent him after the wrong prisoners, the ones who left with the blacksmith. Tell her that she needs to be ready. Can you do that?'

Elaine nodded. 'Yes,' she said. 'I can.'

But she was already forming a better idea.

Sixty-One

'Where are the prisoners?' Edwin demanded.

'I don't know what you're talking about, mate,' said the blacksmith. He was sitting inside the forge next to the enormous hearth, eating a thick slice of bread with bacon and dripping.

'Don't call me *mate*,' said Edwin. 'I'm the King of two nations! I am Your Majesty!'

'King of two nations, eh?' said the blacksmith. 'In that armour? It doesn't fit properly, and the helmet doesn't match the rest of it. I can kit you out with a new suit if you like. At a very competitive price.'

'I've got an entire army waiting outside!'

Leo's troops were following Edwin so far, though their loyalty was grudging at best. There had been too many witnesses to the agreement to have a duel for them to disbelieve that Leo had lost, extraordinary as it seemed to them, and Edwin was Tuft's only living heir. The death of Noah had been harder to explain. Edwin claimed that he'd killed himself out of grief for the loss of his King, and this had appeared to placate the men, though who knew how long that would last. Surely one of them would figure out soon enough that cutting oneself in half is not a standard form of suicide. Edwin feared a coup. He knew he'd have to keep the army busy to stop them from turning on him, and that was just one of the reasons he was now planning a war on Camelot. He had Tuft's army under his command, just about, and Puddock was already preparing for battle. So why not start at the top? Arthur and his bloody Round Table! So smug, so superior, so infuriating! Sir Dorian was just the beginning. Edwin would take them all down, one by one by one if he needed to. Just as soon as he found Martha. Oh, and sorted out the conscription and the training and the marching and the rest.

'In that case,' said the smith, 'you'll be needing a lot more armour than that. As it happens, I'm running a special offer at the moment. Buy nine suits of armour and the tenth is free. If you wait while I finish my butty, I'll get you a loyalty card.'

'I'm not interested in buying any armour!'

'That's only because we haven't found the right deal for you yet.'

Edwin took a deep breath and tried again.

'I'm looking for three men.'

'Well, I don't work in that kind of business myself, but I can ask around.'

'No. Three specific men. Escaped prisoners. One is – do not misunderstand me – one is actually a woman. He just looks like a man.'

'It's not my place to judge. The customer is always right.'

'The others . . .' What had the army captain told him? 'There is an inferior knight of some sort, and a coloured squire. I believe unconnected to one another. But they are of lesser importance. The man who is really a woman is the one I need to find. Let us beat around the bush no longer. You will clearly do anything for money. I will make it worth your while.'

'That's as may be,' said the smith, 'but I still don't know what you're talking about.'

'But I do,' said a voice behind Edwin.

He turned. At the door to the forge was a beautiful damsel, dressed in a shabby grey dress. In this hovel she was an apparition, a pot of gold at the end of a grubby rainbow. Edwin could see sadness in her eyes, which pleased him. Sadness made women more vulnerable.

She curtseyed low. 'Your Majesty,' she said as she straightened. 'May we speak in private?'

'You see, that's the way to talk to a king,' said Edwin to the smith. He turned back to the girl. 'I'll do more than speak to you in private,' he said. Then, to the smith: 'Piss off.'

'It's my forge,' grumbled the smith, but he popped the last bit of bread in his mouth, and got up to go. He gave the damsel a look that seemed intended to be meaningful, but she didn't react.

'You know about the man who is really a woman?' said Edwin, after the door shut behind the smith.

'Yes, Your Majesty,' said the damsel. 'I believe the person you are referring to is your wife.'

Edwin tried to emulate his late brother in feeling surprise but not showing it. He did not succeed. 'Carry on,' he said.

'My name is Lady Elaine du Mont,' said the damsel. 'I've been travelling with your wife, Queen Martha, for these past few months, during which time she has been in disguise as a man and using the name Marcus. She is not the prisoner you've followed here. I can take you to her if you wish.'

'What's the catch?' said Edwin.

'The catch?'

'Nobody ever does anything just for the sake of it. There's always a price. How much do you want?'

Elaine shook her head. 'I don't want money.'

'Really?' said Edwin. 'You look like you need it.'

'No,' said Elaine. 'I need something else.'

'Of course you do. Spit it out.'

Elaine looked around, but there was nobody else in the forge. 'Can I count on your discretion?' she said.

'Count away,' said Edwin.

'I am expecting a child. The father is irrelevant, a former guard at my parents' castle, long gone now. I had a fiancé, a knight of King Leo's, but he ran away from his responsibilities and no longer wishes to marry me. It seems to me that you need to find your Queen and dispose of her discreetly, and yet you need an heir. Meanwhile I need a husband and a father for my child. I will take you to Martha, you will kill her and marry me. And then you will raise my child as your heir. That is my price.'

Elaine was attempting to appear calm but Edwin could smell the terror on her like a dog. She would certainly be a stunning Queen on his arm. Not to mention in his bed. And knowing the secret of the child's parentage would make her easier to manipulate. But the child would not be his. And there was still the question of the legitimacy of his rule.

'How about this,' said Edwin. 'You take me to Martha. I bring her back to Puddock and keep her as my wife until she bears me a child. Then I kill her and marry you. Your child may live with us if you insist, but it will have no rights to succession.'

'I take you to Martha,' said Elaine. 'You bring her back to Puddock and keep us both away from sight until my baby is born. Then you kill her, claim that my baby is hers, and raise him to be king. You don't have to marry me, but please, I beg you let me see the child.'

'That's very selfless of you,' said Edwin.

'Not really.' Elaine held Edwin's gaze for a few moments.

'The heir to Tuft and Puddock will be my flesh and blood,' said Edwin. 'There is no negotiation on that point. My original offer is my final offer. Your child will have wealth, but he will not have power. Though perhaps we will make him a good marriage one day. That is the best most younger siblings can expect.'

Elaine considered the offer, then nodded. 'I accept.'

Sixty-Two

With Elaine as his guide, Edwin retraced his steps until he was back at the border village where he had killed Leo. It was a two-bit village now, but Edwin planned to build an enormous monument there to his triumph. People would come from miles around to admire it. It would be the jewel in the crown of Tuft. Or Tuft-Puddock, now that he was King of both nations. It would be Tuft-Puddock-Camelot soon. Then Tuft-Puddock-Camelot-Grint. It was getting to be a bit of a mouthful. He might as well just take all of Britain.

Not that he would be invading Grint just yet. He didn't want to waste valuable troops. And for ludicrous reasons, you weren't allowed to take an army with you when you crossed the border into Grint.

'Really?' he said to the customs officer. 'I'm not planning to do anything with them. Just a bit of marching. They need the practice.'

'You have to leave them here,' insisted the customs officer, a dwarf with a peculiarly hairy face. He looked vaguely familiar to Edwin.

'I demand that you let them through,' said Edwin.

'Sorry. No can do.'

'Leave them,' said Elaine to Edwin. 'You're not going to need them.'

'It's a matter of principle,' said Edwin. 'I am the King. I will not be refused by a jobsworth dwarf.'

'King or not, they're not coming in,' said the dwarf.

Suddenly Edwin remembered. 'You're the dwarf from the Puddock border! Didn't I send you back to the castle for incarceration?'

'That's right,' said the dwarf, who seemed a lot less impressed with Edwin this time round.

'I knew you wouldn't actually go, you dwarves are all the same. Liars the lot of you.'

'Actually I did go,' said the dwarf. 'I met a nice man there called Sir John Penrith. We practised our French together. *Mais oui*. I told him you sent me to be imprisoned, but he set me free. I don't think he likes you very much. Obviously you'd sacked me so I couldn't go back to the Puddock border, but well-trained customs officers can always find employment. I work for the Republic of Grint now. You have no jurisdiction over me, and that army stays in Tuft.'

Edwin was preparing to kick the dwarf into next week, but Elaine turned to him. 'Just leave the army behind. Remember, you're here to rescue your wife.'

'No, I'm not really, it's more like –'

Elaine silenced him with a flash of her entrancing eyes. 'You're here to rescue your wife,' she repeated. 'The people of Puddock will be enraptured by your bravery. Do you really want to share the glory with this pack of grunts?' She gestured to the troops with a sweep of her elegant arm.

Edwin was impressed. This damsel was smart. She might actually make a good wife for him. A listening ear and a quick wit could be useful attributes in a queen – or princess consort, as he was planning to call her.

Edwin left some soldier or other in charge of the army, and he and Elaine travelled on alone. It was pissing down with rain now, which he'd have thought would be better than heat with the armour, but because the helmet didn't match the breastplate there was a gap at the back of his neck where cold water was trickling in, and it was starting to accumulate in puddles around his hips. He should have got a new suit from that fat smith when he'd had the chance.

'It's not far from here,' Elaine reassured him, picking up on his discomfort. A very good wife. She even looked lovely with rain plastering her hair to her face, God damn her.

The village she brought him to was a dreary old place. How could people tolerate living in villages? They were so dull, and all the bloody same, give or take a church or a tavern. When he ran Grint he'd torch this place and plant himself a pleasure garden.

At Elaine's suggestion, they sheltered from the rain in a hay barn in a farm on the edge of the village, while they made their plan. Edwin removed his armour and stood in his sodden under-garments pouring rainwater out of the various pieces.

'We'll wait until night,' said Elaine. 'They'll be asleep in their beds. Then you can go in and take her.'

'They?' said Edwin, stopping midway through tipping out his elbow guard. 'She's not alone?'

'No,' said Elaine. 'There are others.'

'How many?' said Edwin.

'Only five men,' said Elaine. 'All trained in combat. Six, if you include your wife. One of them is a giant. I think you've killed him once already.'

'What?'

'And a woman,' Elaine continued smoothly, 'but she is adept with a sword, having spent a number of years in that form herself. And maybe the Damsel at the Door, if she's still there. I'm assuming she can do magic.'

'I can't go up against that many!' said Edwin, aghast. 'Even I, I mean.'

'But they'll be asleep.'

'And if they wake?'

'If you're quiet they won't wake.'

'And if she screams?'

302

Elaine didn't say anything but she looked downcast. Edwin was disappointed. He'd thought she was intelligent. He should have known not to expect too much of a woman.

'You go instead,' said Edwin. 'She trusts you. Go to where she is, find some kind of excuse and bring her back here to me.'

'I'm not sure that she trusts me very much,' said Elaine. 'She'll be wondering where I've been all this time.'

'She trusts you more than she trusts me. And the others – they won't suspect you, will they?'

Elaine shook her head. 'No. At least, I don't think so.'

'So go,' said Edwin. 'You'll be perfectly safe. You'll be long gone before they realise that anything is wrong.' *And if not, well, never mind.*

Elaine turned to go, then turned back. 'But what if she won't come with me? She's in the form of a man now, she's stronger than me, and I'm with child. I don't think I can overcome her.'

Edwin groaned with exasperation. 'You'll be fine.'

'But what if I'm not fine?'

'Have you no courage at all? Look, take my sword, and if there's any trouble don't hesitate to use it. Just don't kill her, and don't damage her womb. Understood?'

'Yes, Your Majesty.'

Edwin handed Elaine the sword from his pile of armour. Elaine curtseyed, opened the barn door, slipped out into the rain and closed the door behind her.

Edwin waited. The rain drummed on the roof of the barn like the fingers of a thousand bored men.

Then eight people jumped out from beneath the hay, weapons drawn.

'Surprise!' said Martha, pulling back her bow, an arrow pointed straight at his eye.

Sixty-Three

'What shall we do with him?' said Martha.

Edwin was bound and gagged in the middle of the barn. The others sat around him picking hay out of their hair and clothes.

'Kill him,' said Conrad. 'I'll do it myself if you like. Tit for tat.'

Edwin whimpered through his gag.

'That is the obvious choice,' said Martha.

'Annul your marriage to him first, though,' said Elaine, who had joined them. 'You don't want to be known as a husband-killer.'

'That stigma never goes away,' agreed Humphrey, who was sitting very close to Elaine.

'Can I do that?' said Martha.

'You are the Queen,' Jasper reminded her.

'Oh yes,' said Martha. 'Well. Edwin, consider our marriage annulled.'

Edwin tried to say something through the gag but it came out as more of a spit.

'Of course that means I can't rule, now that I'm un-married again. Oh well. I suppose I'll have to change the constitution.'

'Absolute power has its uses,' said Jasper.

'So shall I go ahead?' said Conrad. 'Get it? A head?' He mimed pulling Edwin's head off. Edwin tried to squirm away from him but his bonds were too tight for him to move.

'I'm not sure,' said Martha. 'I don't know if I have it in me to kill in cold blood.'

'Apart from unicorns,' Humphrey reminded her.

'You could put him in an iron mask,' said Karim.

'He's not bad-looking,' said Alistair. 'Seems a shame to cover up that face.'

'You can't see his teeth under the gag,' said Martha, 'but to be honest, it's more that he's ugly on the inside. And I'm not one to talk. I was a pretty lousy-looking female, and now . . .'

'You look all right to me,' said Karim.

Martha flushed a little.

'I can restore you to your previous form, if you like,' said the Damsel at the Door, who was no longer the Damsel at the Door but the Beauty in the Barn.

'Really?' said Martha.

'Yes. Restorative magic takes a while but it is possible. It's a bit like untangling a knot. Fiddly but doable.'

Martha, hopeful but worried, couldn't help but glance at Karim.

'I told you before,' said Karim, 'some people don't mind either way. And you should be you.'

Martha smiled. 'Thank you,' she said to the Beauty in the Barn. 'When we have time, I would be grateful for that. But right now it's not the most pressing matter at hand.' She pointed the tip of an arrow at the captive Prince of Tuft.

'If it's hands you're interested in, I could pull his fingers off, stick two up his nose, the rest in his mouth, and we can watch him suffocate,' suggested Conrad.

Edwin shrieked into his gag. Again he tried to move away from Conrad but he only managed to tip over.

'I have another suggestion,' said Leila, as she watched Edwin flail. 'Now that I'm a person again, there's a vacancy for a magic sword.'

'That seems quite generous,' said Humphrey. 'He killed a child.'

'Amongst others,' said Conrad.

'Have any of you ever been a sword?' said Leila. Unsurprisingly, none of them had. 'It is not in the least bit generous. It's a prison worse than . . .' She looked at her brother. 'Worse even than an iron mask, I think. And he wouldn't be any old sword. He'd be magic. There can be certain restrictions put on what he can do.'

Martha looked at Edwin, who was sweating a lot for someone who was drenched in icy rainwater. 'Only to be used in the defence of the innocent, for example,' she said. 'To remain a sword until his soul truly repents?'

'Exactly,' said Leila.

'Could you do that?' Martha said to the Beauty in the Barn.

'Sure,' said the Beauty in the Barn. 'Transfiguration into swords is one of the first things you learn at the Lake. Oh, Edwin. I bet you wish you'd been nicer to me now.'

Edwin's face began to turn faintly yellow.

'And you're going to need a sword,' said Elaine. 'There's still an army on the border, loyal to Edwin and Leo. I don't think they're going to turn round and go home just because you ask them nicely.'

'It sounds like I'm going to need more than a sword,' said Martha. She looked around at her friends. 'I'm going to need knights. What do you say?'

There was a pause.

'You want me to be one of your knights?' said Humphrey.

'I want you all to be my knights,' said Martha. 'First I need to prevent a war with Tuft, and then there's so many things I want to change at home. I want Puddock to be a place where you can live safely, brother. I want it to be somewhere where everyone can live peacefully. I need your help to do that. I need all of you to help.'

Jasper turned to his husband and raised his eyebrows. Alistair thought about it for a moment, then nodded.

'Without a doubt, yes,' said Karim.

'And we'd all be knights?' said Conrad, with the beginnings of a smile.

'All of you. Though the Lady of the Lake might prefer a more supernatural role. Say, the Crone at the Castle? I can promise you an excellent apprentice.'

'Less of the Crone, thank you,' said the former Lady. 'Though I suppose I might consider Sorceress of the Citadel.'

Martha turned to Leila. 'Lord knows you've served me long enough, and that against your will. You are, of course, free to go – as indeed you all are. I can see you might dearly wish to leave. You owe me nothing. But, Leila, should you choose to stay, I would like you as my personal guard. There is nobody I trust more.' She glanced nervously at her brother as she said this, but he nodded his encouragement.

'I would be honoured,' said Leila.

'What about me?' said Elaine. 'I can't possibly be a knight. I haven't a clue about how to fight, and I've got a baby to bring up on my own.'

'You're not on your own,' said Humphrey. 'Not if you don't want to be.' He reached out and took her hand.

Martha felt a surge of warmth as she watched them. Maybe a hint of the old jealousy too, but nothing that mattered. 'There's more than one way to fight,' she said to Elaine. 'You've got a great head for strategy. I could use an adviser like you. Are you in?'

'I'm in. For now, anyway. I have some plans of my own. I want to go to Africa. I want to see where elephants come from.'

'And people,' Karim reminded her.

'And people,' Elaine agreed. 'I want to show my child the world. I might even take a knight with me.' She squeezed Humphrey's hand. 'But Puddock first. For as long as you need me.'

'So it's settled,' said Martha. 'Thank you all. I could not wish for better companions. Now, much as I would like to celebrate, first we'd better figure out what to do about this army, before they cross the border looking for the . . .' She glanced over to where Edwin had been, where now lay a beautiful golden sword with a pearl-studded hilt. 'Ex-Prince Consort. Right. Who's got any ideas?'

And thus began the adventures of Queen Martha and the Table of Equally Valued Knights.